IERAPETRA

or His Sister's Keeper

Joachim Frank

Printed in the United States of America
Hardcover ISBN: 978-1-961624-92-4
Paperback ISBN: 978-1-961624-93-1
Ebook ISBN: 978-1-961624-94-8

**Canoe Tree
Press**

Canoe Tree Press is a division of DartFrog Books
301 S. McDowell St.
Suite 125-1625
Charlotte, NC 28204

www.DartFrogBooks.com

In Memoriam Renate 1944 - 1998

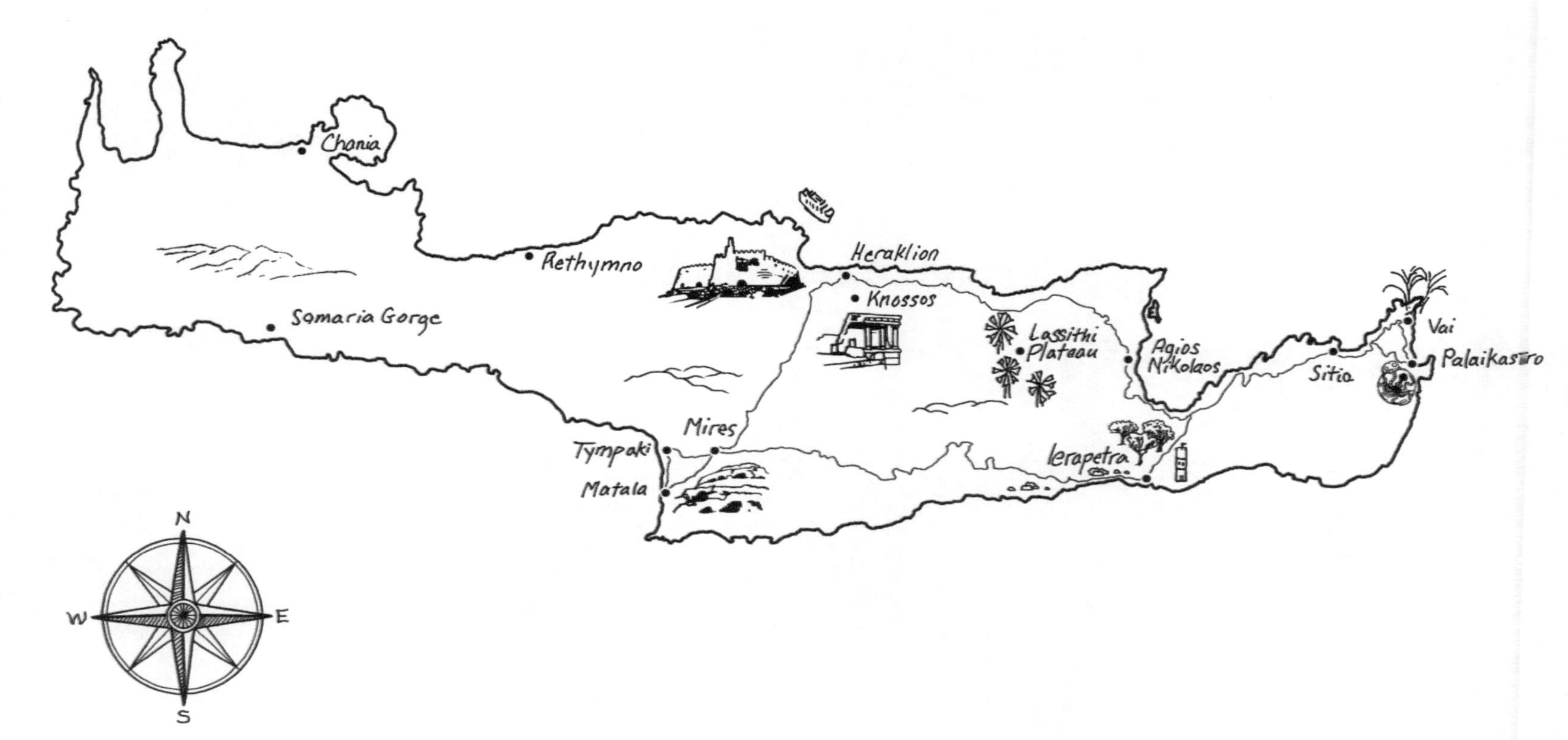

Chania
Rethymno
Heraklion
Knossos
Somaria Gorge
Lassithi Plateau
Agios Nikolaos
Vai
Palaikastro
Sitia
Mires
Tympaki
Matala
Ierapetra
N
W
E
S

Her Letter

It's been twenty years, almost to the day, since my sister died. She suffered through a long illness; in the end it had galloped mercilessly, uncontrolled, to its conclusion. By then her auburn hair had turned a dirty gray, her arms were bony spindles, and her eyes were transparent windows allowing a view all the way into her brain.

The picture on my desk shows Monika wearing a floppy, wide-brimmed sun hat reminiscent of one I saw Marilyn Monroe wearing in a famous photograph from the fifties—not the one where she stands on the subway grate, though. Monika had a large collection of hats, which grew by leaps and bounds as friends and family fed her habit. It reminded me of Imelda Marcos's infamous shoe collection. I wonder where all her hats went after they were orphaned. Are they with Peter? Did their daughter Brigitte inherit the collection?

I found one of the last letters she wrote to me by accident. I keep letters like hers in a black Leitz binder, but I had not opened it for years. I'd used a two-hole punch, the German business way, to make the letters fit on the two-pronged fork in the binder awaiting them. The binder has moved with me, along with its companions, to every city and every country I've lived in.

Seeing the hole in its back that makes it convenient to grab it from the bookshelf with your fingers like a hook reminds me of Germany. It reminds me of my father, who kept trial cases in binders like that, who gave me a *Leitz* binder the day before I left for college and told me to keep my financial affairs in order. I have since converted to the American three-punch system, but that binder, my way of counting, and, incidentally, my love of potatoes are still German through and through.

The latest and probably final home of all those binders is my study in the basement of the house we bought in the country. I see a sliver of my backyard through the glass of the door that leads outside, and with it, a patch of the sky. Once in a while a bird flies by, and the occasional chipmunk peers in, standing on its hindlegs but barely reaching the lower end of the glass.

Behavioral science has a concept called *Übersprungshandlung*, which is a German compound word that Mark Twain would have loved. Literarily translated as "over-jump action," it refers to the curious way some animals behave when they are cornered and extremely stressed. Birds, for instance will start to peck at the wall; there is of course no sense in the action under most circumstances, but it's inspired by the need to do *something* in response to a threat of some kind. I guess it's the extra adrenalin driving the body into action.

At any rate, one day last fall—one of those days with an intense blue cloudless sky—I found myself sitting with the opened binder in my lap, reading and rereading two pages written in blue pen. I had the whole weekend to myself and was going through some personal documents I had saved over the years. Going back to them is always an eye-opener, since the crispness of the language gets lost in memory, and summarizing clichés keep invading instead.

It was a simple letter, filled with practical matters. No expression of love at the end or some sentimental greeting, just an acknowledgment of the sender as my sister: *deine Schwester.* Though email has existed for quite some time, people still wrote letters then, and, if they cared for each other, awaited the arrival of the mailman with a pounding heart.

This letter, written by a jittery hand but still in the curly style she adopted in middle school, reminded me of the days in which she held on to the last thread of her life. In that letter, she talked about a movie she'd just seen: *Frühstück bei Tiffany*, with Audrey Hepburn. She said she loved—absolutely loved!—the actress. I'd seen the movie years ago and couldn't remember much except Hepburn's innocent face. She'd always looked like a demure schoolgirl, really. I couldn't even remember the bedroom scenes, of which there were plenty.

I have no idea what Monika found so compelling about the actress, except perhaps a secret desire to break all norms of decency as Hepburn famously did in that movie. It's too late to get an answer to this question, not to mention the many others that my sister never would've answered—not even in her typical monosyllabic way.

I always thought we are not responsible for our siblings: for the decisions they make, their screwups, the way they look at the world. At least, I never saw it as *my* job. That might sound harsh, but I really thought it was too much of a burden, especially when you're young and it's enough of a struggle just to find yourself. Instead, I saw growing up with siblings as some kind of a race, but a peculiar one in that we all began at different starting lines. And in this particular race, everyone takes off erratically and in different directions. My point is, we are all supposed to start taking charge of our own lives before our parents have to worry about us, our inaction, our failure to join the adults in a productive way.

This reminds me of the flea circus I saw in Copenhagen many years ago while traveling with my elder brother and his fiancée. When I talk about this now, fifty years or so later, I'm met with incredulity. *Fleas? In a circus? You've got to be kidding!* But I saw everything with my own eyes. Those fleas were all dressed up in tiny costumes and strapped to miniature carriages that they pulled with unmatched agility and power—for brown little dots, at any rate. If humans had a similar strength—as we learned from the director I'm about to introduce—then we could jump over the Eiffel Tower several times a day without much difficulty.

Given the delicate nature of these creatures and their diminutive size, the costumes were in fact scraps of fabric tied to the body of the fleas with thin silver wires. The carriages, also attached to them with silver wires, were painted with the royal Danish insignia of red hearts and three blue panthers on an orange background. But what immediately caught my attention was the rotating Danish flag on top of the tower. It moved in fits and spurts, driven by a single flea that ran on a circular platform on top. The flea circus director liberally used an enormous magnifying glass to invite us to really see his show and all its subtleties.

As a physicist, I didn't have to ask about why he'd chosen to utilize silver. For those to whom it is not obvious, silver is a metal soft enough to be drawn into thin wire, and noble enough to be chemically compatible with the insect's own delicate body armor. I was still worried about sulfur, though, an element that is abundant in an animal's body and will form black patina on the surface of silver quite soon after exposure. I think gold would have been more fitting, though a bit more expensive, and this was the economy of an operation just surviving from one day to the next, so I can't blame anyone for cutting costs wherever possible.

Still.

Perhaps also related to economy, the flea circus director told his small audience that he let the performers feed from his arm whenever they got hungry. For proof, he raised his right arm to show it was covered in little red bites. His forearm, in particular, looked quite unhealthy to me.

Nowadays, marks on an arm or any body part may be unremarkable, but I'm speaking of a time when people with tattoos were considered outcasts and were looked at with suspicion. At any rate, these red bites were unsystematically spaced out on his skin and lacked the aesthetics of a tattoo—if you believe there is such a thing,

Now to the point of comparison, before I get too carried away and go into trips I have taken *without* my brother, which were actually more eventful. Like the one I took with my friend to the Camargue, where a horse threw me off and dragged me through the brush. By the time we came to a stop, I felt how Achilles must have felt after being dragged in a grand circle around Troy. Incidentally, this is when I decided never to go on horseback again. Or my time in Prague, where a fiery young woman I'd slept with took off with my wallet, along with all my cash. These adventures are still alive in me and soar through my head and my dreams to this day.

So, the flea circus director lined up his little creatures for a race across the table—there was a starting and a finish line on a field he'd meticulously drawn on a green cardboard mat—and everybody in the audience held their breath. The fleas and their curved chitin hulls were all glinting in the light from the single bulb dangling from the ceiling. At that moment, the director raised a small pistol loaded with a fire-cracker and fired it as we covered our ears. Nothing on the table moved, though, and between the loudness of the shot, the expectant audience in the cramped tent, and the lack of action on the field, the whole display could not have been less climactic.

I'd searched the director's face for signs of disappointment in vain, but there was no twitch of a muscle, no acknowledgment of failure to be found. He might have thought of potential punishments to be meted out once the audience was gone and he had the tent to himself, like withholding his arm and making them starve for a whole day. I don't even know if fleas can hear sound. As a matter of principle, doesn't the wavelength of sounds have to be much shorter than the body of the listener? Bestowed with senses of smell and vision, fleas may be able to navigate perfectly in the world they inhabit and, under normal circumstances, do not need this extra level of sensory sophistication.

What I remember best from that afternoon in the flea circus is that once thirty seconds had passed after the pistol was fired, one of the creatures lurched forward, only to come to a rest after about ten centimeters. Then another started moving, much slower than the first one, but with much more persistence. He (or she, or it) gained advantage over its faster competitor, who had inexplicably stopped and was still stuck at the same place. Then a third one took off, almost taking the royal carriage attached to it into the air.

Back now to my relationship with my siblings: to me, the fascinating things about the race in the flea circus were the breaks and hesitations, or the unknown forces that brought contenders to a stall and the counteracting forces that caused them to restart capriciously and at random. Until then, I think I had conceived the world as a giant Cartesian machine, where random lapses were inconceivable. At that moment, I realized these suspensions of the rule of determinism were in fact commonplace.

I don't think I know my siblings at all, even after all those years, nor what makes them tick. We see each other once in a while and take an interest in what we are doing. Why shouldn't we, even if only to compare our predictions and extrapolations about where each was headed in life with the real thing? It's only when something goes terribly wrong that we rediscover our long-buried feelings and remember the unfinished business we still have.

There were initially four of us. I already mentioned my younger sister, Monika, whose memory this book is dedicated to. I also mentioned my elder brother in the flea circus episode; my role then had been to act as a chaperone for him and his fiancée. This was the condition under which our parents agreed to the trip and allowed him to take our only family car, a VW Beetle.

Of course, there was nothing in my power to prevent them from sleeping with each other; they probably did, considering they shared a tent next to my smaller one on every campground we visited. As in many arrangements like this, the mere appointment of a third person fulfills the requirements of society's moral code, no matter what is actually enforced in the end. For me, the notion of them copulating was quite a stretch. It was difficult for me at the time to imagine the kind of chemistry that could make people decide to engage in this degree of intimacy, especially if one of them was my brother. And, in case you are curious, I did not find her the least bit attractive. I still don't know what's behind attraction. Perhaps those of us who are interested in women look unconsciously for our mother's features? But, on further reflection, this wouldn't work as a theory since I shared the same mother as that woman's boyfriend.

Along the way, the odometer passed its 150,000-kilometer mark. We were on a long stretch of the road heading north, passing wide-open fields and a birch tree here and there. My brother stopped the car to take a picture of the odometer to mark the occasion, then one of me with his fiancée posing in front of the car. He sent scans of those pictures to me only recently, after digging through his massive archive.

On that trip, I saw my first northern lights display. I'd stepped out of the youth hostel in a town north of Stockholm to catch some fresh air. The sky rolled and danced: a large-scale Isadora Duncan in motion, clad in garments of blue, orange, and green. I was in awe, but also convinced that for people living in Sweden, this was pretty much a nightly occurrence—no big deal. But when I reentered the hostel and told someone what I'd just seen, all hell broke loose. Everybody rushed outside to see what was left of the spectacle, reprimanding me all the while for not telling them sooner.

The other sibling I haven't mentioned yet is Angelika. Five years older than I, she is brilliant, compassionate, sharp, snotty, well-meaning, and ever so condescending.

When Monika died, the pain I felt was raw and unexpectedly intense. By then I had experienced the death of both of my parents, though ten years apart. Perhaps the reason this pain existed on a different scale was that, by the time the first of my parents died, they were already quite remote. They were no longer part of my life, as harsh as that sounds. In my memory I'd liken my father to a hard, brittle mineral: a piece of quartz from the gravel that once covered the paths in our formal garden. My mother, then, would be a quiet plant—say, an elderberry bush. They both died slowly, fading out over a period of years.

By contrast, I'd always taken my younger sister's future for granted; she would always be around, she was part of my world, and, in a very real sense, part of me. After my father died—still not believing much in artists and their creative contributions to society—she instantly flourished, transformed. She became radiant, outright beautiful, and took on the art of quilting seriously.

I still can't believe that she is gone; it seems like part of an indecent plot of fate. Part of me wants recourse at some sort of high tribunal that must exist somewhere out there, but I don't really believe in high tribunals of divine origin or their ability to comprehend and adjudicate complex matters like life and death. If they did exist, I'd want to put them on notice that all my wrath is forever directed at them for their failure to intervene.

The hospital high on the mountain was supposed to provide her with the absolute best medical care. It was the place where celebrities and their families were sent since their well-being was of uncontested, highest priority. Instead, they botched one operation after the other, and left her a wreck.

The funeral was a strange event, but on the other hand, I had little to compare it with except my father's and then my mother's. What did I find disparate? The somberness of the occasion and the need people felt to chat and gossip. The spaciousness of the park versus the narrowness of the space that received the coffin. The coldness and emptiness inside juxtaposed with the gloriously sunny summer day.

The stone they put on her grave was a poor excuse for a memorial, a declaration of defeat in regards to the task of representing a myriad of memories, sentiments, and both tangible and intangible things that all make up a person's life. If a stone stands for anything, then it signifies the opaqueness of a complex person, not to mention the inability of others—even family and friends—to truly know what's going on inside. There is a reason why headstones are not made of glass. And as such, opaque as they are, they stand for the mystery of human consciousness, which exists in many walled-in pieces that will forever be separate, unable to merge.

Whenever I go through an emotional trauma, I don't recognize its poignancy at first, but discover it much later, in the way that I express myself in writing. Then it stares back at me from every page, and each piece is another discovery of myself. This is how I wound up writing a poem right after my sister died. It dealt with her death in a somewhat tangential and even superficial way, but still made me recognize the deep disturbance, the gravitational waves that gave rise to tremors of language.

I also wrote a short story at the time, which is still incomplete. But now that so much time has passed and I've decided to write a longer piece about her, I thought it should center on one summer when we were young. It was the only time I traveled with her, aside from the trips we went on much earlier with our parents. There is this picture of the two of us sitting in a ramshackle café; I forget who took it, but she is beaming with life. With this as my inspiration, I tried to get started on the story several times but was unable to write a single convincing sentence. I finally realized that the "I" was in the way of my endeavor. What the narrative needed was distance—a lot of it—so I needed to tell it in the third person, with myself entirely removed from the story.

The name of my avatar, I decided, should be Reiner. Reiner, as the weak sound of his name implies, is a nondescript person, a man without qualities—much like Ulrich, the character dreamt up by *Robert Musil* a century ago. After giving him some subtle training in gestures, gait, and timbre of voice, I granted him absolute discretion in what he should feel, think, and say. I don't know at this point if he agrees with all the traits I gave him, but it's a start.

Reiner knows a lot about me, except for the stories about the flea circus and the northern lights. I didn't think they would help. He also doesn't know that, without my sister's untimely death, he would never have made an appearance. That would be a lot for an ambitious guy like him to swallow. And, I decided to give him some extra license at the end—up to a point.

PART I

Matala

Chapter 1

"We suffer and we learn.
And we will know the future when it comes.
Greet it too early, weep too soon.
It all comes clear in the light of day. "
—Aeschylus, *Agamemnon*

"Look at them! They are sweating like pigs!" Monika said, pointing at the workers as they prepared the boat for landing, and moved about with a heavy gait.

"It's hard work for sure," Reiner said. "Pigs don't sweat, by the way."

"God! You are *so* literal!"

Reiner and his sister stood on the giant ferry alongside a throng of passengers, eagerly awaiting the clanging sound of the heavy iron door meeting concrete. As it came nearer—the mysterious sliver of land that had invoked stories of demigod heroes from thirty centuries ago—the landscape changed into one made of metal, concrete and dust. But the port of Piraeus, located near Athens, had already prepared the siblings for the clutter and noise of Heraklion, Crete's main port.

"Incredible! These iron chains are thicker than a man's arm," Monika said. "I'm so excited!"

"We'll have a great time, little sister!"

She glanced at him with a frown, but it quickly turned back into a smile. Yes, he was just kidding. Only three years separated them, and at her age of twenty, all of their differences in maturity were close to diminishing. In fact, traveling alone with her for the first time had made him look at her in a new way. Tall, with wide-set blue eyes and auburn hair, she was striking, and unlike anybody else in the crowd on the ferry.

Without noting the significance of setting foot on the land of the legendary Agamemnon, king of Mycenae, and without paying much attention to the taxicabs, street vendors, tourists, housewives laden with

"

grocery bags, vendors' voices, screeching brakes, honking cars, and braying donkeys, Reiner and Monika made their way from the landing to the youth hostel nestled in the middle of town.

The first stretch of the road was a vast construction site that liberally bellowed dust into the sky and caked their gums with the bitter taste of bitumen, reminding Reiner of resin tapped from a pine tree. There was no sidewalk; cars and mopeds buzzed by just centimeters away.

"Jesus! Where exactly do they want us to walk? This is dangerous," Reiner said.

Stopping at a couple of street corners, he unfolded the map they bought in Piraeus to make sure they were still headed in the right direction. He had to hold it at an angle to prevent the breeze from wrapping it around his chest. The map showed only the main roads, and all in Greek, so navigation was going to be difficult.

"I'm tired," Monika said. She had not slept on the ferry as she'd intended, and now she was visibly crumbling with every step.

"What do you want me to do about it?" Reiner said.

He was slightly annoyed with her, and the prospect of having to give her exclusive attention for the whole next week began to sink in. But then he caught himself and considered that his irritation was probably nothing more than a byproduct of his own weariness after the long journey.

Being her keeper was an honor; it was evidence of the trust their parents had placed in him. It all started with Mutti worrying that her daughter would fall into lecherous hands. There was so much lust stored up in Mediterranean men, she'd heard, and only Reiner's presence would shield her daughter from the worst.

"Yes, yes," he had told his mother, half joking because he thought she was blowing the situation out of proportion. "Trust me, I will not let her out of my sight. *Kein Problem!*"

They found the hostel on a narrow side street, marked with a flimsy triangular sign, and approached the reception desk. A tall, wiry man with intense black eyes and a goatee asked them a lot of questions in a combination of Greek, German, and English. Reiner thought he looked a bit like Don Quixote—at least in the way Cervantes's warrior was depicted on the cover of children's books.

"Hello, *yassou! Wie geht's?* Where from are you?" He looked at the passports they handed to him. "Ah you come from Germany, I see! Where are you headed to?"

"We want to see the place with a thousand windmills," Reiner said.

"Lasithi Plateau? Nice, but windy as hell. I think this was the whole point of putting windmills there, yes?" He laughed at his own joke, and Reiner acknowledged it with a quick smile. "And actually, there may be just a few dozens left, if you are lucky. You can see them from the bus driving through. There is no point getting out. What else?"

"There is this gorge we've heard of," Monika said. She didn't mention Matala, the one destination they were looking forward to the most. Matala had a famous beach and caves populated by hippies from all over Europe. Some had even come from as far away as the United States. Matala was on the southern coast of the narrow island, at the end of a road running straight out of Iraklion.

"The Samaria Gorge, of course! Beautiful place out west. But before you go anywhere, don't forget the palace of Knossos. Just a couple of hours from here." The man turned around and pointed to a poster on the wall with an assortment of ruins. If there had once been a palace there, only rubble was left by the time those photos were taken. "The king of kings, Agamemnon: the biggest attraction of all." Going back to the business at hand, he checked a roster of available rooms. "Is it OK for you to be separated? We have one dorm for girls and one for boys, then a little dorm in between for married couples."

"We are brother and sister," Reiner said.

"That settles it. You won't mind being split up." It was an order, not a question.

He pointed to another poster on the wall that outlined a litany of things they were not supposed to do while staying at the hostel in Greek, French, German, and English: bring food into the dorm, smoke, drink alcohol, bring someone over to sleep with (*consort*, the flyer said in English, and *beischlafen* in German), speak loudly, keep the lights on, or use a flashlight for reading after ten o'clock in the evening. Except for the last part, nothing sounded too onerous, and as Germans, they were used to following rules.

The man showed them the three dorm entrances, separated from one another by gender and marital status, as was indicated by the crude symbols painted on the tops of the doorframes.

"Let me guess. Two rings intertwined is for married couples," Reiner said.

The man simply put his thumb up in response.

"I need to stretch out," Monika told her brother as they parted. "See you in an hour?"

"Maybe later than that," he said. It had been a long day.

Reiner dumped his belongings on the upper bunk bed, just in case he had to share with another traveler, and sorted out his bathing suit and towel. He fished the notebook out of his backpack and opened it up. The empty page stared back at him in the dim room; the blinds were drawn all the way down to keep the heat out. Thin pencils of light, like legs of a spider, stretched out onto the walls from the sides of the window, advanced on the floor, and inched up to the top of the mattress he was sitting on. He'd never kept a diary before, but had read those left behind by a lot of famous writers and artists. Goethe's *Italian Journey*, for one, was drilled into him in high school.

He'd decided that keeping a diary was a way to become a writer himself, something he had always dreamed of. It would work like a bootstrap; he would write down things from memory, and, upon rereading his entries, would take issue with the way he expressed it. So, he'd redo it all in a more refined, embellished way, then continue on in these cycles of incremental improvements. At least, it was a start. He was certain he would never reach the perfection of Goethe's writing, or come up with anything resembling the master's sketches of Italian landscapes and buildings. Reiner knew he was constitutionally bad at drawing. People he tried to draw looked almost willfully naïve and pathetic. They also looked stressed, as if they were squirming to escape from his incompetent hand. Their eyes and ears were often misplaced, and their arms always bent at strange angles.

Agamemnon, he wrote and then underlined to mark it as the title of his first entry. *Palace of Knossos. Just two hours by bus from Heraklion.*

Right then he remembered the joke his brother had told him several times when he was younger, about a refined man who would say *Agamemnon* when he meant to say *angenommen,* the word for *assumed* or *accepted* in German. By retelling this joke—not just to Reiner, but also to his friends and classmates—his brother had wittingly (or perhaps unwittingly) shown that he'd adopted their father's disdain for highfalutin people and swindlers, or *Hochstapler,* the likes of Thomas Mann's *Felix Krull.* Their father's poor opinion was nurtured by frequent exposure to a rich cousin who had a big belly and a pompous way of speaking, and who would stare at you with unwavering eyes that betrayed his conviction of superiority, until you turned your face away.

Angenommen, Reiner added to the title. *We will soon see Knossos, the palace of King Agamemnon,* he continued. *Wir sind angekommen/ we have arrived/ in the awesome land of Agamemnon.*

A beginning had been made, and beginnings were notoriously hard.

In high school lessons, Agamemnon the king had always come across as a legend, and it was difficult to believe there was still a tangible place to be found on this earth, replete with historical artifacts, where he had actually roamed and held court. Reiner was tempted to visit the palace and look for a piece of ceramic to take home with him—just a sliver!— but he knew it was strictly forbidden and could land him in jail. This was why the whole idea of going to Knossos had lost its attraction for him.

In the end, what counted was the brittle stuff in your hands, the tangible proof that there was a chain of molecular traces going all the way back to the time three thousand years ago.

Chapter 2

"We're not gods; why then expect to enjoy a lifetime of
unbroken happiness?"
—Aeschylus, *Agamemnon*

Reiner awoke to the distant braying of a donkey and found himself lying on his notebook, bathed in sweat. One of the pages was folded over, its edge torn.

In his dream, a snake had slipped into his shirt as he was asleep in the grass of a large meadow. When he jolted awake, still in his dream, it was pitch-dark and he was frightened, unable to recall how he got there. Just before he awoke for real, he had reached back to dislodge the snake.

It took him a minute to collect his thoughts in the strange surroundings of the dorm. His notebook, which was supposed to survive at least two weeks of traveling—depending on the number of impressions he accumulated and the time he would have to put his thoughts on paper—was off to a rough start.

After washing up and exchanging his sweaty shirt for a crumpled but clean one in the common bathroom, he met up with his sister in the lobby. Two hours had gone by. She yawned and still looked tired and a bit disheveled with her hair in disarray, but she wore a bright red T-shirt that seemed to signal her readiness for adventure.

"I'm hungry," she said, "like a wolf!"

She opened her mouth wide and growled at him, but it did not amount to anything remotely frightening. Nor did Reiner find it funny as she'd intended.

Here we go again. Another problem to fix.

"I fell asleep," he said. "When I woke up, I didn't know where I was until I heard a donkey."

"When you hear a donkey, you could just as easily be in Spain," Monika said. "Or Italy, for that matter."

"Ah quibble day." He looked at her with a frown. "How do I deserve this?"

They asked the Don Quixote look-alike at the reception desk for a place where they could get a quick bite, and where to find a bus that would take them to the beach.

"When you leave the building, go to the right. At the next corner, there is a fig tree. Go straight. At the next intersection after that, take a left and look for a narrow walkway to the right. At the end, you see a drugstore called Philippides."

And on it went, one haphazard landmark after the other, all rattled off in the man's Greek-tinted German singsong as his goatee danced up and down in time with his narrow chin.

"Right, fig tree, left, right, Philippides," Reiner repeated. "That sounds simple enough."

They walked a few blocks, trying to follow his directions, but none of his them made sense in practice. If there had ever been a fig tree, it was long gone. They did find a drugstore, but its sign said it was called Nikalaou, a far cry from Philippides. Just when they were about to give up, a delicious whiff of grilled food wafted their way. They followed the scent to a little stand draped with triangular blue-and-white flags.

A heavyset man with big, bushy eyebrows greeted them with open arms, as if they were his old friends. "You German?"

Reiner and Monika looked at each other, equally surprised, before Reiner asked, "How did you know?"

The merchant gestured to his right eye with his finger, hinting at his detective skills. "The clothes you are wearing, my friends!" he said. Continuing in his Greek touristic version of German, he added, "*Khartoffeln!* Potato patties, my friends! Delicious, freshly baked, authentic Greek potato patties!"

He handed a piece on a toothpick for Monika to try, and she nodded her approval.

"Fantastic," she said. "Let's get lots."

"Give me ten." Reiner paid with the first coins of the drachmas he had exchanged for Deutschmarks earlier on.

"Sure my friend."

The merchant wrapped up the pile of potato patties so they could eat them on the bus. Reiner was weary of being called *friend,* which he considered to be something of an insult to the very concept of friendship since, in his mind, it was something that developed over weeks, months, and years—certainly not seconds. In Germany, *Sie* only yielded to the brotherly or sisterly *du* after a long time, usually in a heartfelt ceremony involving at least two glasses of wine and—in some northern regions—an additional ounce of salt to stand in for so many joint breakfasts, lunches and dinners.

Following the man's directions, they found the bus stop not far away, but had to wait more than half an hour in the glaring sun.

"What did they do with all the trees?" Reiner mumbled, more to himself than to his sister. "The roads are mostly naked."

"They built ships," Monika said. "I heard somewhere that Greece was covered with forests until they started building ships."

"Pathetic," Reiner said. "Ships for the Argonauts, ships for the Peloponnesian War. And now look what is left!"

"The Trojan Horse! That was all wood, too," Monika said.

"Of course. How could we forget? That alone probably took out a dozen good cedar trees."

They laughed at their own jokes and high-fived. The other people waiting for the bus, farmers by the look of them and not privy to the siblings' historical insights, looked askance at them.

The bus was half full of tourists all heading for the beach. It rumbled along the coast past the outskirts of Heraklion, where partially finished apartment buildings were propped up left and right on concrete stilts. The siblings ate the potato patties and got the oil all over their hands; they had to wipe them off on their clothes because the street vendor/ detective had not given them paper napkins. Some of the mess dripped onto the red plastic seats they were sitting on, but nobody seemed to care.

The whole urban scene passing by outside the bus windows was quite disorganized, the very opposite of the kind of city planning they were used to, but on the outskirts the effect was magnified by the sight of scorched earth and trash—bottles, flattened cans, plastic bags, worn and mud-encrusted shoes—lining the road left and right.

Reiner saw a brown stray dog running along the border of the asphalt as if to assert an unalienable right to a narrow but potentially infinite domain on that side of the road. The bus narrowly avoided the animal; either the driver was distracted, or he was unwilling to respect the territorial claim.

Chapter 3

Despite the bright sun it was windy and cool on the treeless beach. The water was deep blue, but the wind ruffled the surface into miniature whitecaps. The wind was so cold that Monika decided not to change into her beach clothes. Instead, she crouched down and started drawing figures into the sand: circles and squares, and some lopsided squiggles that could have been either octopuses or windmills or water spiraling down a drain.

Reiner watched her doodle for awhile. "Are you sure you don't want to swim?"

"I don't want to freeze my ass off, thank you very much."

The water was frigid at first, but soon his body felt as if it were connected with the vast body of the Mediterranean Sea. A sense of deep satisfaction set in as he moved through the water with rhythmic breast-strokes. He kept his hands slightly open because he enjoyed the sensation of the water slipping though the spaces between his fingers almost like honey. He swam for a long time, and there came a point when it seemed he could easily go on for an hour or even longer.

Then he saw Monika wave at him, a tiny figure on the beach moving her arms like a windmill, and he swam right back. He felt whole; every step on the warm sand felt right.

"Why did you wave? Were you worried?" he asked.

"No, I just felt like waving. How was it?"

"Terrific. Try it yourself," he said.

"Are you kidding? I'd freeze my butt off."

"At first, but there was a point where I was the water and the water was me. I could have gone on forever."

"Yeah, right. And leave me here to fend for myself!"

"Ah, come on. You would manage," he said.

She often liked to depict herself as helpless, and he felt he had to set her straight from time to time, even if only in jest.

After drying himself off and walking around a bit, sinking into the sand with each step, he felt very tired from using muscles that he'd neglected to use for years. He had always avoided swimming pools at home because the monotonous back-and-forth swimming was terribly boring. The only upside was seeing the girls in their minimal outfits, especially after bikinis made their debut in the province of his home-town. So, sometimes he would just take a few token leaps into the water, then dry himself off and sit on a stool at the milk bar under fake palm trees to sip one of those blueberry shakes and watch the girls emerge one by one from the changing room. They similarly treated the pool as a mere decoration of their hangout spot and giggled their heads off when someone paid them any attention.

Today, though, there was nothing to look at except the beach itself and his sister, who didn't count. He put his shirt back on, smoothed out a patch of sand with his hands, stretched out face down on his towel with the image of Brigitte Bardot in her role in *La Vérité*, and fell asleep in no time.

* * *

When he awoke, Reiner found it difficult to move. The backs of both of his legs had turned crimson and were in a serious amount of pain.

"Ti-po-ta," Monika spelled out, trying out the singing sound. "*Tipota, tipota.*"

She was sitting next to him, leafing through the little Greek-English dictionary she had fished out of his backpack.

"My legs are burnt," he said. "Badly. You should have woken me up. But what does *tipota* mean?"

"It means *nothing*. It also means *anything*."

"Makes a lot of sense." He managed to smile in spite of his condition.

"And this business about waking you up?" she said. "Sleeping without any cover was your decision. Am I supposed to check your knees every minute?"

"Every *second*. That's what sisters are for."

"Yeah, right."

The dull ache on the back of his knees was almost unbearable by then, especially when he stretched them as he got up and started walking. They found the bus stop and waited three quarters of an hour with two older women who had a brown goat on a leash. The goat regarded him with its shifty eyes, and he wondered if it thrived on *schadenfreude*, as if the animal sensed his agony and drew some sick comfort from it.

Goats were such strange, alien creatures anyway, like fur draped over a leftover scaffold and hastily nailed together.

The two women tried to talk with them in Greek, but gave up after a lot of gesturing.

When they got back to the youth hostel, with Reiner walking the final stretch next to Monika with his knees bent like a monkey's, he eased onto his bunk bed and assumed the fetal position. He barely took notice of the bustle in the hostel from the last ferry of the day spilling its human cargo into the port.

"What am I supposed to do now?" Monika asked, folding her arms in front of her chest, still in her red T-shirt. She had simply followed him into the boys dorm, ignoring the strict rules. She was all energy now, but she'd also done nothing with her day except lie on the beach fully dressed and study the dictionary.

"Just leave me be," he groaned. "I don't know what to suggest. Walk around a bit, have a look at the town. Buy yourself an ice cream!" He lifted his head as an idea came to him. "Actually, since you are asking, you can get me some type of ointment for my skin."

"I don't speak a single word of Greek."

"You know that one word: *tipota*."

"Right, I'll go into a pharmacy and ask for nothing. Or for anything."

"Some people actually understand a bit of German because there are all these tourists around," he said. "The merchants pick up a few words, that's just good business. Remember the guy who sold us the patties? Just try German! But speak slowly. Oh, and before I forget, can you get me a postcard for Almut? And a stamp?"

"You want me to buy you a postcard for your girlfriend?" Monika asked, spreading her hands out in surprise. "What kind?"

"I don't know, just something showing something from here."

"Knossos? The palace?"

"Sure, that's a great idea. Except there are only ruins left. Perhaps one of those pictures with people dressed up in costumes, dancing? Or mosaics from somewhere—mosaics always look fresh like they've been done yesterday."

After Monika left, Reiner lay motionless, his eyes trained on the low ceiling he could reach with his outstretched hand if he wanted to, and pondered the extent of his stupidity. He could have put the towel over the back of his legs. He should have known something about the fierce intensity of the sun in Greece. But, he was also still mad at his sister. She had watched his legs turn red and done absolutely nothing about it.

The light seeping in between the blinds on the window had shifted upward and crept up onto the mattress. The sun, muted and screened off, had still managed to follow him into this dark room, mock his pain, and laugh at his pathetic victimhood.

He had visited Greece once before, on a reckless trip three years ago with two of his friends. They drove an old, pale blue Peugeot all the way down the coast of Yugoslavia. The outdated car in its bent, *katzenbuckel* shape had reminded him of the hunchback of Notre-Dame. Most of the main highway was a dirt road with loose gravel. One of his friends was from South Africa but had a Dutch-sounding name and eyes like an octopus except for their watery-blue color and their ability to move in their sockets. The other friend was from his math class in college.

That was the first time he had seen the Parthenon on the Acropolis in Athens. But to Reiner, the experience was disappointing because the colossal building reminded him of bombastic high school reading material, and at the same time, his own insignificance. The depth of millennia was unfathomable, and he was unable to empathize with the people who once cared to erect a temple dedicated to Athena—a goddess who lived on a mountaintop close to the sky and was known to quarrel regularly with the other immortals sharing her lofty abode!

He could not relate to any of it in a meaningful way, and neither could his friends.

The final destination of their journey was Ithaca, the island of Odysseus. But it, too, proved to be a disappointment; it was a childless, cheerless, soundless place except for the crowing of roosters in the morning and the braying of donkeys in the afternoon. Slow-moving retirees who had made their money in Australia or America by running diners with Formica tables and plastic flowers made up the largest demographic there.

He and his friends had discovered later—after fights over food as the money was running out, after ceasing to speak to each other because of their differences of opinion on Apartheid, and after the Peugeot finally broke down—that modern Ithaca was an entirely different island, and the real ancient Ithaca inhabited by Odysseus and Penelope was miles away.

He looked at the meager beginning of his diary, and evaluated the thickness of the notebook, the number of empty pages, and the amount of time he had yet to cover. Yes, his dream was to be a writer, but writers needed to have something to write about; Reiner's greatest fear was that he never would.

Goethe—from what he had gathered in high school—had it so much better. Whenever he ran out of things to write about, he could switch to drawing. Whenever he was sick of drawing, he switched back to writing. On the whole, the general distribution of talents seemed extremely unfair.

After a long hour, Monika came back with an herbal ointment she'd been assured had worked on countless others for at least three millennia. This time, she had to argue her way into the boys dorm.

"I'm his sister, for God's sake," she told Don Quixote when he intercepted her at the forbidden entrance.

She helped Reiner spread the ointment on the back of his legs. Even though she tried to be careful that her touch wasn't too rough or abrupt, he sometimes opened his mouth to inhale forcefully to keep from cursing.

"You are a physical therapist," Reiner said. "Your hands should be like silk."

"Your skin is the problem, not my hands."

She told him there were postcards to choose from at the front desk downstairs—the palace of Knossos as a rebuilt model with frescos and lots of warm colors, or dancers dressed in blue and white—but she'd found no stamps.

"It can't be that urgent," she said with a pout, as if daring him to object. "Almut can wait."

Reiner had already assumed Monika wouldn't go out of her way to get something for his girlfriend. He suspected she might not even have tried to find the post office. The two were not exactly on cordial terms. Rather, there was something like respectful recognition of each other's roles in his life. He wondered if this was pretty much a given between sisters and girlfriends across the board but had never talked about this with either woman.

"OK, thanks for the ointment," he said. "I guess I'm pretty useless today. Just walk around some more and enjoy the town for me."

He'd been full of excitement at the idea of spending time with his sister. As long as he could remember, any quality time spent together had only been under the umbrella of their family, their siblinghood an unquestioned, natural condition. Now he'd felt a bit like a selfless knight, taking her out into the world without the familial obligation. Traveling with him, without their parents and elder siblings, she would have a chance to define herself and become a real person, and he would get to know her better in turn.

Until now, Mutti kept saying her hairdo was never right. Her sister criticized her for her total lack of initiative. Her oldest brother mocked her for her failure in math. Father expected nothing from her since she was a girl. This history of hostility and negligence, as well as the memory of Reiner's own criticism of Monika, had accumulated over time and weighed heavily on him. He had often expected her to share his excitement about one scientific topic or another, but her mind had always seemed to work in ways quite different than his, and he suspected she sometimes faked excitement just to humor him.

Actually, the story was a bit more complicated since he had made all his original plans with Almut, who had canceled at the very last moment due to the flu. On impulse, he asked his sister to come along instead, and she was able to switch her schedule around with one of her colleagues. He was glad that things turned out this way; over the years, he had felt guilty about having spent so little time with her.

But it was not just that; it was more the sense that he'd neglected her as a person even as he grew up with her. The coming years, with him living in a different city, would only widen the chasm, so this was a good time—perhaps the last chance—to fix it.

He wondered how Almut was doing now, in her mother's care and probably surrounded by the stuffed animals he had made so much fun of when he first saw them. That was a year after he met her; she'd invited him to her birthday party at her parents' house, and he had seen the whole menagerie when her bedroom door was left open: two bears, a dragon, a stretched dog, and three cats. Sickness always sends a person back into the days of early childhood. He imagined the light coming through her window, landing on her quilt and slowly advancing with the minutes and hours, as had happened to him only moments before. He tried to imagine the boring hours of languishing in a sickbed with nothing for her to do but read a Gothic novel or watch TV. She had given him the OK to go without her, and he had to respect her for it.

"Why should we both suffer? It wouldn't make any sense," Almut had said.

She was right, of course. He would have dreaded watching the summer fly by without his dream of visiting Crete coming true, and he'd sensed that after he started graduate school in the fall, there would be few opportunities to take sufficient time off.

The sunburn had forced Reiner into an awkward position. He was totally unprepared for this state of weakness and complete passivity. In fact, for at least a couple of days, he wasn't sure how he'd manage without the help of his sister.

Chapter 4

The next day, because of the delay in their plans due to Reiner's miserable, self-inflicted condition, Monika wandered off and ran into a student from Germany, a tourist who'd arrived on the same ferry they took the day before. Much later, Reiner was haunted by the idea that his stupid decision to go to the beach without sun protection had changed his sister's fate.

He spent the day quietly, lying stock-still on his bunk bed, afraid to move for fear of aggravating the pain. Occasionally, a newcomer arrived and tossed his bag on one of the available beds. In the evening, Reiner was back on his feet, but forced to walk around in a crouched, pitiful position since the affected skin was still taut and sore despite Monika's ancient-ointment treatment.

At five o'clock, as they'd agreed, he went down to wait for her in the courtyard. Half an hour later, he was taken aback when his sister showed up with a man in tow.

"Reiner, this is Bernhard."

Bernhard was tall, blue-eyed, blond, and handsome in a way that spoke to the evenness of his features, though to Reiner they seemed a bit too good to be true. Based on the movies he'd seen, Bernhard looked like someone belonging to a secret service. They looked at each other briefly and coolly; each said hi, and that was all. Bernhard then excused himself, saying he was staying in a bed-and-breakfast nearby, and presently had to do some errands. His accent carried a hint of the Rhineland dialect, in that the l's in his speech came out in a broad way, and the *Ich* sounded more like *Isch*. Still, on the whole, his German was OK, and not a constant irritant as some dialects from further east were. Reiner was reminded of his own attempts to purge every bit of his heavy native tongue to make himself presentable to the world.

Later that evening, knees still wobbling, Reiner insisted on taking his sister to a Greek restaurant.

"Are you sure?" she asked. "You still look like a lobster and hobble along like an old man."

"I'm sure. Don't worry about me."

They walked along a promenade by the harbor and looked out at the fancy yachts bobbing softly, dreamily, and found a restaurant opposite the massive fortress. The fortress itself was crenelated on top and sat there like an oversize shoebox, stretching the length of three city blocks. It was entirely devoid of windows, but dozens of yellow lights made it look as if it were hovering above the ground like a Fata Morgana. The people moving by on the promenade were reduced to black silhouettes.

The siblings sat under garlands of blue, white, red, and yellow lights strung up between fig trees. Here and there, an octopus dangled to dry. A cat strolled by, brushing its upturned tail against Reiner's legs. The mustached waiter was a charmer, greeting Monika with compliments laced with the few German words he knew and going out of his way to make her feel special. Greek men seemed to have something for blue eyes, Reiner observed. She beamed under his attention.

In the distance, strange music started up: repetitive and entrancing and promising no end. It was as though each moment was played for the listener's comfort, just to reassure them that in fact no time had passed at all. It was music both defying and glorifying death.

"What is it that we are hearing?" Reiner asked the waiter.

"*Mantinades*," he said. "Songs of love and sorrow and return. You like?"

"Very, very much," Monika answered for her brother, returning the waiter's earlier compliments by looking directly in his eyes with a big smile.

"And what is this fortress we are seeing?" Reiner asked.

"Oh, it's called *Koules*. It's been here forever."

The waiter shrugged and asked a colleague who was just rushing by for more information.

"Venetian, sixteenth century."

Necessary but brutal architecture was Reiner's take. He had taken a course in urban design at his *studium generale* as part of the liberal arts program. He had also read a book titled *Architecture without Architects*, and ever since had walked around with critical, knowing eyes, as if he were an expert.

The walls were slightly inclined and built from enormous slabs—too thick to be penetrated by cannonballs. They also were too high and steep to be scaled by 16th century attackers, but no longer posed an obstacle to mountaineers with today's sophisticated gear.

The fortress was faceless, a disturbing apparition he thought he had encountered before but couldn't quite place in his memory. And then it came to him: Ingmar Bergman's *Wild Strawberries*. A haunting image at the beginning of the movie showed the back of a man as he walked down an alley, passing a clock without hands. Then, as the camera switched direction to display the man's approaching face, it was revealed to be featureless and smooth like a baldpate, lacking mouth, nose, and eyes. Reiner could not remember if the scene was part of one of the character's dreams, or some other device embedded in the narrative. He had seen that movie as a teenager on his first real date and had talked with the girl for hours afterward since she did not see the point of the movie. They split up not much later on since there was nothing left to talk about in real life either.

"What's wrong?" Monika asked. "You look like you've seen a ghost."

"Ah, it's nothing," he said. They ordered *souvlaki, tzatziki*, Greek salad, and a carafe of white wine. The waiter brought the wine in an orange, anodized aluminum can and poured it into two heavy water glasses, the ones with vertical grooves carved out all around to serve as grips for one's fingers.

"*Prost*," Reiner said as he lifted his cup in a toast to his sister.

"It's *yassou* in the dictionary," she said.

"OK, *yassou*. Whatever."

Her mention of the dictionary reminded him painfully of the time on the beach, and he squirmed a little in his chair.

The wine had a shocking, bitter taste that made him remember the chewing gum his elder sister Angelika prepared by chewing pine resin droplets they gathered in the woods when he was a boy. The first time she showed it to him, she gave him half of the gum she'd made. Reluctantly, he put it in his mouth; it was disgusting, still coated with her saliva and already cold.

Monika's face crumbled after she took a sip, and she set down the heavy glass. He grimaced, exchanged a glance with her, and called for the waiter.

"What kind of wine it this? There is something wrong with it."

The waiter scoffed. "How long have you been in this country? It's *retsina*: Greek wine and most popular. It is meaning to be bitter."

He went on to tell them how sailors in the olden times had added pine oil to the wine to keep it from spoiling on journeys that lasted for months.

Miraculously, they both started to love it after that first glass. Was it that they had instantly acquired the taste, or was it that they thought they could feel and taste a connection to the legendary heroes of the distant past and their windswept voyages that brought them to distant islands when it was the will of the gods?

"To the Argonauts!" Reiner said, raising his glass. "Think of Odysseus and his many years at sea!"

"To Penelope," Monika countered.

Reiner did not bring up Bernhard. In the back of his mind, he wondered if this strange man would just be forgotten by next morning anyway. He was reassured by the fact that she didn't mention her new acquaintance even once.

They made a plan for the next day to hitchhike to Matala, due south-southwest. They'd picked up a romantic notion about hitchhiking from an American movie they'd seen. It was a logical extension of the ideas of communes and saving the planet; most cars on the road weren't full of passengers, and all the energy already being spent on driving them could be used to help transport other passengers as well. Besides, the idea of meeting strangers for a few hours was quite exciting.

"I want to see real hippies," Monika said, spreading out her arms and waving them in soft, flowing motions. "There were these pictures in the *Spiegel*: the fantastic costumes they wore! I loved those colors!"

"I know, I saw the articles, too. I like the concept: communes and the whole bit. But honestly, some of them are nutcases," he said.

"I wonder how anyone can live in a cave? Seriously? Do they even have toilets?"

"They get high and imagine anything they want. They can easily imagine toilets."

"Well, that's true. But, no matter what they imagine, they need to shit, and the shit itself is real."

Reiner had to laugh in agreement at that. Ripples of the protest movement against the Vietnam War had eventually reached Germany. Universities were a fertile ground for solidarity rallies and the examination of every tenet of society. He had taken part in a circle of students discussing Karl Marx's *The Economic and Philosophic Manuscripts of 1844*, and had gotten really good at arguing its exegesis until he got distracted by a girl. He'd found the language of economic theory and an attractive woman in the same room to be at opposite ends of a gap that was hard to bridge.

With the antiauthoritarian wave came long hair and other signs of alternative living. One of Reiner's friends at college had a ring in his nose and a laughing squirrel tattooed on his left arm. The right arm was still a work in progress then, but his torso featured a stripper posing on Hamburg's Reeperbahn. Several women in his math class wore no bras under their silky blouses, and that knowledge had taken Reiner's mind off Cauchy's convergence criterion and the special functions of mathematical physics more than once.

Although he rejected the idea of being associated with hippies, long unkempt hair, dirty fingernails, and that overall *Struwwelpeter* look, he felt he'd shared with them a sense of unadulterated freedom, and the need for the natural, the authentic.

So when he first heard about the flower children, he instinctively sided with them. His father, following his own instincts and morals from pre-World War I, found them totally despicable. He had even called them useless parasites of society and whatnot. The most disturbing part of it was how frequently he used the same phrases as Hitler.

Monika, for whom everything beyond the province they'd grown up in was new and exotic, shared Reiner's excitement and sense of adventure. After all, they both came from the same stiff, Protestant town where no misstep was tolerated. It was a place where enjoyment in and of itself was suspicious and taken as a sign of frivolousness, or even a lack of character. He still associated this sour attitude with the stern look his grandmother gave him for any misdeed, any transgression of even the smallest caliber. It was a menacing, thoroughly disapproving look that made him feel he was beyond redemption. With that one look, she channeled God's unmerciful side, His Jekyll, and rained it down on her offspring.

Chapter 5

"The scent of citrus and of brittle pine
Suffused the island . . ."
—Homer, *The Odyssey*

In the morning, Bernhard came to the youth hostel. He walked, in cheerful and unshaven, his hair all over the place. He carried a backpack with a sleeping bag rolled up and fastened on top.

"I'm ready to go," he said. "I didn't know when, so I came early."

Monika blushed and greeted him. "So good to see you! How was your night?"

Reiner looked at his sister sharply, but she avoided his gaze.

"This place was OK, but a bit hot," Bernhard said, oblivious to the silent conversation happening in front of him. "No ventilation."

Apparently, Monika saw no need to discuss this change in plan with her brother. She had not said a single word at the restaurant about Bernhard joining them on any of their adventures. Reiner felt apprehensive and outmaneuvered, but considering he was the reason they'd had to spend an entire extra day in dusty, noisy Heraklion, he thought he was in no position to argue.

That didn't stop him later, however, as they checked out of the hostel, from taking her aside and hissing, "Who on earth is this guy? We don't know a single thing about him."

"He is the nicest guy in the world," she whispered back. "Believe me."

"Don't you understand? You know absolutely nothing about him. He could be a swindler, a moron, a thief."

Monika rolled her eyes, but had nothing to say in reply.

Reiner took another look at the man. Bernhard had a finely shaped nose, but there was a gap between his two front teeth, too narrow to be caused by a missing tooth. He noticed it every time Bernhard smiled. It looked quite silly, sure, but how could he hold it against him? Somehow, this imperfection led him to think about possible moral flaws Bernhard might have, about the precariousness of trusting strangers, and about the risks of running into *otherness* in general.

They walked toward the south end of the city, until houses gave way to a sporadic succession of gas stations, car repair shops, and the shoestring outlets that kept the city's inhabitants as well as the tourists supplied with the essentials.

"One thing you have to promise me," their mother had told them before they left, "is that you never, ever hitchhike. Take the bus, or trains. Too many bad things have happened; one reads about it all the time in the *Westfalentag*."

Sorry, Mutti, but this one has to give.

Her credibility had already taken a hit with her suggestion to pack umbrellas and to guard themselves against Gypsies. Besides, there were just a few buses on Crete, and no trains. And, as far as the *Westfalentag* was concerned, it was not the most reliable source of information.

With Monika positioned on the side of the main road as bait, they were all picked up within minutes by a local man heading south in his small truck. He accepted the extra passengers without objection and opened the back flap of the truck. They settled down on a heap of damp topsoil that carried a faint animal smell Reiner found difficult to place. Perhaps there was some animal dung mixed in as fertilizer? Leaning against the wooden sideboards, Monika sat with Bernhard on one side of the truck bed and Reiner claimed the other. The truck rumbled over potholes in the asphalt road, which was also interrupted by stretches of packed dirt. He enjoyed looking back as they moved, and seeing the road dwindle into a thin thread.

The air was laden with the smell of wild herbs and honey as the warm, arid summer landscape rushed by. A shimmering, blue-green tapestry of light hovered in the air. Reiner closed his eyes and absorbed the many scents swirling around them, unadulterated by his other senses. Rosemary, coriander, oregano, and thyme, all present in ever-changing mixtures: it felt like swimming in a mountain lake, where cold layers alternate with warm, and every stroke brings a new surprise. Reiner took a breath and held it for a few seconds, wishing he could just close his nostrils and take in the spectacle of light without interference for as long as he liked. He felt alive, more alive than he could ever remember.

The driver put a 45-rpm single into a record player that was mounted inside the glove box with a flimsy iron bracket and shaped like a tiny Citroen, or like a futuristic space station model drawn up in the 1950s. The music surged out through a slotted window in the back of the driver's cabin.

Everything they had seen in Greece in the last three days had this shoestring element to it; instead of serious attempts at finding a solid solution to a problem or inconvenience, there were always ingenious yet short-lived improvisations. Greeks seem to live in a world of continuous approximations.

This was the second time Reiner had heard the music of Crete, the hopping, circuitous sounds of the lyra backed by the strumming of the bouzouki. He recognized it from the distant songs they had heard while sitting in the restaurant near the fortress in Heraklion. He had never played an instrument himself but had acquired an ear for exotic music in high school. Once, he gave a presentation on jazz as part of an independent study project; perhaps bebop was the closest approximation to this music, at least in tempo, wildness, and uninhibited joy.

He recalled that his music teacher had a pockmarked face and was always friendly to him. One day, he was just gone. Rumor had it that his love of boys had gotten him fired. Reiner had not even known that there could be such a thing.

From where Reiner sat in the truck, he could turn his head and look through the back window into the cabin. A *komboloi*, a string of worry beads, was suspended from the driver's rearview mirror and swung like a pendulum every time the truck hit a pothole or even slightly changed direction. The beads were a deep honey-brown color, reminiscent of amber death traps for insects found in geological digs. The beads swung about and caught the rays of the sun, refracting and splitting them into an undulating light show.

He caught his sister in an unguarded moment, crouched but snuggled up to Bernhard, arm in arm. Her expression of bliss was not one he had seen on her before. He was tempted to get her attention, but she was occupied, and he had the sudden notion that she was just as entitled to privacy as he was. Respecting it was not something he had learned at home, where parents and siblings stormed into your room without notice.

Monika and Bernhard whispered to each other as if he weren't even there, and the wind and engine noise was too loud for Reiner to hear what they were talking about. He thought he could guess the direction it was taking, though; their bodies shook and moved in unison as the truck cleared the bumps on the road.

Watching them interact, Reiner couldn't help but fixate on the mysterious force of inertia that synchronized people and united them with unanimated matter like stones and shoes. He thought about accidents in which people were flung into the air by explosions and flew along unseen parabolas just like gravel and dirt—as if, in the greater scheme of things, their life forces counted for nothing.

It was peculiar and a bit alarming to see his sister as a desirable woman in the arms of a stranger. Reiner felt removed from the scene, as though he'd been placed on a different planet to watch her and even himself from afar. At the same time, he tried to see her through Bernhard's eyes, or through any other man's, for that matter. Looking at her now, he saw she was pretty in a distinct way, with her blue, wide-set eyes, expressive mouth, and auburn hair. Amazed, he watched as the attention she received from this young man who had brazenly invited himself to travel with them made her light up. Her eyes sparkled, her whole face was animated, and her gestures were more confident than ever.

He had to admit that he was unprepared for the situation. Officially, in the eyes of their parents, he was supposed to be his sister's chaperone, but he'd never thought about the implications of this appointment. It dawned on him that it entailed complicated judgments about the personalities and intentions of strangers. Right now, the pace at which he was able to familiarize himself with Bernhard's character lagged far behind hers, so he felt unqualified to question her actions. The mounting gap between what he understood as his mission and the reality of it made him uneasy.

Somewhere along the jittery, southward journey he must have fallen asleep. In his dream, he wore lederhosen and was taking a walk with Papa and his little sister on a *Spaziergang*, as they always did on Sunday afternoons. Reiner was on the left and Monika was on the right. She was holding Papa's good hand, but he had nothing to hold on to because Papa's other hand had no fingers left, except for the thumb. Wearing his heavy gray *Lodenmantel*, Papa linked them in a way, but also separated them.

They intended to walk through a park to the café on the other side of the hill and have lemonade and a piece of cake. The asphalt was wet, but the sun was high in the sky and the road emitted after-rain steam. Monika was furious at him about something and yelled at him, but he could not understand a single word of the unknown language she spoke. He turned to Papa for help, but Papa ignored him.

Reiner awoke when the truck rumbled to a halt.

"Where are we?" he asked his sister who was once again an adult. Their father was gone, and in his stead was Bernhard.

"About halfway there," Bernhard answered. "I saw signs along the way and checked the map as we went."

The truck had stopped just off the main road next to a small, partially built house. The house's concrete walls were slightly extended by thin struts of rusted steel that pointed up toward the sky in a hopeful sort of way. In the fields stretching out on both sides of the road, blue-green shrubs bore leaves that flickered in the sunlight. Thistles and thorns formed impenetrable shrubs that had caught plastic bags billowing in the wind; the flapping sounds they made reminded Reiner of large birds taking flight.

The driver climbed out of the truck and walked around to the back to explain why they'd stopped. His face, which Reiner had not examined before in their rush to climb on board, was suntanned into a deep honey hue, almost like the color of rust, and thoroughly crisscrossed with wrinkles. What they were able to make out from his gestures and broken English was that he had promised a friend (possibly a relative) to look after the animals kept there: two goats and a cow.

"These goats are so weird, and unashamedly brown! I never thought goats could be anything but white," Monika said as they watched the man tend to the animals, refilling their troughs with water.

"Un-a-shame-ed-ly? What on earth do you mean by that?"

"I mean that the color is so unexpected. It's more fit for a dog, or maybe a kangaroo."

"You make it sound as if they need to apologize," Reiner said, making her laugh.

His sister had a way of observing things as though they had just fallen from the sky. There was a naivety in the way she saw the world, but she also had a poetic touch, and this was the first time, even after having lived with her for so many years, that Reiner truly noticed it.

Living with your siblings could condition one to be blind to their special qualities and idiosyncrasies. Or, there was just no time and space to talk to them one-on-one and develop a sense for who they were.

Bernhard opened his backpack and pulled out a large sketchbook. The Faber-Castell brand gave him away as a serious artist. A few strokes with his sharpened yellow pencil captured the contours of the forlorn, unfinished house, of the old man bent over the trough, and the expectant animals standing by. He spent most of their break perfecting the texture and billowing shape of the olive tree, which cast a sharp shadow over the ochre ground. The light was so fierce, and the shadows of the trees so dark, that the landscape looked like a sketch already. The artist just had to absorb it with open eyes.

But absorbing it was one thing; translating it into a cohesive sequence of strokes with nothing but a pencil was another. This was the most mysterious aspect of art to Reiner: how the hand could magically reproduce a visual image received by the eye, then reconceived and reconfigured in the brain. He watched Bernhard closely and the way he appeared to take in his surroundings. He felt a sort of kinship with him, but because the uneasiness from before was still churning in his stomach, he could not bring himself to compliment his technique.

After a short while, Monika approached Bernhard and placed her hand on his shoulder. Reiner knew about her interest in the arts, in making things with her hands, but it occurred to him that this moment might be the first time he recognized that this was the way she looked at the world, too.

Just then, as if she'd heard him come to this conclusion aloud and understood what it meant for his perception of the soundness of her judgment, she cast her brother a glance that was almost triumphant. Reiner acknowledged her glance with a quick, strained smile.

"I like the light here," Bernhard said, turning toward Reiner. "It makes things seem sort of ethereal."

Reiner agreed with him tacitly about the quality of the light, though in his mind he scoffed at the addition of *sort of.* The phrase took the sheen off the fancy word and made him wonder about the aspiring architect's lack of precision.

The driver came back from his errand, leaving the animals happy and contained, and ushered his human cargo back into the truck to set out on the second leg of the journey to Matala. From the new, assertive way his sister held on to Bernhard, and from the frankness with which Bernhard's eyes met his own, Reiner saw that something had indeed changed, and that he would have to make an allowance for the presence of their new companion in the days ahead. The vacation he had sought to spend with just his sister was already over, and only a couple of days after it had begun.

Chapter 6

One by one, Reiner, Monika, and Bernhard jumped off the truck with their gear and brushed off the topsoil that had nested in the creases of their clothes. Reiner thanked the driver with one of the few Greek words they all had under their belts now: *efkaristo!* The man just smiled, lifted his head, and said, "*tipota*," before rumbling off.

"Ma-ta-la!" Monika cried out as she jumped up and down in the sand like a child. "This is just so beautiful, isn't it?"

They all stood there, letting their eyes wander over the surrounding cliffs and the distant waves swelling and finally spilling onto the beach. From the cliffs, which were staged in a large semicircle, the land sloped off toward the beach. The sea beyond was mostly calm except for the smooth waves turning over as they reached the shore, leaving white froth on the sand. Reiner noticed the delay between the sight and sound of each surge as a measure of distance and scale. The scene was a vast amphitheater, the likes of which few places on earth could match.

The cliffs were perforated by caves looking over the scenery like majestic, all-seeing eyes. This could have—and might well have—once been a grand auditorium for theatrical performances. But now, quite prosaically, groups of people sitting on blankets, wrapped in sleeping bags, or simply lying motionless on the bare sand formed little specks in the landscape, much like touches of a brush here and there in an impressionist painting. There were a few umbrellas, too, adding blotches of colors. Anyone standing or walking on the sand cast a shadow, and all those shadows were united in a ballet choreographed by the sun.

"Are we going to sleep in one of the caves?" Monika asked.

Reiner and Bernhard exchanged a look.

"Not sure about that," Reiner said. "Where would we do our business? Remember the conversation we had about toilets?'

Hearing parts of other conversations as he and his companions headed toward the water, Reiner picked up fragments of French,

German, Spanish, English, and Dutch—the native tongues of tourists from every corner of Europe. Other than German, he spoke only English, but recognized a few other languages by their cadences and a few more common words. There was a French hippie who had a ring in his nose and wore rimless glasses like John Lennon, but otherwise he looked much like a poodle because of his unusually curly hair. And there was a woman speaking Dutch who wore a transparent blouse and nothing underneath, as well as a blue skirt with seahorses on it that reached all the way to the ground.

They arrived at the *kafeneio* on the beach; it was a little wooden hut with an extended roof made of dried palm leaves and supported by stakes planted in plastic barrels filled with concrete. They sat down at one of the tables in the shade. Thin shards of light filtered in from above, but the roof protected them from the simmering heat. They ordered the only items on the handwritten food menu: a Greek salad with an omelet, and a kilogram of *retsina*. Ordering wine by its mass, not its volume, was a new experience for Reiner, but it seemed to make sense since wasn't mass the only true currency in the universe? The owner served the *retsina* in an anodized aluminum can and poured it into their water glasses.

"*Yassas!*" they all toasted and Reiner relished the taste of bitter pine oil again.

"So, what is it you study?" Reiner inquired, leaning forward on his elbows though the four-legged table was a little shaky.

"Architecture," Bernhard replied softly, taking his gaze off Monika for only as long as necessary. Monika continued to look at him with dreamy eyes, paying no attention to her brother's interrogation.

"And where do you study?"

"In Bonn."

"Where in Bonn?"

"At the university."

They ate in silence as the sun neared the horizon. The cliffs around them had turned orange, and the water azure, just as the brochure back home had promised. Reiner thought Bernhard was putting himself at a bit of a disadvantage with his monosyllabic answers. He was peculiar; not exactly shy, but he seemed to lack interest in conversation, as though he regarded Reiner as nothing more than necessary ballast in a larger scheme. Reiner sharpened his focus so as to be ready to quip in retaliation if it came to that. He reconsidered his passivity, and decided to take his parents' chaperone mandate more seriously.

His opinion of architects was ambivalent. The *Bauhaus*, with its functionality but total absence of charm, was the result of a revolt against decorative elements that bloomed a century earlier, but he felt the revolt went too far. Too many contemporary architects had come up with radical plans for urban redesign, experimenting with peoples' lives on a grand scale. Someone had told him, for instance, that at one point in the history of the German post-war school of architecture, trees were no longer considered a legitimate element of habitat or composition; instead, they were regarded as superfluous, romantic holdovers of the past.

"Do you like trees?" he asked Bernhard.

Bernhard put his fork down and regarded him with wide eyes. "Do I like *what?*"

"Trees. I can't point at any particular example here since it's all rocks and sand."

"I know what trees are. I thought I didn't hear you right. This is like…excuse me, but it's like asking me if I like nouns."

"Well, not exactly. You are an architect and build tangible things, not sentences. I'm asking you how trees figure into your work?"

"I'm not an architect—not yet. But once I am, I will integrate trees in my blueprints. They were here first, after all."

That answer, so close to his heart, won Reiner over. He lifted his glass and toasted him. "To trees and all other firstcomers!"

Bernhard seemed surprised by the change from initial coolness to something bordering an embrace.

"Can I say something completely unrelated?" Monika said, leaning forward. She'd been quietly picking at her omelet while they discussed the merits of trees. Reiner and Bernhard looked at each other for a quick moment, and both nodded at the same time for her to continue. She smiled. "There was this plant I saw on the way here. You know how much I like plants. I saw agaves in bloom for the first time: a big stem, a shaft coming out of nowhere, a kind of sudden spurt upward to the sky. It was so fantastic! I wished I could plant one at home."

Her outburst was greeted with silence. An agave houseplant back in Germany? Holy shit! She'd need to cut a hole in the ceiling for the flower mast to poke through. Reiner didn't feel like lecturing her about climate zones, and he sensed Bernhard was holding back as well. He also may have gotten a bit distracted by the obvious phallic allusion, but thankfully didn't spell it out for them. Reiner felt that, whatever the reason, their prolonged silence had to be hurtful to her.

"There are actually places in Germany where they can grow," he finally said. "Like Heidelberg: tropical plants do quite well there."

Monika gave him a thankful smile.

It was at this point that Bernhard, perhaps inspired by his share of *retsina*, began a speech with no relation to the subjects at hand. It made more than up for the curtness Reiner had noted before.

"Where I come from, we dress up as fools in early spring. "For a few weeks, everything is upside down." He spread his hands out, turning his palms up, then down. "I think it's a release of some sort because most of the year people are responsible and boring. Maybe the wine makes me think of it now. So, last year in spring—not this past spring—I dressed up as a chicken and went to one of those balls of the butcher's guild or the shoemaker's guild or the God-knows-what guild." Here he had his shoulders raised, apparently for wings. "I was all by myself because I had just split up with my girlfriend, and I ran into a woman dressed up as a rooster. We sort of acknowledged the coincidence with some forced clucking and—"

"Are you still split up?" Monika's face had grown pinched during Bernhard's rambling speech.

"My girlfriend? Yes, of course. When I split up, I split up for good. I'm now talking about that woman dressed up as a rooster."

"You were cross-dressing," Reiner said.

"I didn't think of that! So, she takes her mask off, and you know who she was? My math teacher from high school."

"Does this story have a point?" Reiner asked.

He knew it was a hostile question, but it was the type of banter he and his sister had learned from their older siblings at the dinner table.

"The point is, we took our feathers off and danced together like wild. And she was my tangent, and I was her cotangent that night, if you will. All those years of listening to her teach math and I never knew about the fire inside of her."

Reiner exchanged a glance of bewilderment with Monika. *Cotangent?* This man might very well have been a good artist, but he sure peddled in disjointed anecdotes.

It had grown dark as the sun hastily followed its trajectory in the southern latitudes. They paid what seemed an excessive amount of drachmas for their meal and walked up the beach toward the cliffs to find a spot in the shade to drop their sleeping bags. Reiner felt the *retsina* in his bones as he navigated the sand's unexpected indentations and elevations. At one point, he stumbled and fell, but the sand and the bag he carried cushioned the impact; he got up quickly and laughed as he brushed the sand off his shirt.

Bernhard's sleeping bag was expansive, and Monika slipped into it with him without a word to or a glance at Reiner. Reiner lay on his back in his own sleeping bag a few yards away from the young lovers, looking at the sky above. It was the first time he'd seen the stars shine so brilliantly. They came out one by one in the darkening, cloudless sky, and hesitantly started to form discernible patterns.

He heard whispers, but failed to catch a single word. The presence of a man right next to him in a sleeping bag with his sister was awkward, and he didn't quite know how to handle it. Then he thought of Almut, and it gave him a sense of perspective. If she were here with him right now, he would sure as hell welcome her in his sleeping bag, and nobody in the world would talk him out of it. He wondered if there was a public phone somewhere on this beach so he could call her and see how she was.

At any rate, the next day would bring some kind of resolution. As his mother always said, "Tomorrow the night is over."

He fell asleep, breathing with the rhythm of the sea.

Chapter 7

The sounds of the waves were still with him when he woke; it was as if a mere second had passed since he last heard Monika and Bernhard whispering in their nest. Reiner was bathed in merciless light, and the side of his sleeping bag facing the rising sun was hot. The sea was a pale blue, its surface undulating with large patches of white foam.

Turning over, he saw no trace of his sister or her beau. There was nothing but a shallow indentation—the imprint their sleeping bag had left in the sand—and footprints around it leading everywhere and nowhere.

He was fully awake now, his mind racing through the possibilities. They were both healthy, strong people, unlikely to let themselves be kidnapped, and there was no sign of a struggle. Clearly, they'd left of their own volition. With a sinking feeling, he crawled out of his sleeping bag, got to his feet, and looked around. It occurred to him that they might have gotten no farther away than the *kafeneio*, but when he looked down toward the beach, he saw the place they had occupied the day before was deserted, the chairs still upturned on the tables.

Just then, he spotted a piece of paper nearby. It was unsecured, not even weighed down by a stone. He was thankful for the complete absence of wind when he read the note scribbled in handwriting he instantly recognized.

Dear brother,
> *We'll be on our own for a bit. I will see you when I see you. The island is not that big.*
> *Love, Monika*

He felt sick to his stomach until he came up with a simple explanation. *Of course, they had just walked down the hill for a stroll on the beach.* He would have done the same thing, had he woken up early. As to her reference to the size of the island, he took it as a joke.

Reiner rolled up his sleeping bag and packed his belongings. As he walked down the beach, he passed colorful assemblages of blankets and clothes and the heads of hippies sticking out of their tents, either still asleep or just stirring. They were *schlaftrunken,* or *drunk from sleep.*

The *kafenio* was just opening up, and the potbellied owner was already hollering instructions to the waiter. A cup of coffee was what Reiner needed most just then, and one appeared in front of him almost as soon as he sat down.

Slurping his little cup of strong, Greek coffee, he considered what to do next. The walk they might have gone on was evidently taking them much longer than he'd expected at first. Either way, they would not have brought their luggage with them for the stroll, but stored it somewhere like the *kafeneio.* He looked around but could not see any familiar bags. On the other hand, they might have stashed their things in one of the caves.

The possibilities grew endless, and some of them were starting to scare him. He tried to calm himself down. Monika and Bernhard were reasonable people, people with sense. Bernhard, for one, seemed mature. His sister had less common sense maybe, but she wasn't stupid. *They would be all right.*

Soon, though, he saw people on the hill getting up and collecting their belongings to seek shade as the sun started its merciless journey to the center of the sky. That's when he recognized his mistake; he should have interrogated his neighbors first thing that morning, one by one, just like they did in detective stories.

Once he set his mind in motion, he was unable to stop it. *So many women had been lost over the years, then found—be it on the wayside, in the brush, in the swampland, or in the deep forest covered by ferns or milkwood or those large green elephant leaves that nobody knows the name of—in pieces in plastic bags or refrigerated, then tagged in a morgue and all this other forensic bullshit they go on about on TV.*

Everything had changed in the span of a single night; he couldn't quite believe it, but his vacation had just turned into one singular pursuit: tracking down his lost sister. Crete, despite Monika's assertion in the note and the fact that it appeared as a tiny speck on a map of Europe, was a gigantic piece of land that encompassed plains with ancient wind-mills, rugged mountain ranges perforated with gorges, rolling hills with thousand-year-old olive trees, and miles and miles of beaches. It had once housed the entire kingdom of Minos!

True, it was possible to travel the island and run into the same tourist twice, but he knew that he didn't have the time he would need for a search, and he despaired. Wasn't the labyrinth, the device designed to make people lose themselves, invented on that very island? There had been only one way to outwit the labyrinth: unspooling a thread you had the presence of mind to bring with you in the first place.

Siblings, he'd once read, were sometimes connected by an invisible thread; they felt its tug even at great distances and each would always know where to look for the other. But he doubted this kind of connection existed between him and Monika. She had always been a quiet, passive presence, and he never had a clue what was on her mind. Perhaps the story about the invisible thread was true only for identical twins?

Two hours had gone by, and there was still no sign of them. In a burst of frustration, he got up from his chair and started pacing. The pressure built, and before he knew what he was doing, he grabbed a stone and flung it into the water.

"*Scheisse!*" he shouted. "*Verdammte Scheisse!* Why is this happening to me?"

The people sitting at the next table looked up and examined him warily—probably searching for additional signs of a mental disorder.

If she really took off in such an irresponsible, careless way, he had every reason to be angry with his sister. As far as he could tell, Bernhard was reasonable. But what if he'd missed some sign that not all was as it seemed? The mere couple of days they'd known him were not enough to ascertain what sort of person he was. What if Bernhard had left her to her own devices? Weren't architects known for their scattered, artistic minds?

But they had taken the map with them, he realized. They would not get lost. He was glad about that part, at least.

Chapter 8

The Tympaki police station was a concrete, single-story building shaped like a shoebox, with the Greek flag as the only embellishment if one discounted the wooden boxes with herbs and flowers that were also mounted out front. That day, the blue-and-white flag was sagging due to a lack of wind.

He had taken a bus to Tympaki since the owner of the *kafeneio* told him it was the second-order administrative unit responsible for the one hundred sixty-seven souls, not counting hippies and other transient travelers, residing in the municipality of Matala. There were only two buses that ran each workday, and he had missed the earlier one.

In Matala, Reiner had been unable to find an authority figure of any kind, even on the local level, except for the owner of the *kafenio.* He was some kind of ombudsman appointed for straightening out local quarrels, but was considered to be a few notches below the level of competence that Reiner's situation required. Several local people pointed him to the eminent authority of the Tympaki principality for burglaries, missing people, and worse.

He entered a room painted all in white, with a low ceiling. It was barren except for a table with a typewriter and two chairs, one on either side. On the wall there were the obligatory portraits of King Constantin II and Prime Minister Giorgios Papandreou. Next to the typewriter stood a vase with a bouquet of plastic flowers, which were covered with a fine layer of dust. A gecko stared at him from the very top of the wall, its head tilted in a way that only geckos can perfect. It was motionless, like a piece of stucco.

The police officer, seated at the small table, wore a blue uniform jacket over a pair of gray, shapeless pants. Above his leather belt, he represented the Greek government; below it he looked like a tramp.

"*Ti kanete,*" Reiner said.

"What brings you here?" the police officer said in passable, though heavily accented German, probably picking up his visitor's origin from the sound of his greeting.

The officer made no move toward the typewriter, nor did he bother to take down Reiner's name. Instead, he leaned back on his chair, and even went so far as to tilt it back a bit while he listened to Reiner's story.

"So, your sister and her boyfriend are missing?" he said.

"Yes, I woke up this morning, as I just said, and they were both gone."

"Sit down, my friend."

Reluctantly, Reiner sat on the small chair at the table across from the officer. The act of taking a seat seemed to convey a lack of urgency before he'd even had a chance to really make his case. At the same time, to be addressed as a friend alarmed him. Was it a ruse intended to deprive him of his own independent judgments?

"How long has your sister known this boyfriend?" The officer placed his folded hands behind his head, his elbows extended and slowly moving like lazy wings.

"Two days and two nights, counting the night during which they disappeared."

"We don't call this long here in Greece, my friend."

"We don't call it long in Germany, either."

The officer gave him a long, pensive look. "You know what I think? I think they took off for some privacy." Smirking at Reiner, he put his two index fingers together, rubbing them against each other in such a way that meant one thing only in the Mediterranean: incessant copulation, for the sheer fun of it.

Reiner jumped up from his seat at the obscene gesture. The officer all but explicitly said that his sister was nothing but a whore, and as such not worthy of a municipal investigation. It was meant as an insult, for sure. No Greek man would tolerate being accused of having a loose woman for his sister.

"I'm wasting my time," Reiner fumed. "But listen carefully. The government of Greece should be concerned about the fate of its tourists. There will be a lot of bad press if something—*anything*—should happen to my sister."

The officer closed his eyes and pressed his hands together in front of his chest, finger by finger, as though preparing to recite a poem that was part of the national canon. "The Greek government, I can assure you, is well aware of the hazards that tourists face when they refuse to heed traveling advice."

Reiner trembled with anger and frustration as he spun around on the spot and stalked out of the door. He knew he would not help things by striking the pompous civil servant, so he left it at that.

He found a *kafeneio* nearby and ordered a sandwich and a coffee while he contemplated his next move. There was so much going on in his head, and he was suddenly struck by the disparity between the turmoil he was experiencing and the emptiness of his diary. One should reflect when given some time to sort things out in your mind.

On that impulse, he took his notebook out and tried to describe the encounter with the police officer, but his temper kept flaring up, and in the end, he had to add another failure to the growing list for this day alone. Between bites of his sandwich and sips of his coffee, he did manage to jot down a few observations:

[Tympaki. Re.: after police report]

The worry about M: if anything, the encounter with the police leaves me more worried than before about her fate. He was pathetic. Perhaps one has to bribe officials here to get anything done? But this might also get me arrested. Besides, the amount of drachmes I have on me is pitiful; if this man is in the game, he is in on it in bigger ways than I can afford.

The King of Greece: what a strange holdover of the past! We had this man— Kaiser Wilhelm, with the crippled arm (I saw it in an old photograph)—who was chased from his throne after WWI (the war he helped start, which left Europe in shambles and cut my father's hand in half). But what was, and continues to be, the business of German royalty all over Europe? Is this still über alles?

The gecko on the ceiling: motionless for more than half an hour. It was quite suspicious. A mechanical contraption with a camera inside? Do they have cameras that little nowadays? Perhaps it's just a mic. It would be an ideal angle to record a conversation from.

The pen in his hand gave him the idea to use one of the postcards that Monika bought when he was in sunburnt agony, and send it to Almut. This was the first opportunity he'd really had to do so. But soon after he started writing on the back of the Knossos Palace, he ran out of space and decided to continue on a blank sheet torn from his notebook. He told Almut about the landscape, the scent of herbs and flowers, the peculiar plants, the intense sun, and the Matala caves, but he left out one detail: the disappearance of his sister. It would not do to raise any alarms when there was still a chance Monika would show up soon anyway—maybe even as soon as the next day. Moreover, he was worried the news would reach his parents.

He stuffed the postcard and the letter into an airmail envelope, then looked for the post office to get the right stamps for the extra weight. He found it on the other side of the plaza, but when he arrived at the small, neoclassic building with two ionic columns by the entrance, he saw a sign it was closed for the day.

Chapter 9

When he was still in elementary school, Reiner and Monika had played together, even though he was so much older than her. Playing with a girl was OK at home, but elsewhere, this kind of thing could damage one's reputation among the other boys for good.

They would pass the time collecting goldstones—pebbles of quartz covered with shimmering fool's gold. Each equipped with a glass jar, they used to crouch on their knees on the gravel in the backyard, looking for stones that glittered in the sun. Their knees would get hurt and even bloody in the process, but the pain was something he accepted as the price of the experience of doing something together; Reiner was sure his sister felt the same way, even though they never talked about it. Each successful pick would result in a tinkling sound as the stone landed in one of the jars. When a jar would start to fill up, the stones would land on the others with quiet thuds. There was competition in this, sure, but also a sense of a common purpose.

She was a good sport even though she was little and quite a bit slower than he was. But sometimes, when the bottom of her jar was barely covered, Monika would lose interest for no reason. And yet there he was, still all fired up and prepared to go on forever—or at least for the rest of the afternoon. Only now did he realize that it may have been just the tinkling sound that interested her in the first place.

He remembered being annoyed by her lack of perseverance; he would scold her for withdrawing from a project as important as this one, but all she did was shrug and walk away. In truth, he had no idea what to do with a jar full of goldstones, except maybe put it somewhere in the basement so that they could both look at it whenever they wanted to admire the collection.

Another grand project he tried to draw his sister in on was the pencil puppet play. At that time, there was a fad being promoted by stationary stores—like the one across the street from their parents' house—that involved pencils with removable heads that looked like kings, queens, jesters, and ordinary folks. These pencils were twice as expensive as normal ones, but they were so much more fun.

Reiner bought the special pencils with his pocket money: fifty pfennige per week. He decided to put together a whole puppet play, and outfitted each of the characters with little garments made out of fabric left over from the annual visit of the seamstress. Twirling the pencil between one's hands made the tiny dresses fly up like Marilyn Monroe's on that subway grate in 1954—photographs he would see much later. He drew Monika into his confidence and tried to inspire her. She took an interest in it…at first.

The premiere of the puppet play was planned for their mother's birthday, in June. Monika put the pencil between her two hands, trying out her own twirling with the queen, whose face looked so serious it was as if she perpetually disapproved of the world around her. Over the course of a couple of weeks, the completion of the dresses and the puppet play became a joint project, and he enjoyed her initial enthusiasm. They talked and whispered about it every day.

"Mother's birthday is less than a week away," he sternly told his sister one day. "Three are still naked, and that's not OK. You've got to do your bit, you know."

"Yesterday you said two," she'd said, her brows knitted.

"That's because I had to buy another one," he said. "The play absolutely needs a count with a mustache."

He depended on her participation as coauthor, codirector, and dress rehearsal audience, all in one. She'd added ribbons to the dresses of each character for extra personality, cutting them from leftovers in the bag by the sewing machine, but then when it came to devising a plot, she was of little help.

Much later, of course, he realized that he had expected too much of her; it was silly to expect all of that from a six-year-old. Still, his feeling of disappointment had never truly left him; it translated into his notion of her as a consistently unreliable partner, an idea that proved difficult to shed.

PART II

Sitia

Chapter 10

Reiner knew that successful detectives—such as Hercule Poirot, Father Brown, and Sherlock Holmes—had the ability to put themselves into the minds of the person they were trying to track down, whether that was the perpetrator of a crime or the possible next victim. Even though he assured himself after initially panicking that, in all likelihood, he was not dealing with a crime, Reiner thought of using Sherlock Holmes's preferred method.

He tried to remember the few conversations between Monika and Bernhard he'd witnessed, but they were all a blur. Next, he thought about the landmarks on the island that a future architect might be attracted to. Nothing except the Minoan Palace in Knossos came to mind, but he concluded that that was the least likely place they would choose since it would force them to turn around and go straight back to the area around Heraklion, reversing the bumpy, tiring ride they took the day before.

An idea came to him at last while he was having a late lunch right across from the inhospitable police station. He had *moussaka* with tomato salad and a carafe of *retsina*—the usual. Mentally scanning the conversations they held in Germany while planning this trip, he recalled that Monika kept changing her mind about what to pack. How many pairs of shoes, how many sandals? One jacket or two? How many sweaters? How many bathing suits? Do they wear bikinis there? How many dresses? Will it get cold, and what will I wear then? In this regard, she was so impractical and inexperienced; her initial choices would have filled two large suitcases, which would have been impossible to drag along.

While they sorted out these and other questions, they'd discovered two special places through the travel section of the public library. They had talked about visiting Sitia—a town close to the easternmost tip of Crete that was known for its warm climate—and Vai beach—a coastal hamlet with a thousand palms.

"It says here that Vai literally means *palm trees*," he'd told Monika, who listened with a great deal of excitement.

"I want to go there. It sounds *so* romantic," she'd said.

That book on Greece was published twenty years earlier. All of the pictures were in black and white, and the one for Vai showed a sandy beach bordered by hundreds of palm trees, a vast sea, and no people in sight. The nearby town of Sitia stood out with its thirteenth-century Venetian fortress on top of a hill.

It was the recollection of her excitement and that word she'd used—*romantic*—that convinced Reiner that Sitia and Vai were the places she and Bernhard would visit first. The idea of *romance* must have been quite abstract to her, gleaned from books and movies, but in her current situation, she would probably feel as if she were being engulfed by it in real life. And for the first time, she'd been free to choose where and when to stage a romance of her own. With the imagination of his newly discovered detective mind, Reiner bestowed Monika's boyfriend with a passion so ardent and blind that he would follow her wherever her whims took her.

And this was how Reiner convinced himself that Bernhard was indeed a decent fellow at heart, and that his only fault would be his inability to stand up to or disappoint her. Reiner was still worried, but it was caused more by her inexperience in a foreign country than her boyfriend's potentially sinister intentions.

Reiner stayed overnight at the only hotel in town after downing three shots of *ouzo* to get ready for the night. He fell into a bottomless, dreamless sleep, the mental and physical exhaustion of the past day having wiped him out.

In the morning, he had the solid breakfast that came with the room. Overall, things were looking up. In a way he could not account for, the belief that his sister was headed for the *beach of the thousand palms* had become a virtual certainty.

His plan was to take a bus from Tympaki to Mires, then change to a bus going from there to Sitia via Ierapetra along a route that hugged the southern coast. Ierapetra intrigued him, as it sounded like a word that would gallop in one's mouth like a stubborn donkey, but also like the promise of something approaching magic—perhaps even paradise.

Chapter 11

After the searing midday heat passed, he boarded the bus to Mires, just as planned. The bus was overcrowded, and there were bundles of chickens tied to the roof by their feet and fluttering madly. The windows were wide open, and the scent of thyme and rosemary was everywhere.

He sat next to a woman from Spain, a black-haired beauty so striking, he felt initially paralyzed. She did not speak a word of German, and he commanded exactly ten words of Spanish, all of which had to do with arriving and leaving and eating, so they were of no use under these circumstances. He started a half-assed conversation in English instead.

"So, what will you do in Mires?"

"I shall find the boyfriend of mine and shall meet himself there instantly."

She turned and looked at him, all innocent and bright-eyed and more than making up for her mistakes in grammar and diction.

"Find your boyfriend? Where is your boyfriend coming from?"

"Munich, I think. Not so sure."

"But if you think you will meet him in Mires, you must have a reason to believe he will be there."

As he tried to hold up his end of the conversation, he had become aware of a particular scent, some kind of ethereal sun oil—perhaps it was her shampoo? Or, in an interpretation he imagined and preferred, it was a sweet fragrance emanating naturally from every single pore of her body.

"Plenty reason to meet boyfriend. Why fuck ask, please?" She had the mouth of a Ukrainian teenager.

He was a bit intimidated, but still driven by curiosity. "But why do you think he will be in Mires if you don't know where he is coming from?"

"Because why he make promise?" she said triumphantly, as though she'd caught a fatal flaw in his reasoning.

At that, Reiner had to pass on debating the matter any further. He looked out at the landscape passing by: bleached, dried brush, the occasional unfinished house standing on stilts as if ready to head off to the ocean out of sheer loneliness or boredom. He enjoyed the glimmering, alternate immersions in sunlight and shade as the bus climbed up the mountains and descended them in turns. Sitting next to this woman seemed to have sharpened his perception of the beauty all around him, as if a switch had been flipped either in his head or somewhere in the sky.

When he turned, he found her sound asleep, her head and the mass of her straight, black hair inching toward his shoulder with each curve the bus took. For the first time, he was able to look at her face and take in the shape of her young body without the rules of decorum or the fear of her noticing his perusal. He felt a physical reaction to her proximity; every fiber of his body responded to her, though he knew he had to keep quiet and motionless so as not to wake her.

When he arrived in Mires, he discovered the last bus to Sitia had already left. The woman—Rosa was her name—apologized for intruding on his shoulder and quickly made her way to the *kafeneio* on the main plaza, where she said she was to rendezvous with her boyfriend. She was still half asleep when they said goodbye to each other with much less ceremony than he would have liked.

Mires was a sleepy, exceedingly dusty town with a short mountain as its neighbor to the north. In the plaza, two dogs lay in the shade of an olive tree, their tongues stretched out and almost touching the ground, which was strewn with brown pine needles. The dogs twitched in their dreams.

He walked along the main road and found himself a cheap, small room with a bed and a chair and a tiny window facing the mountain. As he stretched out on the bed, the crickets outside struck up their incessant chirping. He wondered where Monika and Bernhard were in that moment. Surely they'd just found a room somewhere, much like he had, with a large bed and plenty of light—or darkness—to pick up where they left off in Matala.

At this point, his imagination failed him; the area in Germany where they'd been brought up was puritan to the extreme. As a freshman in college, just a few years earlier, he and a friend had taken his sister to a new nightclub in their hometown. When a woman walked onstage to take her clothes off, one by one, Monika was shocked. Until then, she had no notion that this behavior was even remotely acceptable, never mind how it could be allowed in this town. And how could her brother, of all people, take her to witness it? Of course, he had been exposed more than once to this sort of nightlife in his college town. They never talked about it afterward, probably because they were not in the habit of talking about anything of substance, and this subject was even more taboo than others.

He decided he could no longer postpone the business of calling home. Besides, this call would determine if she'd already contacted their parents without him having to break the news about her possible disappearance. But when he arrived at the post office, he found all of the phones were out of service for repair. The call would have to wait until he arrived in the next town on his journey to the beach with the thousand palms. At least he was able to send off his letter to Almut. The letter should be sufficient to express his concern for her, he decided, so he opted to postpone calling her, too.

Back to his rented room and stretched out on the narrow bed, he awoke sometime later, disoriented. It was pitch-dark outside, and his watch said it was eight o'clock. His stomach growled and he decided to walk back to the plaza for something to eat. Rosa was still sitting at the same place, which was by then lit by a garland of lights. Reiner stopped at her table and saw it was covered with empty glasses and little plates holding olive pits.

"This boyfriend of yours…"

"Is being maybe probably a total piece of shit," she said, looking up to him with those eyes that made him wonder whether this alleged boyfriend of hers even existed.

If he did, wouldn't he move heaven and earth to meet her at this agreed place, and exactly on time? Or maybe he'd get there even a bit earlier, just to be on the safe side.

"May I join you?" he asked, but sat down without waiting for her answer.

It came, if a bit late, in the form of a wave of her little hand. She studied him for a long time with those eyes that made his stomach melt.

"Let us obtain the *ouzo*," she finally said, flicking her hair away from her face with a smile.

"I'll find this waiter guy," he said.

From what he could make out from her confusing story, Rosa had made her way by train, bus, and ferry from Salamanca, where she lived. Her boyfriend was from Barcelona, and he had intended to stop in Munich on business before joining her in Greece. They'd been sending telegrams to each other, with the occasional expensive telephone call in between, and the unequivocal date and time they'd set for their meeting was that day at precisely four o'clock, Eastern European Time. That was four hours ago, and there had been no trace of the *bastard*, as she had already started to call him.

Reiner told her his own story, and his determination to find his sister and her newly acquired companion. By the time he was finished, he could tell Rosa had only listened with half an ear.

"Where are you staying tonight?" he asked.

"I wish stay with my boyfriend," she said. "But my boyfriend has gone disappear. Poof!"

She spread out both of her hands to emphasize her point as the waiter brought *ouzo* in tumblers and small dishes of olives and nuts.

"I have rented a room," Reiner said. "It's small, but you can stay with me. I'll sleep on the floor."

He suddenly felt hot at the thought of all the other sleeping arrangements they could find, but which he had to immediately dismiss. Almut had a firm hold on his conscience.

"God, you be my hero knight!" Rosa exclaimed, raising the little glass of *ouzo* and emptying it in one swallow.

"I take that as a yes?" he asked.

"You OK," she said, smiling. "You cool."

Chapter 12

His room was ridiculously small for two people. Granted, it even was small for one. Reiner and Rosa stood awkwardly by the bed—strangers just a few hours before, now roommates. He showed her the view of the black mountain from the little window, then switched the lamp off so they could see the stars.

The night was moonless, but the contours of the mountain could be traced against the starry sky from the way its mass intruded on the expanse from below. He turned the light on again and offered her the bed just as he had promised, preparing himself for a long night on the carpet, but she would have none of it. Instead, she sat on the mattress in a lotus pose and patted the spot next to her, inviting him to join her as one might invite a pet.

"Be my guest," she said, oblivious to the fact that she had reversed the roles of guest and host.

He decided then that her quirky mannerisms were due to a thoroughly quirky personality, not just her English going astray.

"I barely know you," he said, even as he sat down and turned to face her. "We are straws; do you know that expression?"

"Straws? What meaning is you say straws?" she asked.

"In German, they call a married woman a *Strohwitwe*, or a straw widow, if her husband is away from home, and vice versa. So maybe we could say the same about boyfriends and girlfriends, too. I'm a straw widower, you see?"

"My boyfriend the bastard has forsaken me," she said. "I'm not wife, I'm not straw. I never be a wife with him."

"He must have just missed his bus," Reiner said, taken aback by her choice of that heartbreaking word: *forsaken*. She must have seen it in one of those tiny dictionaries they sold on the street.

"He finded another girl," she said tonelessly. "Girls," she corrected herself with much more venom in her voice. "A fucking, fucking harem!"

She stayed in the same position for a while, then leaned into him with her eyes closed, pivoting around on the shaky mattress. He put his arms around her and kissed her on her forehead; it was the least he could do, it was as simple as that. At least, that's what he told himself. Perhaps this was the way it would be between them that night and however many more.

"Rosa?" he said, his heart pounding.

"Yes?" she whispered.

"I have to tell you about my girlfriend back in Germany." He swallowed hard.

"Far away," Rosa said dreamingly, waving her hand as one would when saying goodbye to a friend. "I need not know."

"Still. She is very important to me."

"She don't find out, never." She reached up and bent down his head, and kissed him on his lips. He was stunned for a long second, then embraced her and pressed back.

"That's ... that's not the point," he said.

"What is the point? What name she has?"

"Almut."

"Almut. Al-mutt. All all mutt mutt," she sang softly as she stroked his back and his thighs. "I can be your Al-mutt for few days."

He patiently explained that *yes*, he could maybe lie down with her—he actually wouldn't mind it a bit—and do things with her that lovers do... just not the one thing that everything would be leading up to.

"Because, you see, in my experience, loyalties can shift when something like that happens." All this talk about his experience was absolute bogus; he didn't have much of it, but he thought he needed to emphasize his resolve and expectations.

"Loy-al-ties?" she asked.

"If we did this kind of thing, I could lose Almut and gain nothing in the end."

Rosa regarded him with wide eyes as he explained these complications, though without much conviction. Reiner supposed it would sound like decency and common sense to some people, but to others like utter nonsense or even vague superstition. It turned out that Rosa didn't mind; the type of closeness he was proposing, touching without fucking, was what he guessed many women aspired to but could almost never find. She managed to say with her broken English that she'd never come across a man so in control of himself.

But then when he began necking with her, their fingers knew no bounds and she started sighing, and he couldn't believe that he'd boxed himself in like that.

"Would you mind if I changed my mind?"

She just laughed, opened his zipper, and guided him inside her with her little hand.

Chapter 13

When he awoke, the sun was already high and brilliant in the sky. A donkey brayed in the distance. Donkeys, he had read somewhere, were intensely and single-mindedly horny pretty much all the time.

Rosa was watching him; she smiled when he opened his eyes and stroked his hair. "Reiner."

"Rosa," he replied.

He felt her warm body, the body his skin remembered well. Saying her name and hearing her softly call his was another reaffirmation of their closeness. They *knew* each other now, and they would never be strangers again. Biblical knowledge—he never really understood before what it meant in all its poignancy. Now he realized it meant knowing the other person in her totality—each gesture, each crevice, each pore—but also acknowledging that there was much more unspoken knowledge hidden beneath the surface.

The first bus to Ierapetra and connecting to the one to Sitia had already left. They crossed the dusty plaza holding hands, and he was satisfied to see the envy he stirred up in the eyes and hearts of the local men who had nothing but a *komboloi* to play with. With her complexion, she could be easily mistaken for a Greek woman, but her clothes pegged her as a tourist who had come from afar.

They sat down at a table at the *kafenio* right next to the bus station, then ordered coffee and sweet pastry as a start to killing the three and a half hours they had before the next bus.

"So, what's your favorite movie?" he asked.

"*Breakfast at Tiffany's,*" she replied without a second of deliberation. "Audrey Hepburn in that role, just great! Seen it much times."

"Mine is Jean-Luc Godard's *Breathless,*" he said.

"That is mine *numero duo*: Belmondo, Jean Seberg."

"Is it really? No kidding!"

During a lull in the conversation, a light brown dog of uncertain breed got up from his spot in the plaza and walked over to them for attention. Reiner patted the dog's head.

"You're still sure you want to come with me?" he asked.

"What else? Rot here? You my fucking hero!" she said, laughing and clasping his hands with hers.

"Literally!" he said with a laugh of his own.

Reiner's mood alternated between anxiety and exuberance. There was the continued uncertainty about his sister, now the idea of having to take care of this stranded young woman from Salamanca, and on top of it all, his money was quickly running out. But then again, he cherished every minute he spent with Rosa. They kissed and kissed again, reminiscing about the night they'd spent skin on skin in that hopelessly narrow room with the view of the mountain.

He felt her hair again as it brushed against his cheek and inhaled the scent he had first noticed on the bus the previous day, before he had exchanged a single word with her. He felt a wild surge of happiness, as if he had stumbled upon a treasure after countless unsuccessful excavation expeditions. How did the sheer emptiness of growing up and fumbling under his bedsheets compare to this? But then he realized that that included the year and a half he'd been dating Almut and the intimacy with her, too.

They ordered another round of coffee and talked about the days ahead, and what they would do with the endless time that stretched out before them like a vast tapestry. The sound of a bus approaching took them both by surprise; it was much too early for it to be the one they were waiting for, the one headed for Sitia. The bus stopped right next to the plaza, its door opened with a hiss, and in his peripheral vision, Reiner saw a young, tall, bearded man all but sprint toward their table. Rosa's expression abruptly changed to one of panic.

"Rosa!"

Before Reiner could even comprehend what was happening, the man seized her by her wrists, his eyes fierce and angry. She let out an ear-piercing scream. As she struggled to free herself, a shouting match ensued in rapid-fire Spanish.

Reiner, who could not understand a single word, sprung from his chair, knocking it over in the process, and tried to decide whether he should intervene and how he would even go about doing so. The owner of the *kafenio* stepped outside, glaring wordlessly at the scene. He took a few steps toward the table and righted the overturned chair.

"I go with you," Rosa said, turning back to Reiner in the middle of the argument and effortlessly switching her language and pitch. Pointing at her boyfriend, she used her own limited English vocabulary to add, "He cannot English."

Empowered by her conclusion, Reiner confronted the man himself, trying to step between the couple. "You leave her alone! Go fuck yourself."

This four-letter word seemed to finally get through to Rosa's boyfriend, as he stopped moving, then slowly turned toward Reiner to eye him as if he'd only just spotted him.

"Bastardo!" he said, shaking with barely restrained rage. "*Hijo de fucking puta!*"

He spat on the ground, then stalked off to an unknown destination, looking very much like a reincarnation of the Lone Ranger – in a country that preceded the Wild West by more than a thousand years.

"Where on earth is he going?" Reiner asked Rosa. "What a nutcase! What did he say?"

"He say 'son of fucking bitch.' And he is a coward, too." It seemed she had, at least for a moment, cherished the idea of being the trophy to be fought over. Sighing, she turned to the waiter. "Two *ouzos*. Quick!"

* * *

When it finally arrived, the bus to Ierapetra was full of excited children, all just shy of their teens, who filled the air with chattering, shrill voices. As soon as the bus started moving, Rosa was in his arms, crying.

"He came all way," she said. "For me! Oh fuck, fuck, fuck!"

"You mean you have changed your mind? You'd rather be with him now?"

"No, I am supremely totally happy in your arm."

"But?"

"But it is so fairless."

"Unfair?"

"Yes, it is so unfair. Us was a truly couple."

Reiner studied her in silence for a second. He liked her sensibility, her moral fiber, but not the effect it could have on this particular situation.

"Look, you can get off the bus in Ierapetra and take the next one back. No sweat."

He wondered if he really cared one way or the other what she chose. He supposed he should have been upset, but on the other hand, there was still Almut, his sweetheart back home to consider.

Rosa cried some more without saying another word, and eventually fell asleep on his shoulder. It was the same posture she'd adopted on the bus the day before, but now with the difference that they *knew* each other as man and woman. He thought about the ways in which she resembled his sister, but also the many ways in which they differed from one another. She was sweeter in some ways, though at the same time somehow racier. She certainly had a foul mouth! But, there was also the intoxicating scent of her body and the memory of clinging to it the night before.

Chapter 14

On Reiner's right, the ocean was a vast, undulating canvas in a deep blue that would be impossible to render in watercolor—his favorite medium in art class in high school, though his projects always seemed to turn out as big messes of brown.

Wide stretches of the beach were covered with smooth stones the size of bowling balls, but in various shapes. No donkey would be able to walk here. The land on the left of the road, sloping up, looked austere and almost entirely bare of vegetation. Here and there, an agave plant with fleshy, blue-green leaves sprouted a stalk, a mast stretching for impossible heights before sending its offspring out into the world. Reiner had heard that it accomplished this feat exactly once in its lifespan, after which it collapsed and died.

At the time, he thought that was how he wanted his own life to proceed: accomplish something stupendous, then disappear without the pain of gradual decay. A bowed back, wrinkles, arthritis, gout, cancer of the stomach: these were the kinds of things his parents were going through or feared they would in the near future. When he was growing up, uncles, aunts, and grandparents all had disintegrated slowly and persistently due to ailments of every conceivable body part, and sometimes took months, years to succumb to them. They all reacted differently; one of the aunts kvetched day in day out, and one uncle stoically suffered through his pain, having accepted it as God-given.

What stupendous accomplishment would be his? Reiner hadn't figured it out yet, but there was still lots of time ahead.

The occasional small olive tree cast a nervous black shadow on the terrain. Small springs along the way spewed water forth through cracks in the rock, each creating a little oasis of vegetation around it. A bearded shepherd and a bouncy, tiny ball of a dog guarded a herd of sheep that had found something green to chew on. The cacophony on the bus had quieted down, and Reiner dozed off, too. When he woke, he found

Rosa had pivoted so that her head and her warmth were nestled in his lap. As he looked at her face, he felt his lap stirring.

Just a couple of days before, he had been alone with the singular focus of finding his sister. Now, even with the problem still present, the world seemed richer. Nothing was solved, but he was certain he would find Monika. He found comfort in the knowledge that he could consult with Rosa, strategize with her, and listen to her feminine instinct guiding her views on the matter.

Rosa yawned, opened her eyes, still drunk with sleep, and blinked up at him with an unconditional, trusting smile on her face. It reminded him of the night they'd spent together, and he saw how beautiful she was, despite—or perhaps because of—the fact that her hair was in disarray.

"*Buenos dias*," she said, in a long, drawn-out way that sounded like a slowly articulated yawn. "Where are we?"

"I think it's still ten kilometers to the town."

"The town of what?"

"Ierapetra. Nice dreams?"

"I wish," she said as she propped herself up and looked out the window. She yawned again, then turned and traced her index finger across his face: his forehead first, then following the profile of his nose. It was like a proud landlord's survey of his possessions as he walked the circumference of the estate and appreciated the view of the orchard, the vineyard, the horses, and the cattle. "Talk me about your sister."

"My sister? What more do you want to know?"

"I do not know what I want to know," she said. "Surprise myself."

"Well, I'm not sure what to tell you about her," he said. "Where I grew up, just about everybody in the neighborhood had a sister. They were just there. Part of the house, you know? Nothing really to talk about."

She stretched out both of her arms above her head like cats are wont to do after a deep sleep, and he was struck by how at ease she was with him just three hours after sending her boyfriend away.

"Same in Spain," she said. "Girls are less worth. You say, worth-less?"

"Worthless is actually less than less worth," he said.

"You fuck with me!" she said softly, shaking her head with a smile.

"Did you make up your mind?" he asked.

"About what make up mine mind?"

"Whether or not you want to turn around."

As an answer, she just laughed heartily and deep in her throat, which he found instantly likable. He realized that these strange rhythmic sounds coming out of the depth of the body were a unique part of a person, just as the shape of one's fingernails or the color of one's hair. It was not something grafted, or rehearsed. He understood that to like her a lot, he had to like her laughter, and that they both had just passed some kind of test. Listening to her continued laughter, he tried to discern where its tributaries might reside in different parts of her body, from her nasal cavities and her vocal cords, all the way to her core. He wondered if a sharp ear could distinguish all these different origins and the way they were orchestrated to form this symphony in the expression of delight.

He'd been close to few women thus far, and all from his time in college; they all had quirks. Take Almut, for example: he liked her a lot, and she was very pretty, but she was a bit fastidious and also did not listen for more than two minutes to anything he'd say. This was quite irritating, and he had silently hoped that, given enough time, he would be able to lengthen her attention span. Another woman he'd known would listen calmly and discuss the matter at hand in a studious, rational way, but was sloppy and essentially unable to cook. The whole experience with women so far had made him realize that there were infinite varieties of attributes that nature generously mixed and combined within a person. Was Almut really the one for him, or rather a transient companion? Perhaps the true solution was to live a long life and not get stuck with any of them too soon?

As they reached the outskirts of Ierapetra, Reiner craned his neck, trying to find something, anything in the landscape that justified the jumbled name. At last, he saw the large rock formation on the beach, or the *petra* part of the name. His Western, Christian upbringing immediately called to mind Petrus, the Apostle Peter, and the firm rock on which Jesus purportedly thought he could build his church.

"There it is," he announced to Rosa. "The rock, you know? The foundation."

"It is a beshitted rock," she said, pointing to the white stuff the seagulls had left behind on top.

Reiner had to laugh at that. "Beshat, maybe. *Beschissen,* we would say in German, but I'm sure this is all Greek to you."

She looked at him, a question written on her face. She clearly didn't get that last part. The really funny thing was that, in German, the phrase was constructed with Spanish as the language in question instead.

Das is alles spanisch für Dich!

Chapter 15

In Ierapetra, they had to wait three hours for the connecting bus. In the midday heat, the town did not feel so inviting. Hot air hovered over the ceramic tiles of the center plaza. Orange trees lined the streets, the fruit a random, capricious addition to the dark green leaves furrowed with black shadows. Hoping for a place to sit in the shade, they settled on the curb surrounding a fountain that had run dry. The shrill sounds of crickets high up on the trees cut the air. Sweat erupted on Reiner's chest, and he caught a musty whiff from inside his shirt every time he moved.

"I'm tired," she said, slouching next to him.

Then came the sporadic bouts of day sleeping; his chin bobbed repeatedly against his chest. His dreams, each of which must have lasted no more than a few seconds, taunted him with ways he might have spent more of his time worrying about his sister. The activities he counted as normal—eating, drinking—were suspended altogether. He saw her, but could not talk to her because his vocal cords and his jaw muscles were all paralyzed.

When he shook himself awake, he decided to finally call home.

"I'll be right back," he said to Rosa as she stirred next to him.

He waited in a tiny cubicle in the post office to connect the call. Standing there, he could watch Rosa through the small, round window on the door; he still worried she might leave.

After an eternity, his mother answered the phone. "*Hallo, Reiner, mein Gott! Wie geht's?* Wir haben nichts von Euch gehört!" – "How are you? We haven't heard a thing from you!"

"Not too bad," he replied. "This is a really beautiful country."

"I'm sure it is, my boy, but how come we didn't get any letters from either of you? Not even a single postcard!"

There was his confirmation that they'd had no news from Monika either, but he continued to stall anyway. "Mutti, postcards are so passé! I was going to write you a long letter—"

"—and then carry it home in person, like you did last time?"

"No, I was going to send it. I even bought the stamps already."

"Well, yes, with stamps, you know, it's a peculiar thing. They're useless unless you put them on an envelope and put a letter inside the envelope and *then* send it."

"I know, I know. You taught me that a long time ago."

"Give me Monika, my baby. Let me talk to her."

"She…hasn't gotten up yet, I'm afraid. You know how she always likes to sleep long."

Outside, he saw Rosa get up and walk to a spot outside his field of view. Had she changed her mind?

"Then ask her to call me later."

"Actually, we … we need to go if we're going to make this bus."

He was pleased with himself at lying so well, especially to his mother, but also shocked that he could pull it off under these circumstances. The distance between their telephones and the lack of eye contact made it so much easier.

"Well, wake her up so she doesn't miss the bus! You know, Reiner, sometimes—"

"I know. Sometimes I'm a bit slow."

"Right. Now, promise me to call us right away when you get to where you are going."

"Mutti, I promise."

Relieved, Reiner replaced the receiver, paid his charges at the counter, and rushed back to the plaza to look for Rosa. He found her draped over a chair at a tiny *kafenio* nearby, one arm hanging down over the chair's back. It was probably because of the heat, or perhaps her fatigue, but to him her pose was quite sensuous, like the old postcards he'd seen being sold in Paris on the promenade along the Seine. At that time, accepted ideas about a woman's body were quite different—heavy rumps were in vogue, for one—and to him, this was a greatly improved version. This one even appeared in color.

"I did something stupid," he said, avoiding her eyes.

"Let myself try guess." On hearing his voice she had pulled herself together, reassembling her limbs one by one. She said this matter-of-factly, as though she'd witnessed the whole conversation and didn't actually need to hypothesize. "You call your mother. First thing she desires is speak at your sister."

"Brilliant—you got it! So, I had to tell her Monika was asleep, then fib about our bus's departure time to get my mother off the phone."

"The part with the bus is full with truth."

"Truthful, you mean. But it's not, since I'm traveling with *you*."

"You have one only day to find her?"

"More or less. Otherwise I'll be in big trouble."

"We shall do it," Rosa said, taking his hand into her smaller and more fragile one. She said it firmly and calmly, like a mother to her frightened child, and gave him an immeasurable amount of comfort in a few simple words.

"If you say so," he said.

What was happening to him was nothing short of a miracle, a miracle he thought he didn't deserve. He looked at her delicate body and was overcome with a rush of recognition, as if each cell of his skin knew its mate was within reach. But with that came a new kind of anxiousness. He worried about losing her even before he'd truly had a chance to come to some kind of agreement, a plan, or even an idea about the future. For instance, there was a possibility that Almut might decide to desert him. Actually, had she not deserted him already with her inconsiderate illness? She took ill just before the trip, and someone with less trust than he would have questioned her body's motives right away. He felt a little less guilty about postponing his phone call and sending the postcard.

The bus, an asthmatic-sounding, blue-and-white painted chassis on wheels, finally arrived. After three hours of waiting, everything was covered with a fine red dust—dust carried by the steady hot wind blowing in from the direction of Africa. It was the sirocco, the Greek version of the mistral he knew from a high school trip to Italy. The table was red, the empty plates were red; his eyes watered, and he felt dust grinding between his teeth.

"Last chance for you to turn around and go back," he told her.

Laughing, Rosa put her hand on his mouth, presumably to stop his silly talk, and boarded the bus ahead of him. Still holding his hand, she chose two seats in the middle section of the bus, "for a nest."

Those were her exact words.

Chapter 16

They fell asleep in each other's arms. Reiner dreamt about flying along the coast of Africa: a continuous darkness without the interceding light of day. The length of the curvy coastline the plane had to follow was beyond his imagination. The cities down below looked like small, grounded swarms of fireflies. Rosa was supposed to be next to him, but her seat was empty. Still, he heard her talk softly to him in German; he was surprised she spoke his language, and yet it was a strange dialect so he only recognized a few words. The rest was gibberish.

He awoke when the bus rumbled to a halt. Next to him, Rosa was still asleep despite the sounds of lyra and bouzouki music coming from outside. Through the window, he saw hundreds of people milling around at some big festival. Thousands of little blue-white flags were strung up between the trees around what seemed to be the main plaza of the town, and flattered in the breeze.

"Where are we?" he asked the bus driver. Rosa stirred, opening her eyes.

"This is Sitia Extra Municipal Stop. Where do you want to go?"

"Vai beach."

"In that case, you have to stay on to Palaikastro, then transfer to another bus."

"Let's get out here," Rosa said to Reiner. "Looks funny."

"You mean, it looks like fun?"

They hopped off the bus to check out the place. Talking to a few people, they found out that this was the annual celebration of the local Saint: St. Anna, Jesus's grandmother.

"The grandmother of Jesus? Let me think this," Rosa said.

"I guess she's from his mother's side," Reiner said.

"Right. God has not a mother," she said. "He sprang up somewhere, the Bible means."

"Here in Greece they once had many gods," he said. "One for wind, one for the sea, another for love, and so on. They were all busy fighting each other."

He paid a dollar's equivalent for their admission, and she looked up at him with a flare of affection. *Of course, it was their first date.* He paid another two dollars for a carafe bearing an emblem that commemorated this special day: the face of the saint herself looking up at something radiating in the sky. The carafe was an all-you-can-drink deal, meaning it got them free *retsina* every time they cared to go to the filling station. It was run by a huge, drunk bear of a man who was still perfectly capable of getting others drunk.

They walked hand-in-hand around the town square through masses of people, young and old, listening to Cretan music and taking sips from their bottomless carafe. A children's choir sang the Greek national anthem on the makeshift wooden stage with the accompaniment of a bouzouki. They were all dressed in King Otto's Bavarian blue-and-white costumes. The noise of the crowd—shrill laughter, outcries of recognition, cousins meeting distant cousins—all but drowned the choir's young voices.

"Remind me why we got off here?" he asked, though not expecting an answer.

"I felt it like." She gave him a quick sideways hug to show she knew he was kidding.

"I guess that's as good a reason as any other," he said, laughing.

She really was a piece, this Spanish girl from a city whose name sounded like a magic spell.

Then a familiar voice cut through the tumult around them. It sounded like someone calling his name, but he dismissed the possibility at first. Nobody here would know him, he was quite certain.

That was until he had to stop walking because he did not believe his own eyes. He hardly recognized the woman, and yet he knew without a doubt that she was his sister. Monika's features seemed harder, more pointed than he remembered—a bit emaciated, even, though he had to reject this idea as implausible, considering just a few days had passed since he woke up on the beach and found no trace of her or her lover aside from a note. Her hair was unkempt, as if she had not washed it those last few days. The man by her side was ostensibly Greek, judging by his demeanor and the clothes he wore; he was dressed up for the fair with a festive, traditional outfit. After a pause, Monika embraced her brother as Rosa and the Greek man looked on.

"Are you OK?" Reiner asked as he freed himself, then pushed her away to look her over. He was simmering with rage amid feelings of tremendous relief. "Who is that? What happened to Bernhard? Where did that moron go?"

"I'm OK," she said. "And this is Iannis. He took care of me. Bernhard is just a complete asshole. I should have known about people from the Rhineland. Catholics!"

"*Arschloch*," her companion repeated in broken German, making a circle with his thumb and a curved index finger. The gesture drew an odd contrast with his refined appearance. "Big, big asshole!"

"You should have listened to me, goddammit. So, what happened?" asked Reiner.

"He just started withdrawing. He was so weird. In the end he stops talking to me altogether. And then when I confront him, he says—I still can't believe what he said," Monika huffed, "'You know, Monika-dear, it was all a big mistake.'"

"I love the 'dear' part," Reiner said with a sneer. "What a fucking asshole! Architects! Didn't I tell you about architects?"

"You got along with him fine," she said sharply, taking a step away from him. "You were almost buddies by the end of that night, the way you talked."

"A big mistake! That is great to hear!" Reiner said, ignoring her last remark because he refused to believe that he had any part in this. His sister stared at him for a short moment, then broke into tears. But he wasn't going to let her of easily. *Tears were cheap currency.* "What on earth got into your head? It's as if you don't give a shit about me, or our parents! You are the most selfish person on earth! I was scared shitless. For all I knew, you could have been dead."

"I-I don't know what to say, how to explain…" She made a low wailing sound as if all her air had left her lungs.

He looked at her uneasily, resisting the urge to comfort her. All it took was recalling the shock of discovering her gone, the indentation of the sleeping bag on the sand. He recalled the sleepless night—the one before the recent exhausting night spent with Rosa—the humiliation he suffered because of the implications made by the police officer in Tympaki, the lies he had to tell his mother on the phone. His sister had been reckless in every respect, and she deserved to feel badly about it.

He resisted for a long time, but when he finally took her in his arms, she sniffled, "Did you talk to Mutti?"

"It's a good thing you ask. I covered for you this morning. I called home when we stopped in Ierapetra. She asked to speak with you, but I told her you were still asleep and that we were just about to take the bus to Sitia. You know, the one I actually took with Rosa."

Monica looked at Rosa without comprehension, as though she'd just noticed her.

"I'm sorry, I forgot," he said. "This is Rosa, from Spain. You will like her."

Rosa gave his sister such a firm handshake that Monika's arm jerked up and down like a puppet's. To Reiner, it seemed the two women were mismatched both in energy and direction.

"I told you this is Iannis," Monika said, pointing to the man she'd arrived with. "He has been good to me in this shit."

Iannis' eyes lit up, and he acknowledged the praise with a slight, dignified nod. "It was nothing. *Tipota.* Anytime. I see she is in good hands now, so I will take my leave."

"Let me at least buy you a drink," Reiner said. "It's the least I can do to say thanks."

"I don't drink," Iannis said apologetically. "A health condition. Nothing personal."

Monika gave him a long hug, then watched as the good man walked off into the crowd. Turning back to Reiner and Rosa, she said, "I can't tell you how lucky I was to run into him."

"I love his costume. You say *coss-tjoom* in English?" Rosa said.

Monika nodded, her head turned and her eyes still following the direction Iannis had taken. Reiner was still furious at his sister, but he didn't know how to properly vent. Then he saw Monika turn to Rosa with a smile. She acted as if nothing had happened, as if she deserved to be welcomed back.

"I thought you would send Mutti a postcard, at least," he said.

"Did *you?*" Monika countered.

"I didn't, but it's more important with mothers and daughters, don't you think?"

She shrugged as the only reply.

"You know, I've been thinking about this Bernhard of yours—"

"Bernhard of *mine?* Jesus! Don't rub it in!"

"*Excuse me,* but you have given me a lot of time to think. I admit that he impressed me with his drawing, his artistic eye. But his shoddy disappearing act made me think about another failed artist. You know who I mean?"

"I have no idea."

"The *Führer.* He got rejected from art school, and in his bitterness, turned on everybody and everything."

"You're comparing Bernhard to Hitler? You are totally out of your mind," Monika said. "Bernhard was a sleazebag, but he wouldn't hurt a fly."

Reiner fell silent, unsure what would get his point across. With his comparison and implied prediction so out of scale, he had inadvertently given his sister the upper hand. He felt a sudden sting of both anger and hunger.

"Let's all get some *souflakis,*" he said eventually.

Chapter 17

They lined up at the concession stand and soon had cardboard boxes containing grilled chicken and lamb wrapped in pita bread.

At the head of the long table in the shade sat an aging priest with a substantial gray beard that had collected a generous amount of *tzatziki* from his meal. He wore the traditional *kalimavkion*, a cylindrical head garment, and a cotton *skufia*, as Reiner later learned. Draped around his neck was a long necklace with exquisitely carved beads. Though there were plenty of empty seats, Reiner thought it polite to ask if they could join him. The priest smiled and made a gesture that dismissed this formality and invited them to take as much space as they needed. Reiner could see in the priest's eyes lighting up that he looked forward to having company.

The priest immediately started a conversation with a few words in English. He wanted to know everyone's name; his was Anastacio. Grinning, he pointed first to Monika and then to Reiner and rubbed his index fingers together, just like the police officer in Tymbaki had just a few days ago. It was Rosa who jumped at the chance to object to this incestuous misappropriation.

"You travel where?" Anastacio said.

"Ah, here and there," Reiner said as he dug in. He was a bit tired and not really in the mood for chitchat.

"Here? There?" The priest frowned.

"With 'here' he means right here, and with 'there' he means Heraklion," Rosa explained. "But also Mires, Agios Nikolaos, and Ierapetra. We have seen lot."

"Yes, Crete is beautiful," the priest said solemnly, stroking his beard with his left hand. "My beautiful home is Agios Nikolaos. *Agios* means saint, Saint Nikolaos is saint of sailors, and Greece is a land of sailors." After a pause, during which he looked around to gauge the effect his speech had on his lunch companions, he lifted both hands into the air and added, "Anastacio means resurrection. This is my second appearance." He laughed at his own joke and then turned to Monika, who seemed to have caught his special interest. "You have siblings?"

"Reiner is my brother," she said with a nod at Reiner.

"He looks not," Anastacio said resolutely.

"Many people say so," Monika conceded.

"They look sister and brother," Rosa interjected. "Blue eyes a kilometer apart, high foreheads."

The priest checked his silver pocket watch and abruptly stood. He mumbled and made motions with his hand that could have been blessings. "I meet now my wife. God be with you."

"He is married?" Monika asked once he was out of earshot. "A priest?"

"Greek Orthodox churches allow it, I heard. But they can only do it once. I hope he took a good shot," Reiner said.

Dealing with priests and pastors of any denomination was hard for him since the incident that happened. When he was fourteen, not long after his confirmation, his discomfort in the Bible circle he belonged to reached a climax. Each member of the circle had to recite a prayer or create one from scratch, then speak it aloud while everyone listened and judged. And every time it was his turn, he had sweated preparing the prayer, and spent so much time making sure it was genuine and sounded heartfelt and original.

After that, he felt elated because the weight had been lifted and an entire week lay ahead, during which he did not have to think about the next prayer.

One day, during his appointed turn, he said, "Oh, God, I'm sure you are not listening since you have better things to do."

The seminary student running the show had cornered him afterward with a serious reprimand. Since then, Reiner had dismissed religion as gobbledygook and had to restrain himself from mocking believers and clergymen ever since. He remembered when he'd renounced religion, but still had to witness his sister's sheeplike adherence to senseless Calvinist rituals when her own confirmation approached.

He kept quiet about his newly found freedom since he feared being reprimanded by his parents; he also did not dare call himself an atheist since that label carried connotations of godless communists like Lenin and Stalin, and the threat of expulsion from the entire congregation. Real atheists had to proselytize their convictions and reach as many souls as possible to save them from needless suffering in this life and, in particular, the afterlife.

It had gotten hot out. A donkey braying in the distance made Reiner smile. He'd come to love the sound as both quixotic and existential: an immodest assertion of importance and, at the same time, a call for attention from all creatures bestowed with ears within braying distance. If there was no reply from another donkey within ten seconds, it meant that the solitary crier would be left alone for at least the rest of the day.

What would it be like, traveling with two women when it was already hard with just one? In that instant, he realized that he'd never shown affection for any woman other than his mother in front of his sister. It would be awkward for Monika to witness his intimacy with Rosa—and for him, as well.

"Let's get some more *retsina*," he said firmly, but it felt a bit like a little boy shouting to compensate for his fear.

"I love your ear loops," Rosa said to Monika, stroking the one nearest to her without actually touching Monika's face.

The silver earrings, each comprised of three circular interlocking wires of different sizes, swung gently at her touch. Reiner held his breath, waiting for his sister's response.

"Oh, thank you," Monika said. And then she repeated the words to herself softly, without looking at Rosa, as if trying to unearth a hidden meaning in them. "Thank you."

He was even more relieved than he thought he would be under the circumstances. In the worst-case scenario, he'd imagined that the two women wouldn't get along and he would have had to spend his time translating and negotiating between them. But here they were, already making real conversation without his help!

"Rosa comes from this place in northern Spain called Salamanca," Reiner told his sister. "She says it has very old fortresses and churches. It also has the oldest university in Europe."

Explaining Rosa's presence to Monika—her existence, her unique qualities—was suddenly the number one goal on his mind. Hypothetically, of course, he tried to envision what it would be like to introduce her to his parents, but his imagination failed him.

"It must be nice to come from a place like that," Monika said.

"Thank you very much so," Rosa said. "But it was not special thing, for me, because it is where I growed. You see?"

"Where we come from, there is just this one castle, and it's maybe five hundred years old. Looks crappy, too."

"That's OK," Rosa said. "At least you have one."

Monika laughed. "I never think to bring up our stupid castle. I guess every town in Germany has at least one."

"Yeah, but some of them are really old—like a thousand years," Reiner said. Though reluctant to reintroduce more serious matters back into the conversation, he sighed and said, "You need to call home before we go anywhere else."

"Oh, shit! My goodness, yes," Monika said. "What am I going to say?"

"That's a good question." He was still angry, and couldn't resist clearing it from his lungs when the opportunity presented itself.

Reiner asked someone for directions to the post office so Monika could make her call. It turned out to be one of the official-looking buildings flanking the plaza and the grand festival. There was a line for the phone booths, and it took a full hour for Monika to advance to the front. Reiner showed her how to dial the prefixes in order to reach Germany, then left her in the booth to deal with their mother.

Alone again with Rosa, he tried to kiss her, but she twisted her slim, sinewy body away from him and said she was tired. For what seemed like an endless ten minutes, he just stood next to her in uncomfortable silence and watched Monika's gestures in the glass box from afar. He could only guess how the conversation was going.

"How did it go?" he asked her when she finally came back.

"So-so," she said, tipping the palm of her hand side to side, her expression withdrawn.

"Come on, tell me!"

"Mutti screamed at me, then started crying."

"Yes, well, what did you expect?"

"I tried to explain—"

"If there is one good explanation, I certainly haven't heard it."

She looked at him with hurt in her eyes and then turned to Rosa. The two women left him standing there, simmering, and whispered to each other a few yards away. Reiner plopped down on a bench by the post office with his backpack and his sleeping bag.

His worst fears about losing control were taking shape. He fished in his bag for the book he had brought with him for just such an occasion, but when he opened it, the letters swam before his eyes and drifted away. They would reassemble again in different combinations, in a different book, miles away where someone else would read them, and that was fine with him just then because he needed to gather his thoughts around something else. He was embarrassed that he'd had to scold his sister and side with Mutti as if he was nothing but an extended arm of their parents' authority—a secret police, as it were. He had fancied himself some kind of knight, someone able to guide and console his sister, but in this first trial, he'd failed her miserably.

Chapter 18

"We're finally going to see Vai beach!" Monika exclaimed at breakfast. "I'm so excited."

"Sounds fun," Rosa said on the tail end of a yawn as she snuggled up to Reiner. She was barely awake, confirming his assumption, almost from day one, that she was not a morning person.

They were sitting in one of those ramshackle restaurants that lined the street. This one had a veranda that was overgrown with grapevines that let sprinkles of sunlight fall through to the tables below. A transistor radio on the windowsill played one of the endless fiddle tunes from the Greek islands. Since landing with Monika in Heraklion, he had acquired a taste for the upbeat rhythms that whipped people into a frenzy at festivals in public squares—so much so that his legs twitched every time he heard it.

They had spent the night in their sleeping bags in an orchard just south of Palaikastro, a little village named for an old Minoan castle on the hill. It was part of the route to get to Vai beach, which was still six kilometers away, due north. The ground was covered in rugged stones, and Rosa had joined Reiner in his sleeping bag. She wasn't tired then, as she'd let him know as soon as she settled next to him. Monika was in the other sleeping bag, on her own. He tried to listen to her breathe, and at one time he thought he heard her cry, but the evening also carried the persistent chirping of crickets, which drowned out the softer sounds of supposedly sleeping humans. Even Rosa's whispers were hard to make out and he had to guess at much of what she said, except for what was made obvious from the way she moved and caressed him. It was an unforeseen reversal of the night in Matala.

They'd all been roused by the birds earlier than they would have liked; in the sleeping bag, there was only so much one could do to cover one's ears, and Rosa had opened her eyes and looked at Reiner, still drunk with sleep, with an astonished expression, as if she had just arrived from Mars.

"You go to Vai?" the waiter said. He must have overheard the conversation as he brought their omelets. "Beautiful place, must-see! Palms planted by Arab pirates long time ago."

"Don't talk nonsense, Giorgios!" the owner of the restaurant said as he walked by to check on his customers' satisfaction. "The first palms were planted by the Phoenicians. Every child knows that!"

"When? Two thousand years ago? Three?" Reiner asked.

"Three thousand is more like it," the owner said.

The siblings and Rosa looked at one another, mouthing *three thousand*. The span of a hundred years was already difficult to fathom, but a period thirty times as long was inconceivable.

After a quick consultation with the map, they decided to walk the rest of the way since the bus would not leave until noon. Six kilometers seemed easy enough to handle, and the morning was still young.

"Rosa, do us a favor," Reiner said, passing his little camera to her. "Take a picture of the two of us. We have nothing to show we even spent any time together."

As he posed with his sister, he experienced a moment of detective's satisfaction: Vai was where he'd expected Monika to wind up when he'd set out to find her and her asshole of a companion a few days before. So, even if he had not stopped at *Sitia Extra Municipal Stop*, he concluded that he would have caught up with her eventually.

Their initial excitement soon faded as the entire road turned out to lack trees to offer any shade. It was a very dull walk across flat terrain and through a seemingly endless field of high swamp grass; a purple haze hovered atop the mass of saturated greenery. The walls of reeds on either side were so high that they could see little else but the part of the curvy dirt road that was right in front of them. The sun stung any exposed skin from high up in the sky, so to stay in the partial shade, they had to walk along the wall of reeds to their right. But, the terrain was unkempt and walking on the grass proved treacherous. Mosquitoes were everywhere, and some larger insects— like beetles and dragonflies—rushed by with only droning sounds as warnings. Searching for exotic palms at every turn, only to be disappointed each time, the three travelers fell into a grumpy silence, during which the attribution of blame grew like a poisonous weed.

Monika was high on the list due to her initial burst of enthusiasm, but in reality, Reiner knew she would have been justified in pointing the finger squarely at him since he had been the one to show her the pictures of this place in the library back home. If Rosa could be faulted for anything, then it was only for failing to veto the plan, but she would be in her right to argue that it would have been two against one at that point.

"I got cramps in my foots," Rosa said, her brow furrowed. "Can we rest for awhile?"

Apparently, she was unused to walking longer distances, and had misjudged her ability to do more than three kilometers without stopping. Reiner and Monika exchanged a glance of exasperation before sitting down with her on the ground. Both were used to endless walks with Papa through the forest, often covering several kilometers without interruption, with lunch in a family restaurant as the reward for when they were done.

Reiner felt his obligations as loving brother to one woman and new lover to the other to be increasingly difficult. While he cherished this renewed closeness with his sister, dealing with this additional person—this virtual stranger and her idiosyncrasies, moodiness, and cramps in her 'foots'—was a challenge he had not planned for. And he saw that Rosa's demands for intimacy were in direct conflict with his own wish to make good on his promise to his sister: that they'd both have a great time in Greece together.

Rosa must have picked up on these unarticulated thoughts, since she'd begun to sulk. Once they were back on the road, she walled herself off and stopped looking directly at Reiner, but sneaked sideways glances as one would at a villain whose respect for values shared by all can no longer be taken for granted.

The dreadful silence went on until, at one point, they heard the roar of an engine. They had to quickly jump to the side of the road to get out of the way of a bus—the blue-gray bus they had dismissed earlier, in fact. It mocked them now by making much faster progress toward the same destination. Reiner swore under his breath; they'd wasted all this time with Rosa's prolonged rest in the middle of nowhere.

"Our map is without scale," Monika said as they watched the taillights of the bus disappear. "I don't know how and why we decided to walk. It was really stupid."

Reiner pressed his lips together and said nothing.

They spent another hour sweating and fighting off mosquitoes before they saw the palms—no less than five thousand of them, according to the brochure they'd picked up in Sitia—standing like a wall on the shore of the deep blue Ionian Sea. It was one of those vistas that was so breathtaking, yet at the same time completely predictable—much like a doctored picture on a postcard. But the sheer harmony of it, and the fact that all of it was tangible and finally right in front of them, made the trio stop and stand in awe.

"It is totally…" Monika started, only to fall short of any descriptors.

"*Fantástico*," Rosa finished for her, breaking her brewing silence for the first time.

All three started to talk at once, giddy at having been proven wrong in their secret but shared and growing conviction that the promised palms were nothing but a tall tale. There was no one else on the beach, and after a quick look around just to be sure, Rosa stripped naked, left her little bundle of clothes at the foot of a palm tree, and ran into the water until she was immersed up to her breasts, immediately accepted by the sea. The sight and glory of Rosa's body made the air around Reiner vibrate, and the earth seemed to take notice. The long, feathery leaves of the palms nearby swayed in slow motion, as if connected by invisible strings. Reiner inhaled deeply, but his breath stopped for a short moment. He and Monika looked at each other in silence for a few seconds, both waiting for the other to come to some sort of decision.

"Hell, I'm in," he said and bent down to start taking his shoes off.

In quick succession, and in less than a minute, he took off his socks, shirt, pants, and underpants. Wordlessly and with her face turned away, Monika stripped as well, and both ran across the beach to join Rosa in purging themselves of all the sweat and discontentment of that morning's dreadful walk.

PART III

Ierapetra

Chapter 19

Reiner sat in the room he'd rented at the very top of a slim, three-story tower made of concrete. The spiral staircase was so tight it seemed more like a harness hugging his body on the way up. Or maybe he would liken it to a tunnel, through which he would be reborn each time he went down and out of the building. This made him think of his mother and how he'd lied to her through his teeth about Monika. He would have to make up for that, so he made a mental note to buy her a very nice present.

Don't they have those beautifully embroidered tablecloths here?

He was the eye in the sky. From his elevated post in Ierapetra, the view of the southern coast of Crete was all rolling, glittering waves of the ocean. The exotic continent of Africa was too far away to glimpse, although he knew that if the earth itself weren't withholding from him the sight of the land beyond the horizon, it was somewhere out there in that same direction. The eye in the sky was inseparable from the firmament and everything contained in it. There was no Reiner anymore. or, on the contrary, everything around had become Reiner, without bounds.

He was paying the equivalent of four dollars a week, in drachmas, to the old, black-clothed, almost toothless woman who lived downstairs. She pretty much left him alone, but he knew there were already rumors in town about that crazy lodger from Germany who had decided to earn money by working outside on the road in the searing sun. The work crew he'd joined was building a trench for the new water pipe that would connect the town's cistern with an orchard. Greeks sought employment in Germany in droves, so the case of a German willing to earn three dollars a day through hard, manual work in Greece was something new and worth talking about in a town with little in the way of news. For instance, the town newspaper—Η εβδομαδιαία πάθος, or *The Weekly Passion*—featured portraits of chickens with outstanding laying records on its cover. In the last week, it had reported the felling of a six-hundred-year-old olive tree owned by the local apothecary. It was an obituary.

Just a couple of weeks earlier, Monika took a bus to Heraklion and flew back home via Athens to return to her job as a physical therapist. Rosa had left him the very next day. She seemed to have gotten used to the intricate balance of their triangular constellation, and after Monika's departure, Reiner imagined that she might have felt he alone was no longer enough to hold her attention. Rosa had often sat and whispered with Monika—girl talk that excluded him. When they hiked narrow paths in the mountains, and they widened for a short while to accept two people side by side, the women were always quick to team up and left him trotting along behind them.

After a couple of days of mourning, he'd accepted Rosa's departure as an inevitable installment of his fate, which would never have allowed him to lay claim on perfection of any sort. He had a few images of Rosa burnt in his memory, kept in a special place: her sitting on the mattress and commanding him to join her, asleep on the bus with her head in his lap, the moment she stripped naked on the beach of palms, and the indescribable glory of her body as she waded into the sea. In all probability, he would never see her again, but he also accepted that the sadness he felt at the loss would never quite leave him; it would become part of him.

But there was something else that stayed with him. During the time he spent with his sister that summer, he had witnessed her exuberance, her boundless joy in this light-and laughter-filled country once she felt free and was able to make use of that freedom. He had also witnessed her apprehension as the day of her departure drew close, at the idea of getting back to the confines of her life at home. Unlike her, he was between jobs, between two significant phases of his life, between the exam that had earned him a bachelor's degree and the start of his graduate studies, which left the entire summer open for play. Unlike her, he was in no real rush to go back to Germany, except perhaps to see Almut again. On the other hand, she had made no effort to contact him.

The day before, he'd taken off from work because the blisters he had earned wielding the hoe had broken and were raw and bloody on his palms. The water that ran in thin, lukewarm streams out of the showerhead burned the raw flesh like fire. He had found an ointment in the pharmacy across the plaza to soothe his pain but was barely able to apply it since moving his fingers hurt on both hands.

Immobilized, lying propped up on his metal bedframe bed, he looked out the window into the distance, taking in the waves and, to the right, the cliffs on the shore that lent their name to the town. He was surrounded by a continuous blanket of light that glistened on the water and covered the beach and the cliffs and the flat roofs of the buildings. He felt the boundary between this abundant light around him and the light within vanish. It occurred to him that if it were not for the pain in the palms of his hands and the worries about his sister, his person might simply cease to exist, only to be submerged into another all-embracing consciousness.

Steps audibly vibrating the iron staircase and then a knock on the door interrupted his reflections. The knock turned out to be perfunctory, since Maria, the landlady, entered without waiting to be granted entry.

"*Kali mera!*" she greeted him with her high-pitched voice.

"*Kali mera, einen schönen guten Tag,*" he replied as he sat up, not bothered to hide his confusion since this kind of intrusion had never happened before.

She set a bag down on his little desk, all the while speaking to him quickly, without allowing for the fact that he did not understand more than a few words of Greek. She only had a few German words in her vocabulary, words that German tourists had left behind for her like crumbs. Her gestures, though, were vivid; she pointed with her finger to her mouth, then to the beach, then to the fields he had worked in, then to his hands, and finally down the staircase below. She waved her arms and pulled a little bottle out of the bag.

From all this he could make out that word had gotten around about the sorry state of his hands, mostly because it was the consequence of his decision to take on work for which he was blatantly unfit. The little bottle of medicine contained a high concentration of alcohol and a pinch of resin and spice; when he took a sip, it made him sputter and cough, and it somehow reminded him of Southern Comfort minus the dash of sweetness.

The most important part of her message, if he'd interpreted it correctly, was that nobody expected him to come back to work. The fact was that the blisters would take a week or two to fully heal, and by that time, the aqueduct was supposed to be finished, the water turned on and running. He knew that nobody had taken his determination to work with the hoe seriously, nor had they found it believable that a German would have to rely on the measly wage for his upkeep.

She pulled an ointment out of her bag that smelled of mint, and when he pointed at the tube he'd bought in the pharmacy, the one he'd been using to dress his wounds, she became agitated and gestured for him to throw it away. Evidently, she was very much concerned about his health, which he found quite touching. But he also saw the helplessness brought on by his open blisters compounded by his inability to express gratitude or to ask questions about the natural medicine she'd brought with her. He made a mental note to put more serious effort into learning Greek.

In the meantime, he bowed to her small figure, mumbling *efkaristo* over and over again. She gestured and giggled and smiled with her almost toothless mouth and then commenced with her delicate footsteps backward, down the staircase. He knew that for her, going forward would be suicide.

Chapter 20

That he was unable to work was a blow to Reiner's plans to travel to the southwestern part of the island, to the wild mountains and gorges and then back up to Chania on the northern coast. He had just enough cash to last a week, even if he just lived on tomatoes, feta cheese, and bread. When his sister left, he'd asked her for her remaining travelers checks and promised to pay her back once he got home, but all she could give him was one worth about twenty deutsche marks.

He spent a restless night with the palms of his hands burning. When he finally fell asleep, he had a most peculiar dream. A man rang the bell of his apartment back in Freiburg and delivered a box. When Reiner opened the box, the rabbit inside looked him in the eye and spoke French in the distinctly Parisian way, saying *ouich* where *oui* was called for. He pleaded with the animal to speak in German, or at least English, but it looked at him in a blasé way—the way rabbits do only when in a privileged position as revered pet. He tried to stroke the rabbit, but it returned the favor by biting his hands. What he found most odd, though, was that a single rabbit could bite both of his hands at the same time.

Upon waking, he found his blisters were still extremely painful. He took them as a reminder of his bad judgment in the past, such as the utter stupidity of taking a job involving hard manual work, and as an omen for more stupidity to follow.

He tried in vain to remember the face of the man who'd made the delivery in his dream, but he recognized the signs of anxiety and knew they could all be attributed to uncertainty about the road ahead. He would enter graduate school in the fall, but the truth was that he had little confidence in his own talent for research. So far, he had only done courses offering what were called Mickey Mouse exercises: experiments designed to train students, but that lacked any other useful purpose.

Outside, the sea reflected the moon where it hung low on the horizon below a dark bank of clouds. He heard the sounds of raindrops hitting the window. It took him a while to reconcile these observations. Then he saw a rainbow, a clear rainbow, on the opposite side of the moon. It was painted in very pale colors, or perhaps a succession of several shades of gray with only the faded colors added by his imagination.

Whoever heard of such a thing: a rainbow in the middle of night? Was there such a thing as a moonbow?

Goose bumps broke out on his skin. He had the urge to talk to someone, a real person. God was ut of the question, though now he saw some merit to being a believer.

He thought of climbing down the spiral staircase to wake his landlady, but dismissed the idea when he imagined her plump little person, frightened and clad in an embroidered, white cotton nightgown, lying in her bed below a large ebony crucifix. He knew it was impossible to talk with her, of all people, about the sight of a rainbow at night. Even if she actually grasped what he claimed to have seen with his own eyes, she might try to exorcise the spirit that gave him this vision by waiving a *komboloi* at him, or perhaps a portable version of her crucifix.

Instead, he stood by the window, holding his hands against his chest so the pressure could ease the pain, and watched the rainbow as it slowly intensified, developed a weaker, concentric echo, then faded away.

What if nobody else saw it? What if nobody believes me?

It was another version of the question of whether or not a tree falling in the forest still made a sound even if nobody was around. In his mind, he prepared a vivid description of what he had seen and a plausible explanation for it that would not violate the tenets of physics. In doing so, he also prepared a defense against the mockery he would surely face when telling the story.

He sat down at his desk, switched the lamp on, and started to write down his impressions, but quickly found he was unable to hold the pen because of the pain in his hands. The moonlit night, the faint colors of the rainbow, the paradox of natural events, his distress over the absence of witnesses—all of this he felt he must commit to writing. But first, he needed to wait for his blisters to heal.

Chapter 21

"A gray rainbow, but the gray shades were actually faded hues of the colors there should have been. You know what I'm talking about?" Reiner raised his arms and moved them around, forming a semicircle in the air as if that would help him describe what he saw.

"Rainbow? At night?" Achilles laughed as he went through the day's batch of mail. "You were drunk? Too much *ouzo!*"

He wiggled his finger, which was stained black from handling the mail, in mock disapproval.

"*Retsina,* actually," Reiner said. "But that's not the point."

"*Tipota,*" Achilles said after checking the mailbox and then shrugging his shoulders in regret. "Nothing today."

Achilles was the clerk at the post office: a little agile man with a mustache and a permanent smile in his eyes, as if it were ingrained after he heard an unsurpassed cosmic joke. His status in town was high since he played the bouzouki at all the events held in the plaza. Reiner visited him every day to ask if any letters had come for him, and Achilles had taken an interest.

There were no letters today: none from his parents, his sister, or his girlfriend. Right after Monika left, he wrote a long letter—perhaps the longest he had ever written considering it covered six light blue onionskin pages to save on airmail postage—spelling out his disapproval of her actions in Matala. Although his letter did not accuse her explicitly of ruining his vacation, in hindsight, it came close. It was also peppered with snide remarks about Bernhard, which he now regretted, especially since she still had not replied. In his head, he'd reviewed what he wrote, and had since lost confidence in the accuracy of his memory regarding the exact phrasing he'd used and the precise words to which she might have taken offense.

He made a note to change his habits and keep copies of his letters from then on. But since carbon paper was difficult to come by in this country, the only way to start this summer was to write the letter twice: once on the page to be mailed, and once in his notebook.

He raised his hand, waving goodbye to Achilles.

"No more dreaming! No more rainbows," Achilles called out to him as he left, sticking his head out of the window of his cubicle. "Easy on the *ouzo*! And get some sleep!"

Reiner stood in the plaza for a while, unsure how he would spend the day, which had only just begun. The sun was still low; the midday heat was still three hours away. Going back to his room atop the little tower was a depressing thought, as it felt like a prison now. His thoughts were with the crew out in the field; the first leather bag of cool water would just be making the rounds, the handles of the pickaxes would rest against trunks of large trees, the men would take out their handkerchiefs and wipe their sunburnt faces and necks, and fat Georgiou would tell yet another of his obscene jokes.

But Reiner could not allow himself to wander in that direction; he couldn't face the questions that they'd surely holler at him, or even the good-humored comments that would be made by these able-bodied natives who could work hard for eight hours and still have enough energy left to sit at the bar and drink and chat well into the night. He decided to take a walk westward on the dirt road lining the stone beach. He'd go past the large rock, the *petra* part of Ierapetra, and head well past the point he'd explored when he first arrived.

Driftwood, pieces of plastic, orange crates in various states, and broken chairs were scattered along the beach. It was innocent trash of the local people—nothing to get too upset about. The glistening white stones covering the beach were almost round and a bit bigger than tennis balls in size: painful to tread on barefoot or when wearing sandals. Not even a donkey—a *yathuri*—could walk there. Its hooves would slip, having found no purchase. The whole beach was deserted as far as he could see. Perhaps this was the reason why the town did not bother to clean up the accumulated debris; it was poor, and there were other tourist attractions to spend money on improving. But Reiner didn't mind seeing the chaotic assemblage of disjointed objects that the waves, those ubiquitous matchmakers, had brought together.

He thought of how he would describe the beach to Almut, and how she might react. They had never been on a trip together; this would have been the first one. The whole relationship with her was still bewildering, and even the idea of calling her his girlfriend sometimes seemed unreal. That is why he did not talk about her with anyone, especially not his younger sister.

Almut was a bit fastidious, so she might have seen the objects on the beach as a disturbance of order and not as a mess that was beautiful in its own right. She would have had the urge to carry it all away to the town dump and then take pride in her civic accomplishment. He was a bit worried about this contrast to his own reaction, but took comfort in the idea that he could educate her, that all they'd need was time for some sort of course in junk art appreciation he could teach her; true closeness to him would be both a reward and the final goal.

But the fact remained that she had not written back to him. Not even once. There was a gross asymmetry to this situation. Wasn't he the one who was alone, craving for the next best substitute for companionship—no more than a letter!—while she was surrounded by friends in her natural habitat? The very idea that she did not seem to appreciate the effect that her silence had on him made him apprehensive. Or rather, he recognized the tension, and for the first time was determined to attribute it to her.

Maybe she was the kind of person who couldn't express her feelings well in writing. They'd never had to test this before, and that would be a plausible reason for her not to write, but she should have realized he would still want to receive *something* from her at some point. Something material—even a postcard. He was tempted to chalk it up to a lack of imagination, maybe even compassion. He made up his mind to call her, to confront her when he was back in town.

Rosa would be different in this situation, he was certain. She would assert herself and write to him passionately. The thought warmed his heart since it made him think about her little grammar and diction mistakes, the gems that were so much part of her and her temperament. If he ever crossed her path again, he would have to be careful not to spoil it by correcting her too much.

Walking a bit further, he got distracted by the sight of some stones on the beach, which lit up in the sun as if they'd made direct contact with white-hot, glowing embers. He even thought he heard hissing sounds, the kind hot iron makes when it hits water. But it was probably just the waves splashing on shore and then sucking and luring the stones into the depth of the sea. He wondered if, were he to immerse himself in the water, he would hear the stones hitting one another. It would be a thoroughly pleasing sound, he thought, a sound that would travel quickly under water, modulated with echoes and twangs much like Hawaiian guitars, plus the much lower pitch and sound of gulping, as though a giant were buried alive there with his head sticking out to swallow some water with every breath.

* * *

"Almut? Are you still sick? I miss you so much," Reiner greeted her on the phone.

"I'm over it now. It was no fun at all, just boring as hell. I envy you. Why didn't you write? Not a postcard, even. Did your sister fly back already?"

"I wrote you a long letter. Perhaps the mail takes longer to get there in summer? Just you wait a couple of days. It was a really long letter, passionate. And yes, my sister went back after her one week of leave. Don't you guys ever talk?"

"About what? You?"

He walked back from the post office, a little ashamed of himself for all the blame he'd heaped on her during his lonely walk that afternoon without one iota of true evidence that she deserved it.

Chapter 22

In his tiny temporary abode, at an altitude well above the rock Ierapetra got its name from, he looked down and saw the lights of the boats fishing for *kalamari*, or squid. The animals they caught would turn into purple, rubbery, five-armed carcasses to be hung on clotheslines along the beach for the purpose of attracting diners to the local restaurants.

Reiner realized that, without the reinforcement that came with speaking his own language, or at the very least English, he would continue to be insubstantial in Greece. Concentrating on people he knew, imagining conversations he could have with them when he got home, would help restore his sense of self. This absolute need for reliance on others was an entirely new experience.

He'd once scoffed at stories of people stranded on uninhabited islands, which all acquired a strength that bordered on superhuman, and now he understood their true struggle to remain themselves while isolated. Few people would survive with their senses intact, and he knew he certainly wouldn't be one of them. That is how he came to reconsider the encounter with his landlady a couple of days before, why he regretted not having sat down with her for a few shots of *ouzo*—after which her physical appearance and age probably would have been more bearable. He could have come up with this idea just for the sake of maintaining good rapport with her, but it dawned on him that he actually needed this human contact for his own sanity's sake.

That people needed each other to survive not just because they relied on each other's goods and services, but for physical intimacy, empathy, and touch was an amazing discovery that inspired him to think back on whether or not perhaps his family was atypical in some way. In fact, he could not recall an instance of physical contact with his family members except the obligatory shaking of hands every morning. But of course, his memory didn't reach back all the way to the time when he'd been held as a baby or a toddler by his mother and grandmother. Grabbing his diary, he began writing whatever came to mind.

[Ierapetra. Re.: early childhood]

There is this early memory of lying awake next to Mutti one afternoon. She was trying to get me to sleep, and it's one of the first times I can remember experiencing total powerlessness. The curtains were translucent, and where they overlapped, they produced moiré patterns that changed abruptly each time I repositioned my head. But with every one of my movements, the noise from the rustling of the pillow and the cover kept my mother awake, and she would admonish me, gently at first, to keep quiet. I would be able keep quiet for a minute at a time, but then again started stirring. All the while, I was unable to understand why I had to spend this perfect hour of the day in supervised confinement. I heard other children's voices outside; they were probably playing hide-and-seek or some kind of ball game, and they were unfettered, enjoying their freedom.

Eventually, Mutti lost her patience and hushed me by hitting the down cover, which made a muffled sound as her hand barely missed my leg. It filled me with terror since I didn't know what might come next, but I instinctively expected worse.

* * *

On the morning of his third day in the rented room, he heard clanking steps on the spiral staircase. His landlady appeared at his doorstep with the news that Christos Maniatis, son of Theophilus Maniatis and a distant cousin of hers, sought German lessons. Later, he found out she'd made promises about Reiner's amazing instructional abilities without ever having seen him teach a single class. But, since he was desperate for money, he made no attempt to refute her claim.

He went out to the only general store in town and bought pencils and paper. Back in his room, he sharpened a few of them and lined them up on his desk. He also put his clothes in order and made up his bed.

Christos arrived with his mother that afternoon. He was a thin fifteen-year-old with striking blue eyes and blond hair, as Reiner was told some people had in northern Greece. His mother was middle-aged, a bit on the heavier side, and her breathing was labored from the effort of climbing the steep stairway. The boy seemed quite shy, but was on the verge of smiling for their entire lesson, though Reiner soon found that he used that smile to stall whenever he didn't know what to say—which was often.

"He doesn't talk a lot," his mother said. "But he is a smart one; you'll find out soon enough!"

At first, Christos did not acknowledge any praise, then he brushed it off with a twitch of his mouth. Reiner remembered similar scenes with his own mother when he was a boy, and he threw Christos a quick glance of empathy.

"He has some inhibitions, you know," she would say to a salesman in the department store. "But don't be fooled! He is *really* smart."

Christos's mother's eyes darted around, probably taking stock of this strange bachelor's few belongings: a backpack, a suitcase, two books, a stack of paper, and five pencils lying parallel on his desk, three of which were newly sharpened. The bed was in fairly decent order, and there was a picture of a black-haired woman on his nightstand. One poster adorned the wall: a man with guitar and wild hair on a stage.

Meanwhile, her son just stood there and grinned.

They agreed to two weeks of daily lessons, a *tour de force*, which Reiner thought could get the boy started if he was motivated enough. Reiner would have to rely on his limited Greek vocabulary to communicate, and he knew the learning curve would be steep.

But from that very first visit, it became clear that Christos did not seem much interested in learning German. He'd often stare out the window and miss questions. His pronunciation was bad, and it did not improve from one session to the next. Apparently, the German umlauts were instruments of torture. Reiner let it go at first, but his student's progress continued to be dismal and he simply couldn't ignore it.

"Christos, something is not right," Reiner finally said one afternoon at the end of week number one. It was raining outside, and the boy had walked in soaking wet. "Your aunt told me you really wanted to learn German, and I promised your mother that I'd get you fairly conversational in two weeks, but here we are, and your mind is somewhere else entirely."

Christos didn't seem to understand the problem, and that could have been attributed to their remaining language barrier. But then he confided in him, whispering—even though there wasn't a soul around to overhear him—that his sister was actually the one interested in the lessons, and that he was just a go-between.

"Wait—you are supposed to teach *her* what I taught *you?*" Reiner felt a jolt of anger as the boy nodded his head. "But why? Couldn't she come here and take the lessons herself?"

"My mother says it's not proper."

"Not proper because of what? Because I'm single?" he asked, exasperation clear in his voice.

"Yes, I think that is what she means."

"How old is your sister?"

"She's thirteen."

"Jesus, then bring her with you next time. You can be her chaperone."

"What is a chaperone?"

"You'll be with her, watching over her, and your mother won't have to worry."

It was silent for a solid thirty seconds as the boy avoided looking at him. Finally, he said, "Mother cannot afford pay for two."

"I won't charge for two. Just bring her along."

Christos apparently didn't know what to say. Reiner regretted his own show of impatience and for raising his voice during the conversation.

The boy left in a hurry, and Reiner barely caught him in time to call down the spiral staircase, "What's her name?"

"Kanta," was the boy's reply.

That night, Reiner dreamt of a woman with that name. He did not see her face; he just saw her walking on the beach, away from him. Just as he was about to call out to her, he stopped himself. It was futile, or—as the Greek saying went—like talking to a mulberry tree. The ocean would all but swallow his voice with the distance between them. He tried to follow her, but something was holding him back, something that turned out to be as silly as a pebble in his shoe.

He awoke, it was with the realization that the name Kanta might be related to singing, and as he started to recall the dream, he reimagined the woman singing a song from her childhood, confident that no one but the sea would hear her.

And then, with his brain fully awake, all his memories and worries came flying back to him from their nightly nests. He felt a pang of guilt since, in the dream, he'd acted out the very fantasy Kanta's mother was probably worried about, enough to keep her away from tutoring sessions. Reiner was incredulous when the boy brought it up the day before, but his subconscious had been complicit all along.

That morning he took a walk on the beach, his sister on his mind, and put a conscious effort into displacing the figure from his dream. He had not heard from Monika since she left, and he had the growing sense that he had failed her. It all started with his stupid decision to lie down on the beach, white-skinned as he was, and the consequences of that decision begat others, a sequence that rivaled the biblical type in length and led to his sister leaving without experiencing the fun and adventure he'd promised her at the start of the summer.

Chapter 23

Reiner fully expected that nobody would show up at three o'clock the next afternoon. He didn't know if Christos had the wherewithal to convey his message to his mother, and, even if he did, Reiner was not convinced that Christos's mother would change her attitude. But, at ten past the hour, he heard steps on the stairs—more steps than could come from a single person.

Kanta didn't look her age; she looked more like she was ready to start college in the fall. With brown eyes, frizzy brunette hair, and adventure written on her face, she had the radiance of an unbridled woman in a Chekhov story. Reiner took a deep breath. The idea that the presence of Christos as a chaperone could make a difference and influence fate one way or the other seemed ludicrous. This woman—girl, Reiner corrected himself—was obviously in full command of the situation. Christos appeared to know his diminished role and dutifully made himself invisible by settling in the corner of the room.

"I'm Reiner," he introduced himself to the newcomer. "Would you like to sit down? I heard you have taken my classes already, in a way."

"*Tipota,*" she said, shrugging as she took a seat. "He tell me."

"Well, good. We can start with a conversation about the beach."

"I like bitch," she said, smiling so broadly he had a hard time keeping a straight face.

"It's 'beach.' A longer sound than you would use in 'bitch.'"

"Long bitch," she said with a measure of triumph on her face. Then she turned to her brother and spoke a gush of words in high-speed Greek, none of which Reiner understood.

"What was that all about?" he asked Christos.

"She told me to go home," Christos said, his arms folded across his chest. "But I will not."

Reiner did not wish to take her side since he was afraid it would be misunderstood, but he didn't want to take Christos' side either since it sounded ridiculous and outdated to restrict Kanta's education based on Reiner's marital status, especially when the girl supposedly in need of protection was able to defend herself so well. In the end, Christos refused to leave because he was there on strict orders from his mother, and he probably faced trouble at home if he came back early and all by himself.

Kanta treated her brother with contempt, throwing abuses in his direction whenever there was a break in the German lesson. Her brother—as far as Reiner understood her view of the matter—was not man enough to stand up for what he believed in. Reiner couldn't help but compare their situation with the way he related to his own sister. She'd never put him down; in fact, she'd always been the underdog, the lowest on the totem pole at their parents' house.

The next time Kanta came all by herself, and for every lesson after that. Apparently, she had won some kind of battle at home. She was dressed in jeans and a T-shirt over a bra that managed to show the contours of her nipples. Reiner, trying to fend off her charm, forced himself to keep his distance and treated her almost coldly. He dismissed the idea that he could be attracted to her. It was quite absurd, and yet there she was. Since he only knew the basics of Greek, and she only knew her home language and minimal German, communication was difficult. But, he found her a quick learner within the sparse common universe of meaning they built up together, which often resorted to gestures and winks.

"This morning, I went to the market," he said slowly to his pupil, who was seated in all her glory in front of him. "Today, the raisins are expensive. Kanta, say something!"

"Do! Not! Sell! Raisins! Today!" she shouted.

"That's excellent! But it's *buy*, not *sell*. You see, sellers do well when the raisins are expensive."

"What are sellers?"

"Sellers are people who sell raisins. Or, in fact, anything else."

"What is *in fact*?"

"Oh, Christ!" he said, burying his face in his hands.

* * *

The exact reason why she was interested in learning German was unclear until a couple of days later when she mentioned Karl May, the German writer and swindler from the turn of the century. He wrote adventure stories while doing time in a federal prison, which he'd been sent to for grand larceny. His books took place in the American frontier and centered on characters like *Old Shatterhand* and *Winnetou*, and they were all popular among boys of a certain age in Germany. It seemed some of this popularity had spread to other European countries.

At the time that he wrote his adolescent stories, May had never set foot in America or the Middle East, where many of his other stories were set. To Reiner's great surprise, Kanta was a Karl May fan, and she longed to read his prose in the original language, not in the terrible translations offered in Greece. When she mentioned she had a Karl May book in German at home, one of those in a festive leather-fake binding, he asked her to bring it with her to her next lesson. From then on, May's made-up macho stories about heroes in the Wild West became the stuff of Reiner's lessons:

"Mein Pferd war außerordentlich unruhig geworden; es tanzte mit den Hufen; es hatte auch noch keine Büffel gesehen, fürchtete sich und wollte fliehen; kaum vermochte ich, es zurückzuhalten. War es da nicht besser, wenn ich es zwang, den Bullen anzunehmen? Ich war nicht etwa erregt, sondern überlegte, innerlich ganz ruhig, zwischen Ja und Nein. Da entschied der Eindruck des Augenblickes." – "My horse had become unusually restless; it jumped on its hooves. It had never seen a buffalo in its whole life and was scared, wanting to escape. I hardly managed to restrain it. Wouldn't it be better to force the horse to take on the bull? Throughout all this, I was not at all excited, but rather calm inside while deliberating between yes and no. And here the impression of the next moment prevailed."

Chapter 24

Reiner had dropped the habit of checking in at the post office every day. His girlfriend had never written, never responded. He did not expect letters from his parents, either. So, it had been a few days since his last visit and he stopped by without expecting much. But there was a thin airmail letter from his sister awaiting him.

Please call me!
—Monika

Her signature was illegible; the pen had clearly run out of ink midway through it. He hastened to get into a phone booth at the post office.

"What's up?" he said when she answered.

"I'm not doing that well," she said. "Can you keep a secret?"

"A secret? Sure, no problem."

"I'm pregnant, but I don't want to keep it."

"Monika, *mein Gott*! What are you going to do?"

"Nobody here knows about it. I'm going to say I'm taking a short trip to Marburg for a couple of days to see a friend of mine, and that will take care of it."

"Was it this phony architect student? The one I met?"

"Reiner, how can you ask such a stupid question? Who else? Do you think I sleep around? Huh?"

"You need money?"

"Actually, I do, but . . . Reiner? I never thought this sort of thing was going to be OK with you."

He made out from the sounds on the other end of the line that she'd started crying and said, "I'm making a little money now teaching German lessons. It's not much, and I'm paid in drachmas, but I might get a few more students in a bit."

"You are really sweet," she said with a sniffle. "But I need it now, you understand? Or within a week, at the latest."

For a moment, Reiner didn't know what to say. Then he thought of the few things he owned that were still at his parents' house. "My stereo—just sell my stereo! It's not a big deal. You can pay me back later."

"What would I tell our parents? It makes no sense, me walking out of the house with your stereo."

"Just think of something to tell them! Put it in a box and make up a story."

He was in turmoil by the time he got off the phone. His sister had been violated, and he had to make it all go away. Sure, the creep's real violation was abandoning her, which left her no other choices.

Reiner was worried she wouldn't have the stamina to sell his stereo. He should have told her he hated it, that it didn't have a good sound anyway, that it was thin and askew in the base—anything that would convince her it wouldn't be a loss. And then he worried that even if she did have the courage to sell it, it wouldn't be enough. The whole business was illegal, and even though he knew very little about it, he knew that illegal things could be quite costly.

The money he was making was supposed to pay his rent. What he earned from teaching German to Kanta, minus the rent, wouldn't be enough to pay for the abortion. He could stay and recruit more students, or go back to Germany and try to get a better job for the rest of his vacation. In the end, after a lot of thought, he decided to stay since he was unsure about the odds of getting a decent job in Germany on such short notice.

* * *

Kanta had brought honey-drenched sweets with her for him to try. The sweets were individually wrapped and stacked like herrings in a red box. She placed the box on the desk in front of him without saying a word. She was wearing makeup for the first time, and a pair of silver earrings: little dolphins.

"Who made the sweets?" he asked after he unwrapped and tasted one. "They are delicious."

"I did. My mother taught me." She smiled broadly at him, and the speed with which she answered his question made him think that she did not want to share them with anyone else.

Reiner took a deep breath and reminded himself that she was just a baby, that he was her teacher, that the age gap between them was huge.

"Kanta, do you know that I'm going back to Germany at the end of August?"

She looked at him for a few seconds, seemingly without comprehension.

"I'm leaving in a couple of weeks and will not come back," he said, hoping the message would sink in.

Her eyes filled with tears, and he felt awful and helpless. He had never looked at her face that closely; she had freckles, he noticed, and her nose was a tiny bit big.

All of this occurred on a Friday, and he hoped by the following Monday that she would have composed herself. Otherwise, he was not sure how to proceed.

Chapter 25

When night approached, Reiner's loneliness always intensified, and he often tried easing it with a few drinks at the bar in the main plaza. He had even bought his own *komboloi*, so he could swing the amber beads around and catch them in the palm of his hand in a display of self-confidence, just as the local patrons did. It was so important to blend in.

The bar was just an ordinary, nameless *kafeneio*, except that it was decorated with garlands of little light bulbs in all colors of the spectrum—blue and red and yellow and orange and green—which got switched on when night began to fall. All of the tables were covered with a coat of light-blue paint so thick and multilayered and buckled from many years of reapplication that there were places where one could not place a wine glass for fear it might tip over.

Although he hadn't made any real friends, there were a few people who recognized him and spoke to him about the weather and this year's harvest, but he knew that this was just a ruse because the topics they were most interested in were his sister and his girlfriend back home.

"How do you know anything about my sister?" he'd asked the first few times it'd come up. "What do you know about my girlfriend?"

It turned out that everything they knew came from his landlady. Once he made this discovery, it all made sense. She handled letters going both ways and she knew about phone calls, and apparently she shared what she heard or read liberally. It was a way for her to keep her status there, he supposed. There was no privacy in a Greek town of this size; even inconsequential remarks were scrutinized for days in search of meaning and intended or unintended commentary on the town, its inhabitants, and the very state of the world. So, he fed them inconsequential stories about Monika and Almut, but still they wanted more.

"Show us a picture of your girlfriend!"

He pulled Almut's picture out of his wallet.

"She is beautiful. You lucky bastard!"

He was sure this assertion was mainly due to the fact that she was blond.

"Are these all books behind her?" someone else asked.

"Yes, it's a bookshelf."

"So, she is sitting in a library?"

They were astonished to learn of the number of books in a single place, and he had difficulty explaining to them that that photo was taken in his own room back home, not in a formal library.

They were also quite curious about Germany, about the way people dressed there and what they ate. They all knew someone—a brother or uncle or nephew—who had either been to Germany or were in Germany then for some kind of job, and the tales they heard were all on the fantastic side.

By then, Reiner's vocabulary had expanded, although his sentences were still extremely short and simplistic. In spite of the compliments he'd received from the locals, he considered his Greek pronunciation barely passable. But in this minimal way, he managed to paint a picture of Germany that left an impression on his little audience. Of course, they knew all about Reiner's stint as a laborer out in the fields, digging up a trench through the stony, desiccated field for the municipal orchard's water supply. It still baffled them that a German would do hard labor out in the fields.

"Show us your hands!" one of them barked.

"Turn them over!"

They wanted to see the calluses that had formed on his palms from joining the crew for a single week. Every time he turned his hands up, it gave them a good laugh. Reiner was good-natured about it. He sensed there was something pathetic to them about a man climbing down the social ladder, from mental to manual labor, rather than up, as they all were trying to do. Still, he defended the idea in his mind, if not aloud; on that front he had no reputation to tarnish.

They knew quite a lot about him, even though he was leading such a withdrawn life, and he came to understand that it was all thanks to the recollections they had from talking to him in the bar in the evenings, then talking to each other some more to keep all those outlandish tales alive and well. They also knew about the visits Kanta had been paying him lately, and they teased him, wondering aloud if she was—because how she could possibly be?—still a virgin. It was all in good fun, but it made him realize how fine a line he was treading, and that every single move he made was being watched.

One special night, he lucked out. It was the night he would later remember as the Night of Bird's Milk.

"*Yassouisinah,*" a man shouted to him in a deep voice. "Come, sit down with your good friend."

That was Nikos, who was in the habit of embracing strangers, making him an unofficial ambassador of sorts for the little town. He was a heavy-set man but was also surprisingly sprightly when it came to dancing the *Pidichtos,* a dance of deep immersion in a subconscious state, in the plaza every weekend. He would get up from his chair and slowly walk to the middle of the floor, then stand still like a statue. That was the point when the conversations would fall quiet, and all attention shifted to the big man. Gradually, he would start moving his legs and his torso with both of his arms raised, each of his moves somehow anticipating the next beat of the music or follow one after another in a syncopated way. All throughout the dance, his body was in constant tension, and all eyes in the room focused on him as if trying to read his very soul.

Nikos was also the mayor's brother-in-law, and that granted him extra respectability in the community. He never mentioned this, of course, but everyone in the village knew.

"*Yassou,*" Reiner called back as he accepted Nikos's invitation to join him at his round iron table. "*Ti kane?* How are you?"

"So, how are you doing, little Nazi?" Nikos said, laughing loudly at his own joke, as he always did.

Reiner grinned but did not reply; he believed playing along would only amplify the bad habit on future occasions. Aside from this stupid routine, he liked Nikos and his outgoing temperament.

"Rinah, let's get some more of the bird's milk," Nikos droned. "Waiter!"

"Bird's milk?" Reiner said. "Since when do they have tits?"

Nikos laughed again, but much louder. He told Reiner that there was a Greek saying about the rich and how they get outlandish privileges like bird's milk, or ὀρνίθων γάλα—*ornithon chala.* Apparently it went back all the way to this great comedian, Aristophanes, who'd lived more that two thousand years earlier.

When the *ouzo* arrived, Nikos poured a bit of water into the glasses and swirled the mix around, turning the *ouzo* white as milk.

"There you go! *Yassou!* Straight from those little tits hidden under the plum feathers. Sneaky little bitches!"

Chapter 26

The butterfly funeral was a scientific experiment of sorts. In hindsight, it was his first biology experiment.

He was nine years old, and Monika just six. All his other experiments up to that point had existed in the nebulous territory between alchemy, physics, and chemistry, and focused on the nature of different kinds of liquids and solids and their aggressive affections for one another. It was a free-spirited sort of science, devoid of any hypothesis. But this one shaped up to be something bigger.

After his grandmother's funeral, Reiner and his best friend Bömbes had a conversation about what would be left of her—about her bones. They were in the backyard, and as they talked, a butterfly settled on a flower right in front of them. This brought on an argument about butterflies and if they had bones as well. He was in favor of this hypothesis, but Bömbes was opposed. After some debate, they thought of a clever way to find out for once and for all who was correct. They'd bury a butterfly and check the decomposed corpse after a few weeks, which should have been plenty of time for it to begin to rot because butterflies were so much smaller than humans.

So, one day in early summer, after searching through the bushes in the backyard, Reiner finally found a dead butterfly—one of those yellow ones that often settled on the nettles—and put it in an empty matchbox. He asked Bömbes, Monika, and two other friends to join him for the funeral.

"What does RIP mean?" Monika had asked. "Why did you write it on the box?"

"It means whoever is in this box is dead," he'd said. "That's what they write on coffins."

In preparation for the funeral procession, he asked his sister to sneak out the little velvet pillow from what used to be Grandma's room upstairs. It was a precious, fluffy thing she used to keep around her all the time, and it was a miracle his parents had not thought to bury it with her.

While his sister was on her errand, he tiptoed into the house to take the brass gong and its felt-covered mallet from the hallway: the one that his parents used to summon guests to dinner at parties. He showed Monika how to strike the gong in a dignified way, and Bömbes offered to bring a trowel from his grandma's house to dig the grave.

The procession lined up in the backyard: at the front, Bömbes carryied the trowel, followed by Reiner carrying Grandma's blue pillow in the crooks of both bent elbows, with the little coffin lying on top. Next came their other two friends, who kept pace but chatted the whole way. At the very end of the procession was Monika, banging the gong solemnly with every step.

After they arrived at their destination—a lovely spot behind the black current bushes—Reiner asked Bömbes to take his trowel and dig a hole in the soft ground. Then, following a speech in which he praised the accomplishments of the butterfly—such as laying eggs and providing aesthetic pleasure to the human eye—they carefully placed the coffin in the ground.

The next day, their mother noticed Grandma's pillow was missing and started interrogating Reiner and Monika. Reiner rushed out, only to find the pillow soaked from rain that had fallen overnight.

"It was *your* job to bring it back," he scolded his sister.

"Since when?" she said. "The whole funeral was your idea."

"What business do you have taking Grandma's pillow into the backyard? And what funeral are you talking about?"

Their mother was furious, and neither of them got any pocket money for two weeks.

Several weeks passed, and at the end of that summer, when Reiner finally remembered the experiment and tried to locate the grave, the path was overgrown and there was no trace of the matchbox or the butterfly. They gave up after digging in several places. Perhaps butterflies did not have bones after all. Or, perhaps this one didn't. Besides, how did a whole matchbox rot and leave no trace?

Monika was too little at the time to appreciate the significance of the project and the ambiguity of its outcome. He was certain she never brought it up later in conversation. Of course, he had not brought it up either; other things came up that seemed much more important. But now, after what seemed a million years, he made a mental note to ask her next time he had a chance if she remembered anything about it.

Chapter 27

The Monday after that weekend, Kanta did not show up at the agreed-upon time for her German lesson. Normally, when school was over, she would just walk the three blocks from there to where Reiner stayed.

Nervously, he waited for her, but he was also curious about the clothes she would wear since by then he felt he'd seen her entire wardrobe. The lavender blouse with flowers was his favorite.

Fifteen minutes passed. He started pacing in his little room, eyes on the floor. As he recalled her distress when they last parted, he felt a hollow pit form in his stomach. After half an hour, he considered the suddenly real possibility that he'd lost her for good. But how could she? He was surprised and overwhelmed by a surge of sadness, and realized he had fooled himself into believing he'd kept his heart in check.

One hour after his appointment with Kanta should have started—about four in the afternoon, when the sun was still hot—two other girls and a boy arrived. He'd never seen these teenagers before, but they demanded to speak with him. One of the girls was petite and plain. The boy was good-looking, if a bit stocky, with curly black hair and a classically straight Greek nose that Reiner recalled seeing on antique vases. The other girl, who had long, blue hair and a tattoo on her clavicle—what looked suspiciously like the statue of David if one viewed it from an angle that emphasized his buttocks—took the lead in explaining their presence, probably because she was the only one who knew a few words in English.

"Are you *Kyrios* Rinah?" she asked. "You must be. We are here for the lessons. In German, Kanta tell."

She nervously tucked her hair behind her ear, which had fallen into her face while she spoke to form an all-blue curtain across one side of her face. The other two students simply stood by, mouths agape, looking at him as one might a rock star.

"*Kali mera*," he said, offering them the only three chairs in his room. "Tell me your names."

"Adelpha," the girl with the blue hair said.

"Pandarus," said the boy.

"Ecatarina," the other girl said, and Reiner could tell she was the shyest presence in the group by how soft-spoken she was.

"Now, where is Kanta?"

They all tried to reply at once, and all he could make out was that Kanta told them about the opportunity to get German lessons, but that he wouldn't be around for much longer. At first, he thought they had shown up out of mere curiosity, but it was clearly more than that since they'd walked in with the exact fee he charged per lesson in drachmas bills they had rolled up in their hands. Kanta must have made a big deal out of his teaching abilities. The thought embarrassed him, and he wondered if they brought their own pocket money or if their parents had invested in their education.

German would grant them the ability to read Karl May in his original language, or perhaps Hermann Hesse's work when they got old enough. But German also stood for the job prospects in the tourist industry—waiters and employees in travel bureaus—and the coveted jobs as government-certified guides.

He had no idea what made Kanta decide to recruit her friends. Had he ever explained that he needed to earn money quickly and for a specific cause? Had he even ever mentioned his sister to her? He scanned back in his head through the time he'd spent with her during lessons and informal conversations—all those hours during which she had sat there, seemingly mesmerized by his lips as they moved in German declinations and conjugations—but he could not remember a single case in which any of that was said. He concluded that Kanta must have had an uncanny ability to read his mind; no other explanation made sense.

From that time on, he had four pupils. Kanta returned the next day without so much as mentioning her peers or how they came to be there with her. She floated in, wearing a bright red dress he'd never seen before, and sat down on the chair he had reserved for her. The world was back in order, and the idea that he'd be able to help his sister seemed feasible.

"*Pós eísai?*" he would always greet his little flock. "*Wie geht es euch?*"

And every time, the different but beautiful ways they mispronounced their German greetings, yet tried so hard to please him, almost touched him to tears.

Chapter 28

Tonight, he was unable to fall sleep—perhaps because the weather was changing, or because of the number of walnuts he ate that evening, or because of unknown and unspecific worries that kept creeping up. He took stock of his life as he lay in bed, watching the light from the undulating reflections of the moon on the black surface of the water in the bay play across the ceiling. The zigzag trajectory of a beam of light had to travel from the sun to the moon, then to the surface of the sea and on to the ceiling, and finally to his open, expecting eye.

What a wonder that, after all this dilution, enough photons were left to reach his retina!

He could no longer remember what precisely made him decide to stay in Greece after his sister left, followed by Rosa's departure. Sure, he was not eager to get back home, where he would sit around until the fall, when he'd have to get started on his thesis project. But the real reasons lay elsewhere: the solitude he'd found, the brilliant light, the magic of the open sky. He had been studying for his exam all spring, and the concentration on esoteric subjects such as Maxwell's equations and Hamilton's mechanics had exhausted him and made him long for an escape. Had it not been for the blisters he nursed over the first few days, Ierapetra would have been paradise.

He had to wonder how this would pan out in the future. There would be serious projects, implicating new equations and lemmas and theorems and propositions—all exhausting in their complexity—and he was not sure he would always find an escape like the one he'd found here on the isle of Crete.

Then he thought of the new, indescribably rich sensations he'd discovered, which were unlike any he'd had experienced before. He thought of Rosa, of the touch of her skin and her scent and the sound of her voice and her irreverence in the face of rules and conventions. He had not thought this kind of intensity was possible between two people—their minds, their bodies, their senses—even though it lasted only for minutes at a time. He wondered where she was and what she was doing at the moment—whether or not by some magic she was awake too, pondering the same questions. As soon as it came to mind, he laughed at the preposterousness of this idea in which he had lifted himself onto such a pedestal.

He wondered if he would ever see her again. Perhaps he would find her pinned down and domesticated in Salamanca with a husband and two children. What kind of man might be able to live with her day in and day out, or keep up with her capricious temper? Could he have ever been that man, and what kind of children would they have had together?

Things had a way of slipping out of his grip, and he wondered if this would prove to be a permanent pattern in his life, or in fact everybody's life? What about Monika and her lonely, intimate worries, or the fact that she had nobody to speak to but one of her former schoolmates? And how curious it was that his sister to be far away for him to feel close to her. While she was with him in Greece, there had always been something driving a wedge between them, despite all their good intentions.

And so he continued with his stream of thoughts, trying to compile an acceptable narrative while tossing and turning in his bed high above the cliffs of Ierapetra.

Slowly, the bands of light moving on the ceiling grew blurry and gave way to another specter. A woman who seemed part Kanta and part his sister rode on a donkey along the beach. The beach was sandy, with large stones here and there. The woman turned around to face him with her lips parted, but no words came out of her mouth. Some of the large stones in the sand were glowing like lanterns, as if a craftsman had hollowed them out and imbued them with perpetual fire.

No, Reiner thought, this must have been the work of dozens of craftsmen, all working quietly and with precision as they followed a grand design. He wondered where they might live and what their stories were. He knew that he was supposed to be consoled by the burning stones, but instead the sight filled him with dread.

Chapter 29

The Need for a Wakeup Call

Spring is here again, or at least the calendar says so; the weather seems to disagree, since all I can see are dead leaves that show signs of wear and tear from snow and abuse by animals both small and large. I can't wait to be outside again so I can fuss with the garden and plant prickly cucumbers, meandering zucchini, feisty heirloom tomatoes, ambitious kale, and industrious peas. There is still some snow along the edge of the forest, where the sun never touches in March. I give it five more days. Wikipedia says ticks are hatching now, and though the babies are not yet infected, it won't be long!

I have put all the photographs in order and put them into shoeboxes I've labeled with a black felt pen, using a font size that anticipates the coming deterioration of my vision. I'll admit that I threw a lot away since they showed the same people in different poses, standing by a grill waiting for all those hot dogs and hamburgers and veggie burgers to cook, or lying on the beach, tanning or napping, or both. These pictures give me the creeps because you know what happened to Reiner (and me) in Heraklion. There are others I threw away because they feature people I don't recognize anymore, even after staring at them for an hour as I tried to place them. This is evidence that my memory is fading, but I also like to allow the possibility that they might have switched my photos with someone else's at the pharmacy where I got them printed.

As much as I like Reiner's work ethic and attitude so far—the way he conducts himself in the face of challenges, his honesty and forthrightness—this business with Kanta worries me. A thirteen-year-old girl he can't get out of his head? Come on! We are getting into dangerous Lolita territory here.

I haven't interfered yet, even though I don't agree with all of his moves, because I believe that keeping my hands off makes me a good mentor. But this is going too far. She's even showed up in his dream, which I think we can all agree was really a symbolic wet dream since it all happens on a beach with the ocean nearby. Meanwhile, little by little, he is losing sight of his sister. Out of sight, out of mind. The last time he lost sight of her—albeit unintentionally—he'd attached himself to Rosa. We can count ourselves lucky that she has since quit the cast of characters.

It seems that, all in all, he has a slight inclination to abscond from his duties and do whatever he pleases unless he gets a daily reminder to stay on track—like a finger coming down from the sky and wagging in his face. But I really can't do this for him every day; someone has to mind the house.

Kanta, I must admit, is something of an irresistible force of nature, and I don't know what I would do if I were in Reiner's shoes. Fortunately for me, this is not the case.

I'm thinking of something drastic to snap him out of it: a wake-up call, so to speak.

Chapter 30

A booming voice coming from downstairs and shrill protestations uttered by a female voice he recognized as his landlady's roused Reiner one morning. He stumbled out of bed, slipped into his blue morning coat, and started down the spiral stairs to see what was going on. Near the bottom of the staircase, he found his landlady screaming, clinging to the handrails on either side, and blocking a big man's access to the upper floors. Clearly, the tiny woman, despite her fierce energy, was no match for the bear of a man, but that didn't seem to be stopping her from trying with everything she had.

"What's going on?" Reiner asked, as best as he could with only his basic understanding of Greek.

"Where is Kanta?" the big man shouted with a menacing grimace. He was bearded but almost bald, as if the total amount of hair attached to his head had been unevenly distributed. "You are hiding her, aren't you, fucker?"

"Wait, there's got to be a mistake," Reiner said calmly, confident that displaying his detachment would keep the situation in check. "I last saw Kanta two days ago for her German lesson after school."

"Don't give me that shit. I know she's upstairs. I'm Giorgos, her uncle. Let me through!"

The man easily broke through the landlady's roadblock and brushed by Reiner as he surged upstairs. Reiner followed but made himself as small as possible as he watched Giorgos start the futile search for his niece in his room, swearing intermittently and making rumbling sounds. He even opened the dresser drawers and the doors to the cabinet, one after the other, as if there was even an infinitesimal chance that a teenager could hide in there. Or, Reiner speculated, perhaps he hoped to find some type of exhibit A, such as red silk underwear, tucked under his Greek-English dictionary.

Reiner waited patiently through the ordeal. There was no point bringing up the issue of privacy, a concept that seemed underdeveloped in the town in general. Uncle Giorgos was clearly convinced of his own high moral ground; Reiner, as Kanta's teacher, should know better than to hang out with her in his single room and therefore spoil her future. As the rumbling and clanging continued, Reiner tried to start some small talk with his landlady, mainly to maintain his cool, but she was so upset she'd started crying. Then, in her high-pitched voice, she began to fling salvos of melodious Greek invectives at the intruder, who was not deterred in the slightest.

Finally, Giorgos seemed to realize he would not find whatever he was looking for.

"OK," he said, ignoring the landlady as he wagged his fat finger at Reiner. "She must have escaped just in time. You lucky fucker!"

Against his better judgment, Reiner laughed at the absurdity of it all, but was still surprised when, after a pause, Giorgos chimed in with bellowing guffaws befitting his ponderous presence. It was clear then that Kanta's uncle had performed the exact minimum of what was required of him to uphold the town's laws of decency; he had gone through Reiner's possessions, drawer by drawer, and found nothing incriminating. This methodic act, conducted in front of a witness, made it possible for him to accept Reiner as an equal, maybe even a potential friend.

* * *

Two days later, Reiner was in for a big surprise when another group of students, this time three girls and one boy, showed up for the German lesson. News must have traveled fast. They arrived, chatting and chewing gum, just a few minutes after Kanta and her friends settled in. He had to ask the noisy newcomers to sit on the floor. Kanta regarded him with the calmness of a woman whose every battle had been won; she also wore his favorite blouse. He was relieved to see her walk in that day since he'd been wondering where she was during her uncle's raid, but was too afraid to ask.

"*Kali mera!*" he said, trying to be casual as he leaned against the desk, which sent the pens and pencils rolling to the floor.

The chatting stopped, and the students all seemed to zero in on his lips. For the first time, he felt self-conscious about his sudden, adopted role of teacher; just a few months before, he had been on the receiving end of wisdom and coping with the aloofness and arrogance of his professors at the university.

He spent the first ten minutes discussing where they might meet next time so everyone could have a chair. They decided on a shaded spot in a nearby peach orchard that belonged to the parents of one of his students: Evangelina, a big-eyed brunette. She just had to ask her parents first.

With that, he began the lesson. "*Me lene Reiner.* My name is Reiner. I give lessons through telling anecdotes."

"What are anecdotes?" one of the new girls asked.

"Anecdotes are short, true stories," Reiner said slowly, mixing bits of Greek with German and English. "Today, I will tell you about Siegfried. You have Odysseus, and we have Siegfried."

A hand went up, and a boy asked, "Your Seeg Freed also travel on ship?"

"No, he walked on land. But he did kill a dragon and bathe in its blood."

"Did he have a girlfriend?"

"Yes, a girl named Kriemhilde. They never got married, though, because of a prophesy she wanted to circumvent." He felt helpless having to condense the *Nibelungen* saga into a few words, but their interest was awakened.

They all tried to say *Kriemhilde* and watched him with mesmerized eyes, waiting for him to recount a tale of romantic love and raging battles in every gory detail. He sighed and wondered how he would explain that the dragon's blood hardened, making Siegfried invulnerable except for the spot between his shoulder blades, which was covered by a linden leaf. Another woman discovered this spot of vulnerability from a hidden place and passed on the secret later to gain an unfair advantage.

It would take months more of lessons before his class was ready for the grammatical conjunctions and subterfuge required to tell this story, and he would be back in Germany by then, in a laboratory he'd visited only once and under the tutelage of a professor he had barely met. This thought alone filled him with unease.

As his young flock filed out of his room, they left crumbled drachmas bills on his desk before bounding down the staircase, which shook violently since it wasn't built for that many people to use all at once.

Chapter 31

A strong premonition prompted Reiner to call his sister the next morning. Not that he believed in premonitions, but this one crept up on him in such a way that he felt it couldn't be ignored. He was convinced there were things in heaven and earth that could not be explained by science. For instance, when he was still in high school, he had woken up one night and fixated on a picture on the wall that was faintly visible in the darkness. The picture then fell out of its frame and sailed to the floor. His heart raced, and each of the hairs on his scalp stood up on end. He never told anyone about it, afraid that reliving the event would make it seem that much more real. Of course, it could have just been that he was unfamiliar with a particular branch of science capable of explaining such an occurrence, or that it had not yet been conceived.

It was still light out; the air was crisp as he walked the four blocks to the post office. He took a deep breath to take in that evening's scents. A few people were out as well, but they were on their way to the market. It was that time of the day, nearing twilight, when the fight between the real and the imagined world was nearing its certain end.

Achilles, the post office clerk, greeted him with a handshake and a weary smile. He was a man of small stature, and he was perched on a high stool so he could more easily reach the customer window of his office. On the white wall behind him hung a crucifix, a picture of his family, and the official portrait of the king.

The loneliness of his uneventful job was written on his face. Stamps, telegrams, telephone charges, money orders, the occasional package to be sent to an exotic place like Luxembourg or Wales: that was about all there was to look forward to on a day in his shoes. Reiner had chatted with him about it a few times outside his place of business, once in the bar.

An airmail letter from his sister awaited Reiner.

Please call home!
  Monika

He stared at the almost empty light-blue page. Her signature was illegible, as if the pen had run out of ink midway through it. He asked Achilles for access to a phone booth.

"Today," Achilles said ceremonially as he flattened his hands on the desk in front of him, "we have three cubicles for you to choose from. Personally, I would recommend number two. It has the best lighting."

Reiner thanked him profusely and did indeed choose the second cubicle. It smelled faintly of tobacco and garlic, which made him wonder what the others might have been like today.

Monika answered, her voice barely audible, and he dove right in with the matter at hand. "I got your letter. Is everything alright?"

"Mutti is in fits. We have no idea when you will come back. We don't even know how to get ahold of you."

"Didn't she get the letter?"

"What letter?"

He'd handed it to his landlady to post, but sometimes letters got lost—or perhaps she had forgotten all about it. That his parents had been in the dark all this time weighed heavily on him.

"So how are things otherwise?" he asked after explaining the possible reasons why they hadn't received his correspondence.

"Mutti's arthritis is getting worse."

"Is she around?"

"No, she's running errands."

"Tell her perhaps I find a cure someday. Tell her I decided to go into biology. By the way, did you ever hear from that scoundrel again?"

"Bernhard? God, no! And don't mention his name again."

"Well, I managed to save some money for you," he said, hoping to make up for his apparent faux pas. "You wouldn't believe it, but they pay real money to listen to me speak German."

"I don't need your money anymore," she said, her voice flat. "I found someone who did it for free. A friend of my friend in Marburg."

"Oh." He caught himself before he could feel too disappointed about not being the one to rescue her. "Are you alright?"

"I am, but Mutti found out. She's furious, though she promised to keep it from *him.*"

Reiner imagined his father's anger would be fierce if he were to find out. He was raised in an evangelical revival family that adhered to strict beliefs. What Monika did in Greece, under Reiner's care—or, as their father would see it, what Reiner had let happen in his irresponsible way—was already unforgivable. An abortion on top of it would send him over the edge!

"He won't find out," he said. "Not from me, at any rate. You'll be safe."

"Whatever happened with Rosa?" she asked, apparently ready for a change of subject.

"I would love to know how she is doing. Perhaps she is back with her unreliable boyfriend. I got over it, I think. I hope."

When Reiner paid his charges for the fifteen minutes and twenty-two seconds indicated on the stopwatch, Achilles asked him what was wrong.

"What could be wrong?" Reiner asked.

"Something must be wrong. It's all over your face."

"Ah, family matters," Reiner said, waving him off.

In fact, he wished he had someone to talk to. About everything. But the post office clerk? In Greek? About abortion? That wouldn't do.

Chapter 32

Somehow Reiner had become a celebrated figure in town. If he hadn't known better, he would have succumbed to the suggestion that he was special and irreplaceable. His landlady bragged about him to anybody who would listen and, as he later found out, played the role of a concierge, deciding who could see him and who could not. Hosting him in her narrow single-apartment tower had apparently boosted her social standing.

Kanta's uncle raised his hand in greeting whenever he saw him on the other side of the street, carrying in his smirk the memory of the mad hunt for evidence of his niece hiding out at Reiner's place. Reiner smiled back, but got the sense that it still would take lifetime for the other man to fully accept him. Parents of his students stopped him on the street, particularly during the weekend at the promenade by the waterfront with all those stands and booths selling red-dyed pistachios, cheap toys like windup rabbits with tambourines, and sweet treats in all the primary carcinogenic colors.

They shook hands with him and called him Professor. He didn't correct them, but usually scratched his head—one of his classic signs of embarrassment—which they found quite endearing. More than a few times, he was invited to a round of free *ouzo* at the bar, which always came with olives or cucumbers or pistachio nuts: a little something always, *tipota*, and the sense of time no longer rushing by, but tiptoeing alongside him like a trusted friend.

"So how is your day, Professor?"

"*Evkaristo*! Thanks, I cannot complain."

"May your day continue to be prosperous!"

"May God guard your every step!"

He didn't quite know how to handle all this attention. By nature, he thrived on recognition; it was compensation for the recognition that was denied him by his family, in which all of the siblings battled one another for favors from their parents. Coalitions were formed and abruptly broken. But here, where he finally found recognition in abundance, he sensed the townsfolk harbored a misunderstanding about the depth of his scholarship (*negligible*) and academic standing (*nil*). They all seemed to have tremendous respect for teachers and what they took on, but he failed to get across to them that he was still a student and had entirely different aspirations for his professional life.

In a way, the attention and adulation he received made him feel more alone than ever; before, he could at least fantasize about meeting people and having deep conversations with them. Now, with all the goodwill in this little town on display, each encounter evolved into a charade of small talk that inadvertently made a mockery of his dreams.

He recalled seeing the rainbow at night, not long after he'd arrived in Ieraptra, and how he'd wanted nothing more than to share the experience with someone until he found poor Achilles at the post office, who'd had no choice but to listen to him and his craziness. Even with all his newfound popularity, he was still unable to truly unburden his soul.

[Ierapetra. Re.: childhood – what on earth do people talk about?]

I often found myself listening to other people's conversations back home. What exactly was the subject matter? What motivated them to talk? What information was passed on? In listening, I'm often astonished by the trite things being discussed.

What do I mean by the word trite? Is it determined in the eye of the beholder? Is this just my arrogance speaking?

As a boy, I would watch and listen to my mother as she made small talk in the grocery store. But take my sister: she chats easily, just like her mother. Is small talk actually women's talk? Is it the need for coziness, a confirmation of I'm-here-are-you-also-here-on-this-earth?

Chapter 33

After he announced he'd be leaving the next week—by way of a bus to Heraklion and then a plane to Athens that would connect straight to Frankfurt, and from there by train to his hometown—a baffled silence fell over the orchard his class met in, interrupted only by the crickets and the melodic cries of a mistle thrush hidden in a nearby olive tree.

The students had gone with him on a flight of fantasy via the *Nibelungen*. Reiner acted out the deeds of Wotan and whatnot's that he vaguely remembered from high school, but in his own class he could curtail or embellish the stories in any way he wanted to without being called on it by some wise guy in class. In fact, Reiner discovered that he loved to look at their young faces—though really not much younger than his own, just at a different station of their lives—and discover a talent he never knew existed. He did in fact have a talent for storytelling, for inspiring others, for teaching. There had not been a single dropout, and this filled him with pride.

"Why do you must leave?"

"Because Germany is my home."

"Can we you visit in Germany?"

"Sure, anytime."

"Shall you back be?"

"I'm absolutely sure. I just don't know *when*."

Their silence and accusing eyes were hard to stomach. Throughout their interrogation, he had avoided looking at Kanta, who was dressed in black as though in mourning and did not ask a single question. Something told him that she thought he had violated her trust, or that she had expectations he could not meet. But then he had to remind himself once again of the absurdity of catering to the unspoken, very likely imaginary demands of a thirteen-year-old girl. Perhaps it was all just in his head?

They all said goodbye—some of the girls with a curtsy, and all of the boys with an awkward handshake—but Kanta was the first to leave.

She had a stoic expression on her face, and she didn't look back once. Reiner guessed that she did not want to cry in front of him. After all of his students left, he walked back to his place, deep in thought.

Yes, he would be back one day, but he would be a different person, and all these kids would be somewhere else: maybe in Athens, Patras, Thessaloniki, or struggling to find their way elsewhere in the world. Some could even wind up in Germany. Ierapetra would be different, too. He imagined a five-story high-rise, a hotel painted in glistening white with balconies facing the beach. His landlady would be gone, and remembered by only a few.

When he arrived at the place he'd been calling home for the last few weeks, he found a box wrapped in red paper sitting in front of the door of his room. It was unusually heavy. Nervous, he opened it to find a cardboard box containing a black, oval stone about the size of a newborn's head, with a thin vein of white quartz running through it like a flash of lightning. There was no message included, and Reiner was again reminded of the man without a face in Bergman's *Strawberries*.

He imagined Kanta walking along the beach, looking for something she thought he could remember her by. Then, after finding what she was looking for, he imagined her walking home, holding the heavy stone in front of her with both hands, and fending off questions from people she ran into in the street. There was no way of bringing the stone home with him, as much as he wanted to, but perhaps that was precisely what she meant by the gift. He would have to decide between leaving it, or staying and embracing both it and her. Its pristine condition, its smoothness, its weight in his hand, its sheer mass: he had to admit, it was the perfect device to inflict guilt on him and to engrave herself in his memories of this place. He was in awe of her cleverness.

"Kanta, Kanta," he murmured, shaking his head. She was thirteen; what would she be like at seventeen?

He placed the stone on his desk with one of the yellow pencils in front of it to keep it from rolling and landing with a thud on the floor right above his landlady's kitchen. Startling her like that would not be nice, especially after all she had done for him.

PART IV

Homecoming

Chapter 34

Fleeting lines of fences, hedges and stone walls between fields, and trees converging in the distance, knotted together on the horizon: as Reiner looked out the window on the train, these images folded over like the pages of a book being read too fast, the contents lost with each turn.

Reiner was on his way from Frankfurt to his hometown. He'd taken the journey many times, and always connected with a train from Freiburg, his college town. He was so used to it, he did not even pay attention to his surroundings most of the time. But on this trip, the train and the landscape it rushed through had taken on a different meaning; the familiar had become utterly unfamiliar under the weight of his experience in Greece.

This sky was a pale blue, not the deep tint that bordered on purple he had grown accustomed to. These trees were lush and green and much too orderly, planted in neat rows; the houses were in perfect condition, not partially built with steel rods sticking out as so many he'd seen in Greece.

Enchanted messiness was missing here. There were no chickens in the street, and the light lacked brilliance; here it was muted somehow, discouraged, intimidated by the weather. Light was trapped in bunkers, under staircases, and in moist corners filled with mildew and sowbugs. He wondered if the Greek gods, in all their splendor, would have wanted to live in this regulated, gray-toned world, and what turn civilization might have taken if it had been forced to make do with tales of love affairs and bouts of jealousy and rage set in places with names like *Worms* or *Darmstadt.*

He thought back to the beginning of his journey and tried to decide if he had learned anything. Books always asserted that traveling educated people somehow.

It was probably safe to say that planning—the sheer concept of it—had not worked. So, this was lesson number one. He'd planned the journey with Almut, and then, after Almut had to bow out, he continued making all sorts of plans with his sister. Almost everything turned out differently than he'd imagined. Monika, to start with, had never planned to meet a wannabe architect, nor had she to get pregnant. And—speaking of making plans—how could Reiner have dreamt up creatures like Rosa or Kanta, each an incredible yet incorrigible girl in her own way?

Lesson number two: girls were iridescent, ephemeral, effusive. To understand girls, one would need a lifetime to study. Thankfully, he was still young.

And while his time in Greece had steeled him against loneliness, it had also taught him the surprising value of physical closeness: not necessarily with a woman, not necessarily charged with erotic fantasies, just with another warm, breathing human being. Even the closeness with his almost toothless landlady in Ierapetra or with the sweaty men in the town's nameless bar qualified for that.

He imagined how he would stroll into his parents' house with the gravitas he had acquired after a long summer abroad. He imagined ringing the doorbell—he had lost his key some time ago and never told to his mother—and, once someone opened the heavy oak door, assertively step across the Italian ceramic tiles with the blue interlocking patterns that decorated the floor in the front hallway. Some of them were loose and had never been fixed even though his mother had complained about them for as long as Reiner could remember, so they would yield and pivot under his foot with muffled clicking sounds. Of course, his mother complaining to his father wouldn't do much good; he couldn't fix anything with his one good hand, the other having been smashed to pieces in the war.

Past the staircase Reiner would go: the one covered with an Afghan runner held by brass rods, one fastened in the crease of every step. Those brass rods had to be cleaned once a year with poisonous metal polish. As a boy, it was his job to pull each rod out of its brass eye on either side, then let it slide down the stairs until its leading end would meet the hard tile floor with a clang, followed by reverberations as the rest of the rod finished sliding off the runner. When all those discolored brass rods lay crosswise on top of one another, like a giant game of Mikado, he had to resist the temptation to put a bit of the polish on his finger—just a tiny yellow drop—and taste it. But then he'd remembered how bored he was whenever he was sick and had to stay in bed.

Finally, he would greet his parents and his older sister Angelika before she even had time to open her mouth and, with one single word, remind him of his place. He would ignore her and look for Monika, take her aside, and find out what happened since she got home. It seemed like years had passed since she flew back from Heraklion, even though it had actually been a few weeks.

The rushing landscape slowed as the train rumbled to a halt in the middle of a wide meadow. He opened the window and craned his neck to look out and see what was going on. At first, he saw no reason to stop. Then he saw it—a flock of sheep that had slipped through the fence separating the tracks from the meadow. Some of them were on the track, unmoved by the sound of the whistle and the cries of exasperation from the uniformed officials. He would be late, but whoever picked him up would get the story ahead of time from the stationmaster; there was nothing Reiner could do but wait.

Would he be greeted at the station by Monika or Angelika? Either way, he would embrace her and lift her up to swing her around as he'd always done in train stations and airports as a ritual of making up for the lack of physical closeness among them for most of their lives. He'd recently realized that he'd always been the one to take the initiative, and that part of it was his perpetual curiosity about females and, yes, the thoroughly mysterious *otherness* of his sisters.

He had first tried it with Angelika once he grew taller than her because these were the only chances he had to feel the pressure of their young breasts on his body. This was just curiosity that had nothing to do with desire, though he realized that talking about this with anybody would get him into a lot of confused arguments, especially in their part of the country since it was suffused with evangelical moral sternness. Monika's were flat, but Angelika's were more substantial, as was obvious from her silhouette and from the one time he'd glimpsed her whole body thanks to the upstairs bathroom door she'd accidentally left cracked open. Her breasts had looked just like those of actresses on sultry movie posters.

The idea of a hug at the end of the journey, he supposed, was part of the joy of traveling, just like the prospect of ice cream after walks with his father.

Chapter 35

Angelika, not Monika, stood on the platform; he hardly recognized her at first in her long blue skirt and the large sunglasses obscuring most of her face. She seemed pale and nervous, and fidgeted more than he remembered. He tried to embrace her and twirl her around, like always, but she froze in his arms and stepped back.

"You look different," she said.

"How so? Is it the beard? The tan?"

"I don't know. Just different."

"Well, I guess that's something to get used to," he said.

They silently walked toward the familiar gray VW in the parking lot.

"You know, it's almost lunch time," she said as she started the car. He sensed an accusing tone. "Mutti made your favorite."

"Which is what?"

Though he was flattered to be honored by a special meal, he didn't want to be defined by all those previous likes and dislikes. He didn't want to have spent all that time away from his parents' house just to return to the exact same way he used to live.

"Why, goulash and potatoes!" Angelika said, taking her eyes off the road and turning her surprised gaze on him.

He didn't want to agree or disagree with her. Instead, he pointed toward the windshield. "The road—mind the road."

They drove the rest of the way home in silence, even when they were delayed slightly by a traffic jam at the railroad crossing, right next the newspaper kiosk where his second girlfriend dumped him two years before. He was struck by the intensity of his visceral reaction to the seemingly innocuous sight. The fight with that girlfriend had been over something absurd: a newspaper article too stupid and insignificant to recall.

At the same time, he was shocked by the vivid memory of his feelings for his past girlfriend, which he'd believed had been purged when he met Almut. In the same way, he traded calm-spirited Almut for Rosa in that little cubicle of a room back in Greece, with barely enough space to turn and with the mountain looming in the background. And after losing Rosa, Reiner realized there was no way of getting back to one girl or the other.

The lowered bars of the railroad crossing were still painted in alternating sections of white and red. It was the exact hue of red he remembered from the times he would have to go to the other side of town for an errand, like buying pencils or books. It was an adventure, and the mechanism for lowering and raising those bars—done by hand by a man presiding over the crossing in an elevated glass box—was so enigmatic, it was the subject of speculations that followed him into the night.

Those memories and the stark, tangible presence of the things that had given rise to them, mingling as they did with his elder sister's behavior and expectations, interfered with the way he had envisioned his homecoming. He had hoped that Monika would pick him up, that they would have fifteen minutes in the car to themselves to talk about her abortion and how she felt before weathering the onslaught of the rest of the family. Instead, he faced Angelika's barely hidden hostility, and had to think of ways to start a conversation with Monika later that night. Perhaps he'd draw her aside, away from the family when they inevitably gathered around the TV.

Soon they arrived at the golden brick house, the house of Reiner's first memories and nightmares alike. It still loomed large, reminding him of the time he tried to capture it with his camera and wound up with twelve pictures instead of one, all distorted one way or the other, and then resisted the urge to paste them together in one grand collage. He always expected the house to shrink in inverse proportion to his own size and stature, back from when he was a little boy and first perceived its overwhelming presence, but now he of course knew that is would remain one size, once and for all.

"*Voilà*," Angelika said as she switched off the ignition.

That single word, *voilà*—a word related to the German *Schickeria*, where every speaker wishes to be recognized for his or her sophistication as a result of traveling far and wide—made the silence that had prevailed during the entire drive seem suddenly quite childish and abnormal. Reiner wanted to castigate himself for letting his mind wander after this business with his family's presumptions regarding his food preferences. He actually found—deep down—the faint memory of once having liked goulash and potatoes. That memory was like the whiff of a fragrance from far away, but he was a boy hidden in many layers, like the innermost installation of a set of Russian dolls.

The heavy oak door opened, and its hinges squeaked just as they always had. Out came his mother to embrace him. Her wrinkled skin was surprisingly warm; he caught himself expecting her body to be noticeably cooler in the same way he anticipated any older person's to be, as though they were all caught in a state of gradual adjustment toward the final temperature of earth.

"Will you give me a kiss?" his mother asked.

His father stood in the background with a broad smile, but he made no effort to step closer and be an integral part of Reiner's welcome home. His presence, as usual, was a presence mainly of mind.

"There were sheep on the track. Can you believe it?" Reiner said before casting a curious glance over their shoulders. "But where is Monika?"

At that moment, his younger sister appeared in the hallway. She looked pale and thin in her light blue dress, and it made him wonder how much blood she must have lost and what kind of pain she must have suffered; he knew little about the procedure she'd gone through since he last saw her. They stood for a few seconds in silence, then Monika took the first step to hug him.

He was at a loss as to what to say to her while the family looked on. Hugging was not common here; he had not even learned how to hug here. It had to be defended as something odd but necessary, and not just for social discourse but also for the preservation of the human race's emotional intelligence.

At length, he thought of something their parents would expect them to say on such an occasion, something that could have been found in an opinion piece in the local newspaper or in a story in *Reader's Digest.*

"So good to see you again."

"Reiner, my crazy brother!" Monika said. "Welcome home!"

He loved being addressed this way. He wanted to be considered crazy, as someone who lived beyond the norms. "It's so strange to be back! Hey, remember that priest?"

"The one in Sitia with the *tzatsiki* all over his beard?"

"Crete is beautiful. Agios Nicolaos is beautiful. Greek people are beautiful," he intoned in a dramatically heavy dialect.

They laughed at the fresh memory, although those events seemed unreal in the present. Their parents and Angelika stood by, clearly baffled, though apparently delighted enough with such a display of harmony between siblings that they all wore slight smiles.

"Well, now, listen," his mother said. "It's late, so I'd better get lunch ready."

"Let me guess," Reiner said, finding his good humor restored. "Goulash and potatoes?"

They moved inside, away from the front door, and as he closed it behind him, Reiner took a quick look back at the neighbor's house. The image overlapped with another one buried deep in his memory, and a shudder traveled over his body as if he'd gazed into something unfathomable, but he knew it originated in his dreams and a part of his childhood, from before his younger sister was even born.

Chapter 36

His mother had put the *good* tablecloth on the table and laid out the *good* china with the silverware made of *real* silver and cloth napkins rolled up in silver napkin rings—the one she'd put at his place even had his initials engraved in it. He knew the silver had been polished in spring as usual because even if it had not been used for the entire year, it had this slight tendency to show a tint that spoke to the sulfur in the air if one looked at it under an angle when the light hit it just right.

The butter on the table was *gute Butter*—good butter, the way she'd referred to authentic butter ever since its scarcity right after World War II. She used the term like a mantra that reassured her and the whole family that the war had ceased for good. There was a time when, once a week, she would mix *gute Butter* with margarine in a big bowl to give the family a sense of the good life again in little increments.

Gute Butter had a slightly different color than margarine; it was more on the yellow side, so Reiner could always tell if it was one or the other, or a mixture of both. He remembered the color and shape of the large porcelain mixing bowl and the white-and-yellow striations in the fatty mass when it was not yet perfectly mixed. The two components would curve around in mad spirals that got thinner and thinner, until they were fractals no longer distinguishable by the human eye. It was satisfying that he now had the words, like *fractals*, to describe observations that had always been relatively precise, but were indescribable by his childhood self. He also remembered the day when the dining room table she'd placed the bowl on broke under the stress of the mixing process, and when he tried to fix it by crawling underneath, the table tipped over again and bumped his head. The bowl did not break then, but much later after developing an irreparable crack.

He had forgotten that all these things existed—except the mixing bowl—but seeing them perfectly arranged and on display in his honor was touching. The only things his mother had not put out for his homecoming were the knife banks made of slabs of crystal glass, which were only used when really important people came over, like the pastor, or a colleague of his father. However, that had not happened in years because the pastor had fallen out of grace for something he said—Reiner didn't remember what it was that it was so offensive—and because all of his father's colleagues had since passed away. Well, all but one, but that one never used to come over much anyway.

"So, which train did you take?" his father wanted to know.

This was the first time his father had spoken since he arrived. Reiner already saw where this was heading but decided to humor him. His father could not help himself; he had an almost obsessive interest in the specifics of transportation. At the same time, he seemed to have no interest whatsoever in how Reiner spent his time in Greece. It was maddening to Reiner because every time he came home from some new adventure, he felt as if his actual person was not valued in this reduced summarization of his journey and the scant interest shown in the stories he brought back with him.

"I took the one past *Dillenburg*," he said.

"It probably saved you some time," his father said, emphasizing the importance of his observation with his somber tone.

"So true," Reiner replied with a weary sigh before turning to his mother for a different, more entertaining line of inquiry.

Angelika beat her to the punch. "Are you going to keep the beard? It makes you look old."

"Old?" he asked. "Mutti, do I look old?"

"Well, you will shave it off, won't you? You will be a doctoral student in the fall, after all," his mother concluded this with the finality all parents mastered at some point.

"But does it make me look old?" Reiner didn't really care about the answer but saw this question as his chance to steer the conversation to more enjoyable topics.

"I don't know, but you can't keep it," his mother said sharply.

"Oh, just listen to yourselves," Monika said. "I, for one, am just glad he is back safe." Reiner gave her a quick, thankful look, and she responded with a fond smile. "Tell us what you did after I took off."

"I gave German lessons."

Lunch stopped. Forks hovered in midair. Mother's mouth hung open.

"You did what?" his father finally said. "German lessons? The way *you* speak it?"

Angelika exploded with laughter, hiding her mouth with one hand and stabbing her fork into the air with the other. When she'd calmed down, she said, "I'm honestly wondering what he could have taught them."

"I can tell you," Reiner said, feeling his temper stir just a little bit. "I taught by using stories about Siegfried and Kriemhilde, for instance. You have no idea what it meant to them. They started from scratch. Perhaps they could even learn something from *you*."

He noticed with satisfaction that he had taken the wind out of Angelika's sails; she appeared to have nothing left to say. Generously, he changed the subject.

"I almost forgot—I brought you some presents."

Wild herb honey from *Ikaria* and boxes filled with unshelled pine nuts from *Aegina*, the tablecloth for Mutti, and silver earrings crafted in the same manner as the jewelry of *Philaenis of Samos*, that philosopher woman of fame: all of this was contained in an extra suitcase he'd bought for next to nothing in the Ierapetra general store the day before he left. It already showed signs of wear and tear from the trip.

"Ikaria, the healing island, is even mentioned by Homer in *The Iliad*," Reiner said.

His parents' faces brightened as he recounted the splendor he experienced, and his mother nodded knowingly at the mention of the old bard's name. She had attended a school for girls that was founded centuries ago, where she had been educated in all the classics, needlework, home economics, and of course the fine art of conversation.

Chapter 37

Reiner and Monika seized their chance to escape from the living room and the incessant droning of the television, its volume turned up so that the sound could reach his father's inner ears through a bulky device that used electronic amplification. The TV had gradually taken over the evenings while Reiner was in high school; in the beginning, it was just the news hour in the evening. Then the news hour expanded, and new channels were added. Heinz Erhardt's potato-shaped face came on every night to add comic relief to the day. His father would sit motionless in his easy chair while his mother did her needlework.

Whenever the commercial breaks came on, his mother muted the TV and turned to her son to ask motherly questions, such as what kind of food he'd eaten in Greece, and if the weather was warm enough because she noticed he had not packed his favorite sweater. Each time, just when he started to respond, the program continued back on full blast, and she seemed to immediately forget her question in favor of the resumption of the barrage of images and sounds. Monika, sitting across from her brother, looked at him and rolled her eyes. He took delight in the rapport he had found with her in their brief time together over the summer.

They found refuge on the third floor after raiding the refrigerator to find a bottle of Riesling, which Reiner wrapped in a dish towel to smuggle upstairs. Monika brought along an opener and two cups because stealing away real wine glasses would be risky.

In February of 1944, a year and a half before the war ended, their house had been struck in an air raid, and the roof had gone up in flames. Having been born a few months after the fire, Monika of course had no memories of the event except perhaps a deep-rooted anxiety. The third floor was still marked by the impact of the incendiary bombs that had set the roof on fire during the final years of the war; some wooden beams were still charred, and the walls still shed pieces of mortar that had crumbled in the heat of the blaze. There was still a trace of that burnt-wood smell, though it would seem improbable after so many years—maybe as improbable as the background radiation still ringing in the universe after the big bang.

For as long as he could remember, the third floor had been an uninhabitable space, and therefore the only place in the house where he would not be disturbed. The family called it *Speicher*, or *the attic*. It had never been rebuilt and made livable after what his parents and many other people referred to as *die Katastrophe*, or the unexpected cataclysmic event that had somehow intruded on their daily lives. As a boy, he spent a lot of time there taking radios apart, and each part—valves, tunable capacitors, resistors, solenoids—was the seed for a new project idea. None of these projects had ever been finished.

Sniffing the air, Reiner found that the smell of dust intermingled with charred wood was exactly the same. What was missing now was the smell of camphor used for soldering, a sweet intoxicating smell that always made him wish he was a valve on a radio chassis and could spend his life there just breathing it all in. The smell of charcoal brought him back to a time when he expected to hear his mother's voice calling him down to supper.

It was cold up there, and he saw Monika shiver, but she did not complain. The chill reminded him of the winters he spent soldering those radios together, the only heat being generated by the soldering iron, and the attic so cold that steam came out of his mouth and nostrils when he exhaled. It was a miracle he never caught pneumonia. He had once been zapped with four hundred volts and survived. After that, he'd considered himself invincible, like Siegfried. He never told his parents since that would have been the end of his radio tinkering.

The only light came from a single bulb dangling from the unfinished rafters overhead. Monika looked around the dimly lit space and peered into former rooms that had been reduced to mere spatial concepts, each marked by four upright beams. The virtual walls spanned by them represented both past and future, but there was nothing there that belonged in the present tense.

"God, I haven't been up here in ages," she said. "There is really nothing here that concerns me. Well, what I mean is, that relates to me. I never knew what you were doing here."

"I didn't either, come to think of it."

They sat down on two stacks of comic books that had been stored up there for more than a decade. Reiner opened the bottle and poured wine into the cups. He remembered those comic books from when he was maybe nine years old; in one of them, Steel Man defied physical laws and walked straight through a house, one wall after the other, leaving his precise profile behind in each of them like a bookworm cutting its way through bound pages. There was little else that he remembered about Steel Man and his life from the speech bubbles, only his terrifying tornado-like propensity to wreck everything along his trajectory.

They drank the wine without ceremony, not unlike taking a drug, as though to fortify themselves with a shield of mild intoxication. Whenever a cup was empty, he grabbed the bottle and refilled it. It took two cups for some of the tension in Monika's face to disappear.

"Hello," she said, looking straight into his eyes as if she'd woken up from some subterranean existence and suddenly taken charge of herself.

Reiner had never seen her in this state, and for perhaps the first time, asked her how she was without it being a perfunctory, surface-level inquiry. As one of the kids—and particularly as a girl—she had no business to complain, and he had no curiosity whatsoever about her well-being. At least, this was how they were brought up. She didn't really have a life of her own outside the explicit instructions of her parents and the directions provided by Angelika, who was eight years older and convinced that, as such, she perfectly understood the world with all its complexities.

But as he asked this question, he was aware of the shift that had happened over the summer. Monika seemed more of his equal, a person driven by her own desires and rationalizations, and ostensibly no longer in need of a guard. He realized that she stood for sisters of other men who might come to the same realization sooner or later, and saw her as a fully grown woman, out of place and out of time with the heap of comic books she was sitting on, pulsing with newly found freedom, and yet still absurdly subdued by her circumstances.

"Lousy," she said in answer to his question. "Marburg was hell. Though, actually, my friend took great care of me. And I have nothing specifically against Marburg, either. But then I had to come back after a couple of days, white as a bedsheet," she gestured as if to surround that last word with quotation marks with her fingers, "and pretend nothing was wrong. I couldn't explain to them why I looked awful or why I cried more."

She shrugged her bony shoulders, as though apologizing for her rant.

"You didn't tell them anything?" he asked.

"Not a thing, no."

"And they had no idea?"

"I already told you that Mutti found out afterward. She read a letter I forgot to put away. She was furious but agreed to keep it from Papa. He would have…well, I don't know how he would have reacted, but it would have been bad."

"But have you heard from *him*?" Reiner asked.

"Him? Who? Bernhard? God, no! I never gave him my address."

"Do you have his?"

"He gave me his business card. On it, he called himself an architect. There was some fancy drawing on it, too, of a building. I threw it away. I don't want to talk about him, OK?"

"OK, I won't mention him again," he said. "That twerp just made me furious." He left her to her thoughts for a moment, but then the silence got to him, and he surprised himself by asking, "And what about pain? Was there a lot of pain?"

"I can't talk with you about *that* sort of pain," she said, turning her face away.

He suppressed the urge to contradict her, but also wanted to apologize for asking such an intimate question. Reiner stopped himself, wondering about the strange order of a world in which this subject was taboo. They had been brought up like dolls with a blunt pubic mound substituting for genitalia.

The horn of a heavy truck blared in the distance, as if conjured up by his memories of the firebombs. Over the years, she had asked him about it; on those occasions, he had to remind her that he was just three and a half when it happened, and that both his memory and his powers of observation were quite limited then. But now, something compelled him to tell her about it, as though she had passed some kind of test and he could finally admit her into the family's innermost circle—a circle of witnesses to events of inconceivable destruction. He also felt that this intimate conversation taking place here, in this odd, cold place in their parents' house, had propelled them back to Greece for another try at sibling bonding.

"You know, whenever I walk into the house, it gives me chills; I felt them again when I arrived here this afternoon. I was little more than three years old when I stood there on the threshold of the front door and saw a whole big house in flames just across the street."

"Which house?"

"The one on the corner of Main Street. I stood there and stood there and could not believe so much fire could be at one place at the same time. I guess it burned so quickly because the whole house was made of wood."

"Who was with you?"

"My—our grandmother. She held my hand and kept me from running outside, but she was upset and her voice was shrill and I couldn't understand anything she said. Or, if I did understand at the time, then I just can't remember."

"But it was not the day ours got hit?" Monika asked.

"Yes, they told me later it was that same day."

"You never told me. It must have been hell."

"The funny thing is, I remember thinking it was quite beautiful, and it was only my parents and siblings with their cries and the hectic rush to put it out that made things so damn frightening."

In recounting it as an adult, he wondered how odd it all must have sounded to someone who had not experienced the event, especially someone from his own family.

"I was born the summer of that same year," Monika said. "So I heard some part of it."

"Babies can hear things from inside the womb?" he said. "I've never heard that."

"The way you hear things when you put your head under water, like in a bathtub or a swimming pool," she said with the authority of a trained physical therapist. "It's muffled, but you still hear things."

For some reason, this bothered him. "How about something else, to change the subject a little? Have you heard about Robert Musil? He wrote a book called *The Man Without Qualities*."

She shook her head. "No, why do you ask?"

"We went through some of it in my German literature class in twelfth grade. The book is about preparations for the celebration for Kaiser Franz Joseph's seventieth birthday. It was at the beginning of this century." At her blank look, he added, "Franz Joseph: you know, the emperor of the monarchy in Vienna?"

"So?"

"In that book, the protagonist and his sister are in love."

She looked at him with narrowed eyes, her nose wrinkled and upturned as she scooted a few inches away from him. "That's so disgusting."

"Well, he's not sure. That's the part where him having no qualities comes into play," he said.

"Reiner, why do you bring it up now?"

She looked at him for a long time, until he couldn't stand it and averted his eyes.

"I…I honestly don't know. I guess I always thought this incest taboo has been way overdone, and to the point that we think something is wrong with us if we feel affection for a sibling. And on top of it, there's all this Puritan crap they still spew here."

Monika shook her head slowly and reached out for the bottle to refill her cup. He took it at a sign that he had clearly overstepped but couldn't account for the reason why he would bring up this confusing book, which he had only read half of and then got stuck for a reason he couldn't even recall. It was true that the mystery of women had first been impressed on him through his sister. There must have been some revelation—perhaps the sight of her naked body as a little girl—that kept revisiting his subconscious in the form of unspoken questions about their respective sexes and destinies.

It would appear that sitting with her in a place where he had spent so much of his time in seclusion had unleashed all of his forgotten questions of brother-sister relationships, all that he had read about what could go right and what could go wrong. The new closeness he felt with his sister had lulled him into complacency, leading to his sharing his most intimate thoughts and feelings.

Just then, he recalled another story he'd read in that very spot as a boy: a short story, or perhaps part of a novel printed in a book that had come apart at the spine. The same smell had been in the air, the same dust, except it was more pungent because his sense of smell had been keener at the time, and the *Katastrophe* had occurred more recently.

The protagonist of the story, a man in his thirties, was stranded in the jungle. His plane had probably crashed, and his companions had perished, but Reiner couldn't be sure because the part of the book— the beginning—had been lost at some point due to the book's damaged spine. In the green hell in which the man found himself, parrots mocked him, screeched at him, and dove down at him, aiming for his eyes—the defense of their young being their sole excuse. Trees stretched out their roots to trip his clumsy advance; he'd eaten treacherous fruit and chewed on dangerous resin bleeding from the purple bark of a tree that reached up into the sky, which made him sick. He had consumed these things without thinking, without the slightest idea of the effects they might have on his body and state of mind. And so, with bleeding feet and his arms and hands lacerated from thistles and thorns, he went on until his feverish mind plunged into total darkness.

That was the first time Reiner had heard about hallucinations, the state where the senses were complicit with the brain in orchestrating a parallel reality.

"Reiner?" Monika's voice came from far away.

For a moment, she was present as part of a vision, as if she'd entered and joined his phantasmagoria: a woman of her likeness implausibly hidden behind a dense, blue-green canopy of lobed and whorled leaves, while he, who had turned into the hero of the half-book, stumbled along in his feverish fantasies. Hearing her voice was a total surprise; she must have traveled hundreds of miles to rescue him from this jungle of his own making.

"Reiner, what's wrong?" Monika said, hovering over him with concern etched in the familiar lines of her face.

His heart quivered, and the jolt pulled him back to the present and to the attic, to the pile of old comic books, sitting right across from her.

"I just experienced the most peculiar thing. Was I asleep?"

"You must be so tired from your journey!"

There was something in her voice, in the way she said those simple words, that gave him unexpected comfort.

* * *

Later that night, he remembered his resolution to continue the diary he had started in Ierapetra, no matter what.

[Home. Re.: refuge in the attic]

Sometimes I think my head is about to burst. How do I account for the years I spent up here? It was a refuge, but from what? What was so terrifying down in the family living quarters that made me retreat? If it was my memory of the war as a young child, then why would I seek shelter in the place that bore physical reminders of when the bombs struck the house? Perhaps it is a perverse fascination with rubble, with chaos and disorder? It this something I need to overcome? I must ask M. if she has this same kind of obsession. She could be the control variable while I figure this out.

Chapter 38

Almut and Reiner agreed to meet in the park surrounding the massive eighteenth-century castle that overlooked the hills of his hometown. On the phone, she'd sounded matter-of-fact, even cold, but that might have been on account of the bad connection.

They'd met several times before on the bench nearest the Two Mothers Fountain. The bronze sculpture referred to an infamous fight over eighteenth-century painter Balthazar Friedrich Neumann: a fat, unattractive baby boy being grabbed by two mothers representing two different cities, each trying to claim him as her own. If he remembered it right, the locations in question were Kassel, where the painter's parents were from, and this city, where he was born by accident after his father got arrested on a false charge as he was passing through with his pregnant wife. The city's claim on Neumann as its son was audacious but rooted in the belief in the contingency of fate; but on that level, both claims had equal merit. The scene invoked the famous verdict of Salomon in a similar fight three millennia ago: divide the goddamn baby so each can have a share!

Reiner discovered that he found it painful to be reminded of his early courtship with Almut, and that agreeing to meet her there, of all places, was a mistake. Besides, he'd never liked Neumann, had never cared for the voluptuous, rosy flesh in his paintings, which didn't resonate with the way he experienced his own desire. In fact, what he'd always liked about Almut was that she was the very opposite image: petite, sinewy, slender, firm, and with small breasts.

He arrived early and took in the French gardens: a mere shadow of Versailles in scale and exuberance, but quite charming if one considered a small-town landscape architect's attempt to imitate the grand model. Bushes of yellow and red roses lined the parallel paths leading toward the fountain. He had been here many times before, going all the way back to the Sunday afternoon excursions with his family, where the castle and its café were considered the destination at the end of long journey by bus and foot. In the far distance was the *Fujiyama*, the majestic name given by the local people to the giant heap of slag accumulated from centuries of iron mining, which sloped down just like the real thing, although it was miniscule by comparison, unable to penetrate or even reach the clouds as its namesake managed to do most of the time.

Reiner immediately spotted Almut thanks to her gait, which was, as always, confident and measured. The impression was reinforced by the formal garden surroundings and the castle, and despite her lack of formal attire, she might have been a lady at court. When they first met, he'd been taken by the regal way she carried herself. But in the present, as she came closer, she looked a bit unreal, as if she'd been cut out of a children's book of fairy tales with scissors.

The paleness of her complexion must have been due, at least in part, to the illness that would have kept her out of the sun for much of the summer. In a curious way, the time he'd spent apart from Almut had been enough to relegate her to distant memory; what he saw before him was a shadow, more of a ghost than a real person. As she drew closer, he experienced a measure of alarm, a premonition of helplessness, and felt the urge to run away. Only a sense of decorum and fairness, and recognition of the trust she had placed in him, kept him in place.

"Almut!" he said, perhaps too loudly.

He hugged her and kissed her, perhaps too passionately, all too aware that it came from a wish to compensate for his absence, both physical and mental, this past summer.

"You called me exactly once in the five weeks you were away," she said as she abruptly freed herself from his embrace. It was only then that he noticed she was not smiling. "I wasn't even sure I wanted to meet you today."

Reiner swallowed hard. "I did send you a letter: the one with the Knossos postcard. But being in Greece, totally experiencing the place, one has difficulties relating back to life home."

"Well, yes, but don't you see that this is the whole problem? I've been part of your life back home—at least this is what I believed—but then you drop me the second I'm out of sight." He fidgeted as she seemed to look right through him. "And by the way, I never got the letter you are talking about."

"I didn't drop you," he said. "You are being a bit melodramatic, don't you think? I did send the letter, and if it didn't arrive then the only explanation is they gave me the wrong stamps at the post office in Mires."

"When you talked to me on the phone—"

"I remember; I was in Ierapetra."

"You sounded…you made it sound as though you couldn't wait to come back. Instead, you stayed as long as you possibly could."

"I owed it to my pupils. You should have seen them."

He felt uncomfortable using what he knew was halfway between a truth and a lie as his excuse. As a matter of fact, the longer he stayed, the more they would have missed him in the end. He was also embarrassed by his choice of term for them—*pupils*—because it sounded so old-fashioned and out of place, especially when he considered Kanta. Also, because he had initially agreed to give those lessons to pay for Monika's medical expenses, but that was one thing he could never tell Almut.

There was no accounting for the way Rosa had derailed him and driven a wedge between him and his girlfriend, just as he had feared right from the start. He decided not to mention her because it would give her undue significance, and there was no chance he'd ever meet her again anyway. And yet, this omission still weighed heavily on him, and even affected how much eye contact he could maintain with Almut. It even affected the tone of his voice.

And so, in a roundabout way, her accusation that he had neglected her became an instant comfort; it felt so unjust and overdramatic, and the credit he thought he was owed suddenly far outweighed his guilt.

"Oftentimes, I think you are not listening to me," Almut calmly said, as if it was a remark she had prepared some time ago and now saw her opening to unload it on him.

Had someone warned him about the outcome of this last meeting with his girlfriend in advance, he wouldn't have been surprised or even hurt. If someone had told him that he would never see her again, he would have felt tremendous relief. He would have concluded that she deserved an altogether better man, one whose feelings were unwavering and more like Ierapetra: solid as a rock. Certainly not a man like him.

Chapter 39

"How did it go with Almut?" his sister asked when they met that night. She'd just got a haircut, and her locks framed her face in a more natural way that also made her seem livelier than she had since he got home.

"Not so good," he said. "We split up."

She asked no more questions, and he left it at that. He knew quite well she had asked only out of politeness, not because she had any particular interest in Almut or his feelings for her. But for some reason he could not account for, he was relieved that his sister hadn't brought up Rosa in any of their conversations since he came home. It was just as well; he was resigned to the fact that he would not see Rosa again, and anything that invoked her memory just postponed the point in time when it would be entirely purged from his brain.

* * *

"Did I tell you I started sewing?" Monika asked with her eyebrows raised, as if she was not sure if she should be ashamed or proud of it.

"Sewing?" he said, examining her closely, wondering if he'd her heard correctly.

As a boy, he regarded needlework as a woman's business, and utterly boring. In the years immediately after the war, a seamstress used to come to their house once a year and made a lot of outfits; whenever she left after three days of work, the entire dining room was covered with fabric in different colors, patterns, and shapes. He always liked the colorful disorder and disruption it brought to the normally tidy room. And he used to make finger puppets from the leftover patches for the miniature theater performances he staged with his sister.

Since his return home, Monika and Reiner had made a habit of meeting upstairs in the attic after dinner. They'd just finished the wine he'd spirited away by tucking the bottle into his sleeve, and while he listened to his sister, he thought of ways to replenish their supply without running into the rest of the family. After some disappointing rounds with Riesling, they moved on with a *Frankenwein*, which was reminiscent of *retsina* in that it was an honest, full-bodied wine.

"Oh, good for you," he said absently.

"You didn't ask me what I'm making," she said.

"So what are you *making* with your sewing?" He knew he made it sound as though he thought she was complaining, but she didn't seem to mind.

She got up and asked him to follow her to the back room. There, she opened a chest of drawers and pulled out what looked like a blanket. As she drew it under the light, it exploded into a kaleidoscope of colors. The piece was magnificent. He looked at the quilt, then back to her face, not believing his eyes. Hundreds of patches met each other in brilliant juxtapositions, bringing shards of an imperfect puzzle home. His sister had made it with her own two hands, and nobody but him knew what she was capable of.

"Why would you *ever* hide something like this?"

"You know our father! He doesn't…he thinks…he feels…"

Reiner knew exactly what she was attempting to say. Women, in his fathers' opinion, belonged in the kitchen. He considered the fact that she had to hide something that was so accomplished absurd, and the order imposed on her stupendously cruel.

Looking back, he saw that his father had made nothing but capricious decisions about both of his daughters' destinies. Luckily for him, Papa had always favored his boys; the result, however, was a two-tiered family, with the two parties always suspicious of each other and perpetually locked in a cold war. The accusing eyes in each conversation always had to do something with education, with opportunities in life, and roadblocks in the way. It was clear to him now that both of his sisters saw him and his brother as misogynists-in-training even in childhood.

For instance, his father relished the occasions when his mother misspoke or made errors in judgment, as if these validated his conviction of her basic inferiority because she was a woman. With a grin on his face, he would pull out a brown, leather-bound notebook from his vest pocket, along with a little pencil that he always kept sharp. He would open the notebook, hold it down on the table with his left thumb, and scribble down his wife's mistakes.

Semper aliquid heret. It was Latin for, "something always sticks." His father's grin and the ritual with the notebook all depicted the patriarch asserting his superiority. And when this behavior was repeated often enough in front of his children, they would adopt the same attitude about a woman's worth. But instead of siding with his father, Reiner had always cringed when he was forced to witness this brand of humiliation. Except he'd simply never said or done anything to try and stop it.

"*Don't,*" he said to Monika, interrupting her before she could finish her thought.

"Don't what?" She asked, her eyes wide with surprise.

"Don't worry about *him.*"

Wordlessly, Monika hugged him. As he returned her embrace, he noted how wiry she felt in his arms. At that moment, he thought about Greece and the separate but similar effects that it had on both of them. He lacked words for the occasion; in fact, he had no way of acknowledging his feelings because this was something he'd never learned to do. Feelings were nothing but constellations of images in his mind that made him either relax or recoil.

The brilliant day they'd spent on the beach in Vai—the beach of a thousand palms, the beach where clothes had lost their purpose and meaning—came to mind, and in a wild, hopeless way, he ruminated on the idea to redo and rewire and revive his family from the ground up. No, he had to take it further and include the stiff, sour-looking neighbors, the whole Protestant town, this whole region of the country. It was a vast undertaking, comparable in scope to the Marshal Plan, remade, but he knew then that they all needed to be recast and repurposed and remade into people with substance and fearless vitality, who would leave proud footprints wherever they stepped, not just flecks of mud.

He knew he lacked the courage and imagination and resources to affect these changes; he knew it was a task beyond even Hercules, and that it would be so much easier to start fresh somewhere new.

So for the time being, he would focus on his sister; she shared his vision and knew how to get by, and with luck, she would escape and survive intact.

PART V

The Visit

Chapter 40

[On my way to Bonn visiting Monika. Re.: exercise in dialog]
  "This is not a table."
  "Sure it is. It has four legs."
  "Lots of animals have four legs."
  "This item is made of wood."
  "It could be a wooden statue of a four-legged animal."
  "But it's clearly a table. It has a horizontal surface for plates."
  "Statues of four-legged animals could have horizontal boards attached."
  "But this one doesn't even look like an animal."
  "Says who? How can you be so sure what animals look like?"
  "I know they don't look like a table. It's a fact."
  "See, I caught you on this one!"

His handwritten notes were getting out of hand; he'd filled many Lisa Frank notebooks, and these notebooks were stacked in cardboard organizers, and the organizers in turn were stacked in boxes he stored away in cabinets. The newer ones were lined up on his shelves.

Today's exercise was in dialog, inspired by a dispute with one of his former girlfriends, who had insisted that insects did not belong in the same category as animals. At the time, the very possibility of such a dispute was absurd, but since then he had come across many versions of the human mind that he found utterly perplexing.

At one point, he'd switched from longhand to typing on the computer, but eventually printed out the pages and scribbled comments and corrections in the margins. Soon after his move to Cambridge, five years ago, he adopted English as his default language. All this writing had started that day in Heraklion, when he was stupidly bedridden in the youth hostel trying to fill that first empty page but came up with nothing except his brother's Agamemnon pun. Then he had scribbled notes about his travels, but they did not say a thing about his sister—perhaps out of fear that she might come across it some years later. He wrote nothing about Rosa because, at the time, he didn't want to jinx himself. Then, after she'd left without trace, he refrained from writing about her for the opposite reason: to avoid reopening his wounds.

The time he spent in Ierapetra alone filled five notebooks with ruminations on esoteric things that sprung up in the solitude of his elevated room while he nursed the blisters on his hands. And then, of course, he'd written about the natural phenomenon that was Kanta, the girl who had the right stuff to be a leader, perhaps even president of Greece sometime in the future.

Years later, he would write about *Gott und die Welt*—God and the world—which was the term his father used for "everything under the sun." Except God had an untenable place in Reiner's own thinking and writing, and served as nothing more than a placeholder for other peoples' beliefs that had woven an impenetrable thicket of half-truths. And this was what Reiner considered to be a polite phrase for what people had been doing for more than two millennia.

[On my way to Bonn visiting Monika. Re.: dreams of soaring]

I used to soar. It was not the primitive high-flying of early adolescence, wherein my body could turn into a cloud with the issue of the inevitable orgasm sprinkling the landscape beneath, just before the ultimate crash, but a mature, steady soaring that required regal posture, my body encased in a nanofabricated, gossamer suit of infinite sophistication, its every inch a sensor. The direction, altitude, and speed of the flight were all controlled by the slightest change in the position of my arms, and fine-tuned by subtle adjustments of my hands and fingers. Sometimes, a mere thought would suffice.

When I set out for the first time to acquire altitude, to see farms, hills, and entire pine forests gliding by beneath me, I dismissed the wet, drifting cloud dreams as something from the past that no longer beckoned to and rewarded me, but now I remember, with the deep embarrassment of the mature adult, looking back to when that was indeed the case. This was the real thing: no longer a dream, but a show of actual power channeled by sheer concentration of the mind.

But what was the essence and purpose of all that writing coming from his blistered hand, and later from his typewriter, if nobody would see it and read it and understand where he was coming from and where he was going? It mirrored the old question of whether or not there could be beauty in a world without people. Maybe there was a slight difference between one situation and the other, but pinning this difference down opened a metaphorical, metaphysical can of worms Reiner didn't want to explore. There was also a difference between the manuscript he intended to write and the manuscript that would eventually take physical form. One was infinitely richer than the other but was predestined to never see the light of the day.

On the way to Bonn via the *Chunnel* Tunnel that had just opened a few months ago, Reiner took in his surroundings. Everything smelled new and plastic; even the train attendants serving dinner looked and smelled freshly made up, and the fact that he could make it in just four and a half hours from London to Bonn without getting on a plane filled him with a sense of confidence in the future. Actually, it was the aftereffect of both the *Chunnel* opening and the fall of the Berlin Wall just five years earlier that bolstered his hopes for the coming of a better world.

He hated traveling by plane, and that was the only reason he had declined a promising job offer from a university in the United States some time ago. But it was less about a fear of flying and more about his hatred for the whole artifice connected with airports: the lines of unapologetically boisterous shops, the lackluster fast-food restaurants, the inconvenience of security, the sardine-like confinement in a *Schicksalsgemeinschaft*—a community of fate—all trembling up there in the air without anybody wanting to admit it.

This was also why he rarely visited his sister, and it was one of the problems the *Chunnel* had solved for him as a sheer miracle of twentieth-century technology.

Still living in Cambridge, he'd gotten involved with a startup to realize his biochemical dream project. The university was gung ho about industrial partnerships, so it was the perfect moment to join in on one, even though it felt weird to be in England, of all places. He had met his wife in Düsseldorf, at the annual vernissage of contemporary arts. Though tempestuous, their marriage had withstood the test of time and the agonizing discussions leading up to Sabine agreeing to follow him into this distinctly different environment. But, as a contemporary artist with lineage to Joseph Beuys, her artistic grandfather, she could not oppose to being close to the forefront of pan-European arts. Since it was an hour and a half by train from the Tate Modern, she could live in bucolic Cambridge without losing touch with the art crowd. Intensely focused on the pursuit of her visions, she had little appetite for travel outside of England or Germany, with the Venice Biennale as the single exception

Monika lived with her husband Peter and Brigitte, their eleven–year old daughter, in a remodeled farmhouse on the periphery of a tiny, secluded village in the vicinity of Bonn. Its name derived from the German word for a particular brand of criminals who were executed there five hundred years ago by being thrown off the top of a tower that still stood in the same field. The first time he'd heard about it, he was in his room high above the ground in Ierapetra, looking out to the sea and overcome with vertigo, realizing that he was prevented from falling only by the thin glass of the windows and a will to live, and to love.

He'd visited her only once before. He'd closed his eyes and listened carefully, trying to imagine the sounds of bones cracking as they met the ground. That was really nothing compared with the reverberations of the big bang; 13.7 billion years after the fact, and they could still be detected in the background radiation bouncing through the universe.

In the modern age, there was an odd mixture of people living in Bonn: young professionals who sought to escape the urban sphere and anxiously watched the hills in the distance for fear of being discovered and overtaken by the modern avalanche of bricks, asphalt, and cement. Some kept bees as a hobby; several others kept horses, cows, goats, and even lamas. These citizens comprised a new brand of rich gentleman farmers who lived off their stock dividends and had a lot of spare time on their hands.

Reiner came by taxi since buses only sporadically visited this forlorn part of the countryside. As they drove in, he saw the infamous tower and that the flat field surrounding it was aflame with bloodred poppies. In the distance, there was the fuzzy profile of the *Siebengebirge*—the Seven Mountain Range. When the taxi entered the village, he saw two dogs on the side of the road licking each other, a young woman dressed all in black walking with measured steps through her garden as if she were retracing similar, but less lonely walks, and finally the remnants of a squirrel that had been flattened by the traffic into the equivalent of thin parchment.

Chapter 41

Whimsical clay figures were everywhere: attached to the fence, to the entrance gate, to posts whose sole function seemed to be to support the tiny sculptures, and to the front door of the farmhouse, which was partially hidden by some tall lilac bushes. Reiner had a sudden flashback to his visit to Florence and the figurines attached to the heavy bronze door of the Cathedral of Santa Maria del Fiore. Even the doorbell was a work of art: a lever crafted from wrought iron and fastened to the gatepost, with a wire running from it through a duct to the chimes inside the house. He knew this was all Peter's work; a shared passion for art that had brought Peter and Monika together.

Once he pulled the lever, the chimes sounded, the gate unlocked, and the door opened. Monika and Peter appeared on the doorstep to greet him. The precision of the sequence reminded him of the clockwork at play within a medieval church tower at noon—the one in Strasbourg perhaps, or in Bruges in Flanders.

Monika looked festive in her flowing blue dress and matching hat—always with the hats! Peter, tall and almost completely bald, wore blue denim overalls.

"So good to see you!"

"Same here."

"You must be exhausted!"

"I made it, though. Actually, I could use the bathroom, and some rest."

"I'll take your luggage," Peter said. "The bathroom is on the left."

"Where is Brigitte?"

"In school. She'll be out at three."

The living room was expansive, with low ceilings that had massive, exposed oak wood beams. On the left as he entered, there was a big, unlit fireplace. Three windows lined the right wall, but they were too small to fill the room with light, even on this bright day. In the diffused light, Reiner could make out several big quilts on the walls. Peter led him into the room and flicked a switch; the wall hangings burst with brilliant colors once they were flooded with light by little low-voltage lamps mounted on the wooden beams above. In less than a second, the room had changed from a drab place into a small but magnificent art gallery. Reiner moved slowly, taking in each piece, one by one.

"This is phenomenal!" he said to Peter.

He'd sensed for some time that his sister had found her true place there, her niche after so many hits and misses. She was a real artist who could be proud of herself. He was relieved, since all these years one idea had persisted in the back of his mind: that he had somehow abandoned her, and that she was still suffering the consequences. His excuse had always been that he'd entered what were the hardest years of his career, which involved a lot of traveling, and that he had a lot of other things on his mind. Now he realized that no excuse was needed; she was on her own feet, she was all right, and she did it herself.

"Where is Monika?" he asked. "I need to speak to her right here."

"She's gone to pick up Brigitte at school."

* * *

He meant to take a quick nap, but when he woke, two solid hours had passed. He found himself in a fog and felt terribly hungry. It took him a minute to sort out where he was and why. The sight of little ceramic people sitting on the windowsill quickly set him straight. After splashing his face with water, he took a quick look in the mirror, hoping to find that the worst of the lines were gone. They were not, but life had to go on.

As he walked into the living room, Monika and Peter greeted him with cheese and crackers and a glass of wine. The quicksilver presence of their daughter welcomed him as well. He had not seen Brigitte since she was little, and now he couldn't believe she was this sinewy, prepubescent girl overflowing with energy. She wore unicorn slippers on her feet and a purple, velvet scrunchie kept her ponytail up at and out of her face. In those soft slippers, she glided across the polished hardwood floor.

She acknowledged his comments on her growth with nervous shyness. But soon, she was engaging all three adults in conversation simultaneously.

"I totally forgot that they were going to take a group picture today," she announced. "I already told Mutti."

"What went wrong?" Peter asked.

"I was supposed to wear a dress," she said.

"You look absolutely fine the way you are," Monika said.

"Did you bring me something?" the girl abruptly asked, turning to her uncle.

"Brigitte, your manners! What a thing to say!" Monika exclaimed.

"Let her be," Reiner said to his sister. "I remember doing the exact same thing at her age." Then, turning to Brigitte, he said, "Yes I did get you something. Are you kidding? Do you think I would come all the way from England empty-handed?"

He retrieved a box from his suitcase. It was a pink, mini-Polaroid camera that came with twenty packs of pictures. Sabine had suggested that the instant camera would be an ideal present for someone of that tender age and gender. When Brigitte pulled it out of the box and recognized what it was, she got excited and started dancing.

"I never, ever thought I would get an instant camera!"

Reiner helped her load in the first pack, and she immediately started taking pictures. She took pictures of her unicorn slippers from a bird's eye view, one at a time. She took a shot of her parents and one of her uncle from the side. She watched as the pictures popped out all in white, then gained faint contours in pastel colors, and finally waxed true. Soon, the peeled negative sheets littered the floor. She showed the pictures of the slippers off to everyone.

"This is so cool!" she said and danced some more with her enviable energy.

"I got you something, too," Reiner said to Monika.

"Uh-oh, I know what's coming," she said as he placed a large, cylindric box in her hands. She opened it, and out came another hat for her collection. It was a wide-brimmed specimen he found the last time he visited London, and was encircled with an embroidered band. "Thanks! This is *exactly* what I was missing."

Monika slowly rotated the hat with both hands, looking at it from all sides. She then gave Reiner a meaningful look and beckoned him to a door at the far end of the room. They were greeted by the strong smell of cedar wood as she opened the door.

His mouth popped open in surprise when she switched on the light inside. It was a walk-in closet she'd turned into a veritable museum of headwear in all kinds of fabrics, colors, and shapes. One hundred? Two? It was hard to tell since they were stacked five shelves high along all three walls of the deep closet. Floppy hats, berets, boaters, buckets, porkpie hats, pillboxes, cloches, ushankas, beanies, two large sombreros that were on the verge of tipping over for lack of support, a cartwheel hat, a Panama hat, and so on: no two were exactly alike. The collection could have served as a training set for small children or extraterrestrials who needed or wanted to learn the very concept of a hat

"You are truly a mad hatter," he said.

"Thank you." She curtsied, pretending to be flattered.

"What is that one?" He pointed at one made of felt that looked like a Fedora's afterthought.

"A sedancasesa."

"That sounds like *abracadabra,* except a bit more like the tango. Where did you get all of these?"

"When I travel, I always go into hat shops. And now people who know about my hobby give them to me as gifts, like you."

"Well, word gets around. Do you wear them?"

"Absolutely. What do you think? Should I just leave them mothballed?"

Reiner took a peculiarly shaped hat from one of the upper shelves and tried it on.

"A trilby! You have class," she said, stepping back to take in the full picture he made. "You should see yourself! Wait, I'll get a mirror."

What he saw was astonishing. The hat made him look like an unapologetic industrial baron. As he looked into the mirror, he tried to refine his stare and stiffen his upper lip. He had never cared much about his appearance, but this was one of those rare moments in which he could understand why some people employed an extra dimension of self to prop themselves up.

"By class, I guess, you mean the upper class?"

Monika shrugged. "No, just class."

When they stepped out of Monika's little headwear emporium, a fire burned in the fireplace and Peter crouched in front of it, adjusting the logs with a poker. Brigitte was sprawled on the floor in her blue jeans and headphones connected to a Walkman, leafing through a large comic book.

"I was worried you'd gotten lost in the closet," Peter said. "Did you try out each and every one of them?"

"Just one. He tried out my trilby. You should have seen him," Monika said.

"After all that, you definitely deserve another glass of wine," Peter said.

Reiner took his glass and sunk into the first easy chair he came across, then raised the glass to Peter. "*Prost!* God, I'm so tired you might have to carry me to bed."

"That shouldn't be a problem between the three of us. Just relax!"

"What are you reading?" Reiner mouthed his question to his niece.

Wordlessly, she lifted her head and showed him the cover of the book: *The Adventures of Tintin in America*. The picture had poor Tintin tied to a pole in front of a couple of teepees. In the foreground, a chief in full regalia swung an axe in the air. His feathered headdress, Peter observed, could well be the single item missing from Monika's otherwise exhaustive collection.

"I love Tintin," he said. "That was one of my favorites. How do you like it so far?"

"It's OK so far," Brigitte said. "It's not really up to date, though."

"What do you expect? It's from the thirties," her father said.

"I know exactly what she means," Monika said. "The mind of this character is always multiplying things into infinity, but I never get a sense of the actual person."

Reiner was too tired to decide whether or not he agreed or disagreed at this point. In his experience, the coziness of fireplaces tended to soften arguments and invited compromise, at least in principle, but here the positions were already established with such vigor and precision that it was safest to stay out of it. Plus, the whole debate reminded him of Kanta and her fascination with Karl May; it all came back to him as if it had been only yesterday.

Chapter 42

On his second day in town, they all went to a park on their side of the Rhine for a picnic. They went early enough to secure one of the highly prized picnic tables right by the river, where they could watch the ducks and branches and debris drift by or get drawn into the shore. Reiner enjoyed the vista, with its majestic weeping willows lining the opposite shore.

"See the meadows on the other side of the river?" Peter said to him. "On the first of May, a lot of people were trapped over there in a downpour: the radioactive rain from Chernobyl."

"I remember the accident happened in April of that year," Reiner said. "But what exactly happened here?"

"Don't you remember? We wrote to you about it. The clouds drifted over from Ukraine and there was this sudden thunderstorm. People were picnicking. It was one giant mess."

"That part I can't remember. I must have been traveling. And then what happened?"

"Some got sick. And then later on—well, it's still going on—a wave of cancer diagnoses—thyroid, mostly. But nothing causal can be proven. You can imagine what juries will do with probabilities versus solid facts."

Brigitte got up abruptly. She had brought badminton bats and shuttlecocks and wanted to play "this minute." Reiner and Monika watched father and daughter from afar.

"Have you ever been back?" Monika asked.

"Back where?"

"Back to Greece."

Of course! The summer they had spent years before under the Mediterranean sky had become a permanent reference point. It was a part of his memory—and hers—that was filled with an atmospheric richness. It was a Füllhorn—the antiquated German word for the horn of plenty found in mannerist Renaissance paintings—a cornucopia of sensory experiences.

"Well, I thought you knew the story," he said. "Just three years later, I was all ready to go again with my girlfriend—"

"Almut?"

"No, remember what I told you later that summer? We broke up since she couldn't deal with the way I enjoyed myself in her absence. Though now I think she had a point." Reiner interrupted himself with a shrug and smirk. "No, it was a different girlfriend by then. Anyway, we decided to go, and, at the last minute, this right-wing junta took over in a putsch. I think it was in April of 1967: Papadopoulos and Pattakos, his right-hand man. It actually reminded me of the Papageno duet in *The Magic Flute* at the time. 'Pa-pa-pa-pa-pa-pappa,' etcetera."

"This rings a bell, but I didn't follow it closely at the time," Monika said.

"We canceled everything: flights, ferries, hotels. We lost most of our money because of late cancellation fees."

Brigitte cut the reminiscing short, her heavily panting father in tow, by recruiting her uncle for the game. Reiner accepted the challenge but was soon out of breath as well. The sun was in his face, but he did not dare ask her to switch sides. She was strong for an eleven-year-old; she hit the balls in straight, fierce trajectories, and he even had to dodge some of them at the very last moment like a coward.

* * *

On the third evening, they finally found some time for themselves. Monika set up a little table in the backyard and covered it with a carmine red tablecloth from Alsace, then set up a ceramic candlestick Peter had sculpted from clay and fired twice and glazed in the kiln he built himself in the garden. There were two glasses on the table, and a dish with nuts and crackers. A tray with olives and a bottle of white wine in a cooler were on standby on a little serving table nearby.

Infinitesimal changes of light marked the evening's passing. It reminded Reiner of the long afternoons they spent as children, back when he was old enough to roam the streets with other boys, but Monika was still under the watchful eyes of their mother and grandmother. A light breeze rustled the leaves on the trees, and there wasn't a single mosquito in sight; the evening was perfect.

"Last time we met like this was at Mother's funeral," she said, breaking the silence.

He detected a hint of accusation in her voice. "I remember the pastor quoting her: the thing about the earth going round and round," he said.

"Yes, that was funny."

"Has it been three years already? That's unreal."

"Yes, you said it: unreal! I never see you anymore."

"Well, I'm here now." He raised his glass. "Let's drink to the event!"

"Sometimes I miss her badly," she said after taking a sip from her glass. "I mean, I visited her so much in her last years, but I hardly managed to talk with her about anything real, anything that wasn't related to food or her ailments. It was like I lost her before she was actually gone."

"I know what you mean, but it was different for me. I was in England all that time, and only saw her once a year at most, so she sort of faded away a long time ago. It's hard to say, but it's true."

"Different for you? Sorry Reiner there is something I have to get off my chest. I worked my ass off, driving there every weekend to make sure she was alright: a hundred kilometers each way. And from you? Letters! You know, that was sort of cheap."

He sure had ticked her off, and now regretted whatever it was that he had said. But calling his letters cheap was overdoing it a bit. She'd bottled something up, perhaps from long time ago, and it sounded like she really meant to hurt him.

"Monika, we've gone through this before." He adopted what he hoped she would interpret as a calm, patient voice. "I had—no, I still have a lab to run, and I basically live there. People make their choices and then they have to live with them."

"Maybe we should just change the subject," she said curtly. "My choice was staying here, and obviously that came at a price. You are lucky you made the choices you did."

He didn't know what to say. This was getting nowhere, and they both knew it.

"Now should we talk about my art?" she asked.

"I would love to talk about your art."

But Reiner hesitated. She was calling his bluff, and now he was supposed to ask questions. This was her way of punishing him, and he would have to tread lightly.

"I told you that your quilts could be in the Tate Modern; I'm convinced they could. Tell me where and how you get your ideas."

"It's all sitting here," she said, pointing to her forehead. "And there." She pointed out to the garden around them. "Pieces of puzzles that wait to be assembled."

"This is the thing I still find hard to understand. My kind of art is fiction. In fiction (and of course in science) I express myself in a sequence of words that express relationships between objects, one at a time, and it's picked up by a reader sequentially."

"What are you getting at?"

"Wait, I'm getting there. In your quilts, the only way you can represent a relationship is through two-dimensional juxtapositions of pieces based on shapes and colors. You actually work in a sequence of time, of course, but this gets lost in the end. There is no record of it. And when it's finished, it all gushes out to the observer at the same time."

"As it would in a painting," she said.

"Right. In all visual art there is no match between the acts of creation and consumption."

A horse neighed in the distance. "That's Paul's horse, four houses up," she said quickly, as if she had waited for a relief from the conversation. "The other one died from something—something to do with the intestine, Peter will remember."

"I love it; it's just like a real village! And you know every soul here."

"So, where were we? I still don't know what you are getting at," she said. "At any rate, I'm probably not the right person to try and answer all these philosophical questions. I just see things in my head and compose using my eyes and hands, and that is all."

"OK, it's interesting this all just comes to you out of nowhere. But never mind my question." He had caught himself in the nick of time. It was not exactly a conversation he wanted to have with her and her down-to-earth, practical mind. People had told him many times that he tended to create unnecessary abstractions. "So, where do you exhibit? Where do you sell your work?"

"I just had a show. I thought I sent you a copy of the catalog?"

"Nope, nothing arrived. Of course, the Royal postal mail in England is a mess sometimes. Perhaps I'll get it by the end of the year."

"Never mind, I'll give you another one tomorrow. Just remind me!" she said with a laugh. "Anyway, I'm part of this group of quilters, all women artists, and we rented a space downtown. We had this big exhibit and I actually sold a few of my pieces."

"Monika, that is fantastic! I hope that one day one of those art critics stumbles in and tells the whole world."

"Well, art critics smell money. And they don't stumble. They know where to go."

"You know what I mean!"

Motion in the brush behind the table interrupted them, and they turned their heads to find Brigitte stepping out into the candle's pool of light.

"I want to say goodnight, Mutti," she said, but her eyes were on her uncle, the legendary man who lived far away and had a mysterious job and made sporadic appearances. To her, he probably seemed like a different person each time.

"You are still up, *Spatz*?" Monika said. "Don't you know that sleep before midnight counts double?"

"Ach, Mutti, you with your double talk!"

"OK, you want my straight talk? That's easy: go to bed right now!"

Brigitte pretended to be offended, then shrugged with a resigned smile for her uncle. She bid them goodnight and stepped back into the darkness to head toward the house.

"She is cute," he said when she was out of earshot.

"I know. So, you want to know about my plans?" Monika said.

"What are your plans?" Reiner asked to cover his shock.

His sister, as far as he knew, made no plans. The Monika he knew coasted along with whatever was happening. He couldn't help but think again about the way she had drifted off without a thought when they traveled in Greece, but it really went back much further. She had spontaneously dropped out of things for as long as he could remember.

"I've been thinking about opening an art gallery."

"An art gallery? Jesus! Here in Bonn? How are going to do that? You'll need a lot of cash."

"I discussed it with Peter. We have good credit since he's in government."

"But think of all the galleries in Düsseldorf! People who seriously want to buy art don't go to Bonn."

"How do you know?"

"I know a thing or two about the art market through Sabine. You know very well Bonn is a *Kaff*—a backwater—especially regarding the arts business."

"All these people from government live here, plus their idle wives, who have nothing to do but sit in cafés and gossip. My gallery will specialize in textile artwork."

"Naturally, with your quilting friends and all that you told me about. Do you have a name already?"

"Rhapso Shop. Rhapso is the goddess of sewing and stitching in ancient Greece."

"Rhapso, like in *rhapsody*?"

"Yes: same root, but the weaving of tunes."

"Let me talk with Sabine about it. She has a lot of contacts still in Düsseldorf. She could put you in touch with people there. But whatever you do, forget Bonn!"

Reiner couldn't help but shake his head. Rhapso Shop? A gallery in Bonn, of all places? It was a nutty idea, as far as he was concerned. He was also worried that Monika would hit him up for a loan; he wouldn't be able to say no if she did. But for the rest of the evening, she kept quiet, her enthusiasm apparently dampened enough by his putdown that she did not want to invite more of his feedback.

* * *

In the taxicab on his way to catch the train home, just as he was again passing the ominous tower on the red poppy field, he took a deep breath. He mulled over the conversation they'd had the night before about her gallery plan, her crazy *rhapso* idea.

Rhabarber. Rapunzel, Ramadan.

Had he failed her by discrediting it so unequivocally?

Ratatouille!

Had she expected moral support instead of the financial variety from him?

Rastafari!

But seriously, had she ever listened to his advice on any important decisions before?

Romulus and Remus! Rhododendron!

He couldn't remember a single instance in which that was the case.

Chapter 43

Mission Misunderstood

It's a perfect summer day, but those tend to go by too quickly. In old age, our thought processes slow down, so we perceive the passing of time as if it were accelerating. That was the explanation I read in the papers recently, anyway. It made a lot of sense, but I wouldn't be surprised if it doesn't go over well with the general public. They told us for years that neurons don't regenerate in adults and now, all of a sudden, we learn that they do it happily all the time. This makes more sense since; even though I'm more forgetful, I do see more connections now.

The tomato plants on the terrace I created in the spring are thriving, except for one that attracted a huge caterpillar about the size of my middle finger. I had to build a mesh fence around the bed where the pole beans grow to keep the critters away. Whatever they are, they go for the bean leaves before the shoots can even think of going up. It could be rabbits, deer, or groundhogs. Between them, there is a telltale that could be cause to use a formulation of Euclidean geometry in order to solve the case; signs that a groundhog is eating your beans include a smooth cut at a diagonal plane on the bitten ends of the vegetation. I assume the inclination of the plane defining the cut is created by the topology of said creature's mouth in the same way that scissors are mounted. But what about the other signs included in this open-ended list of clues? The shape and color of droppings? The types of collateral damage on vegetables around the scene of the crime? Besides, I have never seen so many moles in my whole life, and the internet, all-encompassing as it is, can be mistaken.

The basil leaves are turning yellow—they are not made for this heat—and this is the last year I try to cultivate those ungrateful eggplants. It's the soil or something in the air, because my green thumbs don't selectively turn black from one plant to the other.

Every day brings a new surprise, and it's not always a good one.

I couldn't believe what Reiner did to Monika just now. He visits her once a year at most because he is so busy with his career, and when he actually gets there, he plays the nice uncle to his niece, has all kinds of wonderful things to say to his sister, and they look at her hat collection: all fine. Perfect, I should say. But when he has the chance to encourage her as she embarks on a project so close to her heart, he does the exact opposite and tries to talk her out of it. How could she get something started in Düsseldorf, one of the most expensive places in the country? For as long as her father was alive, she hid her art and her aspirations. Now, for the first time she is settled and can realize one of her dreams, and her own big brother puts it down—the same brother who once encouraged her not to worry about what someone else thought of her art.

To his credit, Reiner does feel some remorse on his way back home, so he knows quite well that they did not leave things on a hunky-dory note. But then he dismisses his own misgivings out of hand. I suppose it has to do with a conviction that the mere thought of remorse is a sufficient foundation for a clean conscience.

Well, he is dead wrong.

Barcelona

Chapter 44

How exquisitely space was divided, how dreamlike the architectural elements were shaped!

Over the years, Reiner had seen plenty of cathedrals: the Gothic variety in Freiburg, for instance, and those in Strasbourg and Reims. Of course, there was the majestic presence of Notre-Dame and the monumental cathedral in Milan, where one could take a walk on the roof and be dwarfed by gargoyle waterspouts even though they looked tiny from the street. All these places, in all their variety and splendor, were nevertheless governed by the same theme and constructed with similar stylistic principles in mind. But Antoni Gaudi's otherworldly vision come true, La Sagrada Familia, was incomparable—almost like the result of a parallel development of sacred spaces over centuries in a parallel universe.

All his life, Reiner had been suspicious about architects, or at least the modern ones. When one has the license to shape human habitats, so much was at stake. The sheer knowledge of this power can lead to arrogance and hubris. But this one was a genius who created unique places of worship and designed apartments and buildings for the citizens of Barcelona to live in. To say he was impressed with Gaudi's work was an understatement.

Reiner was traveling in Spain to attend a scientific conference in Sitges, an old Catalan town about an hour away by train. He had just come from there and was spending an extra day in Barcelona to see Gaudi's creations. Tomorrow, he would fly back home. He always hated flying, but he had no appetite for a fifteen-hour train ride via the *Chunnel*, which would undoubtedly include many transfers along the way.

The conference was exhausting and cheerless, just as most conferences hosting a predominately male group of scientists with singular science pursuit tended to be. After a lofty start on the first day with a keynote speech by an elderly pioneer of the field, the second lecture had opened old wounds between two rival schools, and the discussion had turned acrimonious. The few female scientists in attendance were all spoken for—or at least it seemed that way since they were constantly accompanied by someone, if not surrounded by a cluster of male colleagues.

The only saving grace for Reiner was what happened while he was out and about in town. An international performance festival was taking place, and had immersed the town in a bizarre but immensely enjoyable circus-like atmosphere. He ran into some of the artists on the beach and in a local bar but was frustrated by his inability to speak even rudimentary Spanish.

On the beach that morning, he met one of the petite female dancers; she'd made intense eye contact with him but didn't speak a single word of English. She mirrored his smirk of regret as both moved on along the beach in opposite directions. Unlike animals, humans needed words in a common language if they wanted to move beyond first encounters. Later that night, he got drunk at a bar called San Sebastian since there was nothing else for him to do.

As usual, Sabine had stayed home in Cambridge. She had absolutely no interest in accompanying him on these business trips since she was not a scientist, and during the day, there was usually an abundance of sessions he had to attend; sometimes the evenings were also filled with additional sessions and cocktail hours he would be unwise to skip. In her experience, garnered from the few occasions on which she'd gone with him and they did find time to spend together, he was *always* tired or upset about what a competitor said or hinted at, so she *always* wound up consoling him rather than having any fun with him.

Over the years, they had argued about this almost every time another trip would come up on his schedule, but she had grown stubborn and continued to refuse to join him. Conferences in Germany were a different matter since she still had friends to connect with, although her parents had died some time ago and she was without siblings. This time, he had implored her to come with him after reading all about the many charms of Sitges and Barcelona.

"Sabine, this is the best time of the year to visit."

"To do what?"

"To swim. Dine outside. Go sightseeing."

"The beaches are too crowded and I'm too fat. Plus, I don't have a good bathing suit."

"Honey, you are not fat at all, and you can go to any of the outlets on Sidney Street to get yourself a new bathing suit. And as for dining?"

"Spanish food is overrated. They season everything too much."

"But this is Catalan food, remember? Alright, how about sightseeing?"

"The way these things go, you'll be busy all day and that means I'll be on my own."

It was no use. Feeling as if he'd at least done his duty by urging her to change her mind, he decided he would just enjoy himself without her. But she had really missed out on the international performance festival, which she could have enjoyed three days in a row while he was at his sessions. He had already sent her an email all about it.

Seeing Gaudi's creations had been on his agenda for quite some time, ever since he'd visited the travel section of a bookstore in Cambridge and stumbled on a coffee table book on Barcelona. He had gotten curious about the architectural plans and the mathematical inspirations that had driven their quirky designs. The discovery had sent him to his personal computer at home for a search through the new and exciting worldwide web.

Just ten years before, give or take, the internet had recreated the world, with it as its own panopticon. Browsing through art galleries, museums, and landmarks had become a new habit, one that was only limited by the extent of his curiosity, the scope of his phone bills for the privilege of using the tedious modem connection, and the number of times the running AOL man got stuck. But it was still worth it to hang in there with him and see the pictures stream in from all over the world. He had the sense that he was reliving his life in a much more profound way, and the excitement was still fresh even though surfing the internet had become more routine.

One of the first things he looked up was *mantinades*: the word for Greek songs of love, both requited and otherwise. He had jotted it down in his notebook after the evening he spent with Monika at the restaurant in Heraklion by the fortress. He found many lyrics, and got drawn into one song from 1958 by Nikos Xilouris, titled "A woman in black passing by."

Once upon a time, my love, there was
a beautiful duchess, God bless you

A blond girl, who had married at a young age,
is waiting for her husband all day long

On a Saturday night, dear, on a Sunday
she's begging the sun, the moon

"Sun, moon enlighten him
Go to talk to him for me

He's wandering and sailing in the seas
He's killing and destroying the pirates

On the morning, in the night and during the rain
And he's leaving me alone and lonely"

A galley is sailing, my love, to the north
He got in a fight, my love, in an argument

In a pirate guild
I saw fire lighting up and murder

He wondered if this was one of the songs they had listened to that evening. He recognized the reference to the garments worn by widows all over the Mediterranean, but what was the point of singing about this sad story, and for what occasion could it be most appropriate?

"Walk to La Sagrada Familia?" the concierge said when he asked for directions. "No way! Take the subway! It's on the periphery of the city, *way* out of the way!"

He promptly ignored her advice. He'd always enjoyed walking leisurely in a foreign city because walking allowed him the time to observe and weave together a complete fabric of the city in his head. With the subway as its sole means of public transportation, the city would remain a jumble of disconnected neighborhoods if he relied on it. The sweat and the dust and the thirst he'd endure during the walk were an acceptable price to pay.

After lining up for his ticket inside, he entered the large, window-less entrance hall where a scale model of the cathedral was displayed, along with a contraption that served as a template for the design of its arches. Gaudi had derived their shapes from the deformations of a web of strings under the influence of gravity. The web of strings was loaded down with many little sacks of birdshot fastened at strategic spots. But to get the shapes of arches from that, one had to turn everything upside down. Paradoxically, the lowest point of the trajectory became the very summit of the arch.

A large poster at the entrance included a portrait of the artist in an almost defensive pose—clear, defiant eyes looking slightly off camera, a pouted mouth partly hidden by his beard—as if he anticipated a slew of detractors to object to the erection of this bizarre edifice. Or, a needle, as it were, stuck into God's eye.

As Reiner checked out the model and the network of strings, he enjoyed the different perspectives. Gaudi must have walked around like this, rearranging the reference structures and gauging how this affected the shape of the vertical trajectories that guided his grand design.

When he reached the opposite side of the display, Reiner became aware of a young man standing not far from him, who had followed each of his movements. He wore a T-shirt with a picture of acrobats printed on the front. After some visible hesitation, the man stepped up to him.

"I was seen you somewhere," he said. "On the television perhaps, maybe?"

"Very unlikely," Reiner said. "Once, I was interviewed by the local newspaper in Germany, but it was about my dog."

"Sorry," the man said. After a long pause, just as Reiner was about to turn away, he added, "What you think about the basilica? You like it?"

"It is a fantastic piece of architecture."

"Yes, I like it much also."

The man explained that every year since high school, he'd come up from Valencia to visit La Sagrada Familia. Once, he'd come with his girlfriend, but she didn't like it and that was the end of that. Reiner thought it remarkable that a disagreement about the aesthetic value of a work of architecture and art could overrule all other considerations in a relationship, and started to look at the young man with a kind of respect.

"What about the acrobats?" he asked.

"Oh, on my T-shirt? That one? It was present from her. I wear still it."

Together, they entered the basilica proper with its niches and unexpected walkways and stairways and sudden vistas from the diverse windows. Gnomic creatures hung upside down, but still laughed about being made part of this cosmic circus dreamt up inside the brain of one man who had died half a century earlier.

All along this journey, the man from Valencia—Francisco—was Reiner's guide. He was a self-taught Gaudi expert, familiar with every wrinkle in the great master's life, and full of anecdotes that could have easily qualified him as a professional tour guide with the coveted *Guía de Turisme de Cataluña license*. In turn, Reiner told him about his life as a scientist, but it became complicated with his limited Spanish vocabulary and Francisco's variety of English.

In the end, they exchanged phone numbers and Reiner told him that perhaps – just perhaps – he might take him out for dinner that night as a thank-you for guiding him, but that he would call later to confirm. More than anything, he hated lonely evenings on his business trips, and this man was sympathetic as well as a fountain of stories that had not dried up so far.

Chapter 45

Reiner recognized her immediately, even from a distance, and even though she was smaller than he remembered. He felt his blood rushing to his head.

People's gaits don't change; they have an inborn directness or hesitation in each step, a modulation of motion that is theirs from the beginning. They fully inhabit their body's unique memory, reaching back to their time in the womb. They have gestures they indulge in. People are captives to their bodies; they are captives to the minds inhabiting their bodies. He had noticed it while watching himself; the many attempts to run away from himself had kept him right where he was, as though he were nailed to the ground.

Initially, as the years went by, he had thought of her occasionally. But then the tactile traces of memory disappeared; his skin forgot hers. In fact, he had visited Spain a number of times in recent years without even making the connection. He would have been very upset at the time had he known that one day, it all could disappear and leave little trace behind.

She was just leaving a small hotel on Las Ramblas and it seemed like she intended to take a taxi. Their paths crossed midway on the sidewalk. She carried herself like a lady, one high-heeled step in front of the other. Her pitch-black hair was thrown in disarray by gusts of wind. His eyes immediately noted that she wore a soft bra that was apparently designed to bounce and distract, showing muffled impressions of her nipples. Or so he sensed with his reptilian brain.

"*Qué estás mirando?*" What are you staring at?

It was as though she was equipped with hypersensitive receptors all over her body—body cameras, if you wish. Her voice was still the same: quirky and short, just like the first time she'd spoken to him on the bus, many years earlier, or when she talked with him in the ridiculously small room in Mires. But she'd left out two words in her question—"the fuck,"—which he would have expected to flow like honey from her lips in this sort of situation. Even though she'd spoken to him so directly, she had matured in small ways.

High-heeled fucking shoes!

"We know each other," he said, but what he really meant was, "We fucked each other. We were one under the Cretan sky. We were an item, inseparable, fused. We were hooked up together until the moment you ran away. You hurt me, goddamnit. What on earth was wrong with you? What were you thinking?"

"Know?" she said, stepping closer, her face brightening.

Reiner experienced a touch of vertigo. Her reaction to this word—perhaps an acknowledgment that he had referred to knowledge of the Biblical kind—had a profound effect on him.

"God, it *is* you!" she said, and abruptly, with one move of her little hand, she took hold of his as if thirty years had not passed.

She embraced him, bestowed kisses to both of his cheeks, and he felt her breasts touching his chest; she was right there with him, so close he felt her breath. He had all but forgotten her command of the present, her unbridled energy. He was alarmed and thrilled at the same time as he saw the past—all those years without her—shrink down to nothing.

"Rosa," he said, his voice hoarse. "Holy shit! Where were you?"

"Everywhere," she said, smiling. "And nowhere."

She still looked young; her beauty had deepened like the contours of a portrait quickly sketched initially and then more deliberately redrawn by an artist on a promenade. In fact, she resembled a famous Spanish actress whose name he had forgotten; she had the same full, evocative lips, the same eyebrows almost connecting over the bridge of her nose, the same piercing black eyes.

"What are you doing here?" she said.

"A conference in Sitges. I decided to add an extra day to see the La Sagrada Familia. And you? Do you live here?"

"Yes, here in Barcelona. For the past twelve years."

"God, I could have…we could have…"

"Could have what? What are you talking about?"

Ah, women. Always playing hard to get.

They sat down on a park bench and fell into silence, each looking at the other in disbelief. A thirty-year span was a vast warehouse full of jumbled facts. Or, he wondered if it was indeed almost nothing, depending on the person you talked to and on the mood you were in when you got up that morning and looked in the mirror. Trying to collect his thoughts, he gazed at the speckles of light filtering trough the chestnut trees. He suppressed the urge to ask the first thing that had come to his mind when he ran into her, which was whether she was married or single.

"How is your sister?" she asked.

"Monika? She has died," he said flatly.

He had failed to bring it up right away, either due to laziness or a lack of courage, but now that Rosa had asked the obvious question, he regretted his cowardice and what must have appeared to her as nonchalance. He mentally rewound what he had said and listened to the tone of his own voice; he found it dry and wrong and wanting. But there was really no correct way of saying it, as he had found out on many other occasions since Monika's passing.

In Rosa's presence, a new realization suddenly hit him. He was transported back to Matala Beach, to the morning he had woken up to find nothing but an indentation of his sister's sleeping bag in the sand and a note that could have just as easily blown away before he had a chance to read it. The perils she could have been facing without him and the many possible deaths she might have suffered had raced through his mind. But cancer was not on that list. Cancer worked slowly, methodically. Cancer took its time to gather its weapons and then struck hard.

Rosa's mouth had dropped open in shock. "Oh my God! What happened? When did she die? *How* did she die?"

She grasped his arm, and he would have been the first to admit that he had not expected her to react so strongly. In all these years, he might have underestimated the bond the two women had formed in the brief time they spent together. That made him wonder when and why exactly the two lost touch, but he decided to keep the question to himself for now. It was just as plausible that Rosa was acting purely out of empathy.

He told her about Monika's struggle, the botched operations that left her a wreck, her hopes until the last moment, as they were later explained by her husband, his brother-in law. He told Rosa about her family: the man she married, the daughter they raised, and her artwork that had started to unfold and bloom only after their father died. He told her about his grief when he received word of her passing from her husband on a Saturday night just two years earlier. It was still difficult to talk about it; Rosa started crying at one point.

It felt strange to tell Rosa about Monika's life between their meeting and her death. In her mind, Monika must have been forever young; to round up her story now, to tell Rosa about the growth of her spirit, her marriage and her child, and all the ups and down in her adult life, only for it all to end so abruptly, seemed silly and pointless and even cruel.

"There is one thing I regret, and there is no way to make up for it," Reiner said. "I was visiting her and Peter and their daughter. Monika was very excited about the idea of starting a gallery for fabric art; she went on and on about it. It was late in the evening, and we sat outside with a glass of wine while I listened to her, but what did I do? I tried to talk her out of it! It was a cold financial calculation, and I still think I was right in principle, but what does that mean when you look at a life as a whole?

"I feel like shit. I mean, she was excited about the idea, and I should have encouraged her to plunge into both the excitement and pain that such a risky operation brings. All I talked about was Düsseldorf, and that a gallery in Bonn wouldn't make sense. I promised to talk about it with my wife, who is a well-connected artist, but then I never did. And it's all because I never took risks in my life. It was just one continuous, albeit lucky career. So what right do I have in talking people out of taking risks? She asked me for my serious opinion, and I couldn't lie to her, but then how could I know that she would heed my warnings? How could I know my opinion was still so important to her?"

Rosa quickly grabbed his arm and kissed his cheek, effectively shutting him up. "What kind of gallery did you say?"

As if it mattered. Aloud, he said, "Fabric art: quilts, weavings."

"Too bad. That is terrible. I mean *was*. But I must leave now," she said, standing up. "How about I meet you tonight? Ten o'clock? Los Carracoles: a restaurant you *must* see."

She scribbled the address on the back of her business card, and within a second, she was on her way. Dumbfounded, he stayed where he was and watched her resolute steps as she mingled with the other pedestrians on the boulevard. He looked down at the card and her slanted handwriting on its back. He brought the card to his nose to see if he could detect her scent, but quickly gave up since this was a sense he had all but lost in the last few years.

After walking back to his hotel, he sat on the terrace outside his room with his notebook on the wicker table and looked east, out over the harbor. The water and the boats were bathed in the glow of the sunset. He remembered the times he'd visited Barcelona before, when he was younger; he had never been able to afford a place like this. He had resented the people who relaxed on terraces with tumblers of bourbon in their hands. Now the tables had turned, and he had made it: a jacuzzi with a switchable bubble activator, a bidet he had never used and had no idea what exactly it was good for, a Japanese toilet that sprinkled the user from underneath and kept one's butt warm, a full-length mirror that highlighted every pimple and every wrinkle but also turns with a flick of a switch into a painting of van Gogh. And of course the self-service bar.

Better to enjoy every minute of it.

[Barcelonely, after Rosa left. Re.: emerald]
She is a phenomenon of nature. Men lose their heads and limbs over a woman like that. A word comes to mind: emerald.
The rhythm of the word follows her motions like a waltz: e-me-rald.
Give me more words like that: di-a-dem, la-pis-la-zu-li.
All the precious stones that come to mind, and all the ones that don't.
I'm a grown man. I'm a grown man. I'm a goddamn grown man.
What am I going to do?

On impulse, he put the pen away, in the crease of his open note-book to prevent it from rolling off the table and hitting someone on the sidewalk seven floors below. Inside, he opened the fridge of the self-service bar and found a bag of Norwegian pretzels, a bag of Sicilian corn chips, a bag of potato chips all the way from Madagascar, a can of capers, a marinated stalk of Bavarian asparagus in a plastic sleeve, a can of Basque olives, a too-slim bottle of Alsatian Chardonnay, three bottles of Perrier, a flask of Siberian vodka, a bottle of rice wine from Cambodia, and a slender bottle of Campari—the nearly forgotten drink of his youth.

That bottle was shaped crudely, ironically, in the form of a woman.

It took him a long second to decide, as his thumb caressed the contours of the glass, whether to drink the Campari on the spot, or outside on the terrace, on the rocks. He eventually chose the latter because, these days, he liked to consider himself nothing less than a gourmet.

Chapter 46

During dinner, they caught up on their lives—the other parts, the ones without Monika. The restaurant, located in the Gothic Quarter close to Las Ramblas, was ancient-looking, with framed letters and photographs of actors and actresses and politicians lining the wall. The original chandeliers, from the turn of the century, had been converted from gas to electric. The whole place looked as if the weather had been invited to roam around inside for part of the past century. After studying the menu at length, they ordered a bottle of cava and paella for two.

"One thing I'm not in the mood for is snails," he said, and she nodded in agreement.

They toasted and finished two rounds of drinks: the first in commemoration of his sister, and the second in celebration of their own memories of the time they spent together without Monika on Crete.

It was Rosa who got them started on swapping stories. "Let me see. I went right back to Salamanca; you remember this is the place I come from? I finished business school. There I met an unusual man. He spent his nights with me and his days with copying medieval manuscripts. It might sound funny, but there is a market for this. Big bucks."

"Couldn't that be done digitally?" Reiner asked.

"Sure, nowadays it can. But this was then. No, he did it on real parchment, prepared everything the old ways. Lambskin. He scraped and ground and mixed his own ink. For the illuminations, egg yolk, red from the blood of the field louse, purple from the worm bush roots. These kinds of things. Anyway, he was not my kind of temperament."

"I can see what you mean; copying medieval fonts and illuminations must be a very slow-moving business."

"You are right, though I never made that connection! I actually meant temperament where it counts."

He had to laugh. There was the quirky girl he remembered. "You know, you have become very sophisticated when it comes to expressing yourself."

"You think so?" She seemed flattered. "I worked in an import/export company for years. English was a must."

"You be my hero-knight," he quoted her in a high-pitched voice.

"What the fuck are you saying?" Ah, there she was again—the old Rosa!

"That's what you once told me, just after we met."

She laughed aloud, almost raucously, her head leaning back to make extra room for her voice. A few people at the table next to theirs took notice and stared. "Hero-knight? You walked around all this time with this line in your head?"

"Believe me, there is much more in my head from that time," he said. "But what happened with the guy who stood you up in Mires?"

"Oh, *that* guy? Never showed up again. I'm afraid I don't have a lot of luck with love. I'm not made for that."

While he considered the implications of that, the paella arrived in a large, hot, steaming pan with yellow rice and all kinds of immobilized sea creatures. At that moment, someone, somewhere back in the kitchen, chose that exact moment to dim the lights, preventing them from getting a good look at the meal before they dug in.

"Well, eating in a restaurant involves a lot of trust," he said, making her laugh.

"But what about you?" she said. "What was her name again? All-mood?"

"Almut? That was over as soon as I got home. She never forgave me for not sending her the correct number of postcards from Greece."

"Did you ever tell her about *us*?"

"I actually can't remember; it was so long ago. But I recall when you told me, 'I can be your Almut!'"

"Did I say that? That sounds so…how do you say…*hokey*?"

He acknowledged her interruption with a quick smile. She continued to surprise him with her vocabulary! "I got married much later."

"Do you think I would like her?" she asked without hesitation, as though she had been waiting for this disclosure all along. She leaned forward with her elbows on the table, the fork listing sideways in her hand.

"I really have no idea."

There was a pause in the conversation after that. It was obvious to both that nothing else had to be said, and for the moment they were content to leave that topic alone. He didn't feel like explaining Sabine to her because that was a long story, not to mention a deflection from this evening, which felt special to him.

"Oh, shit," he said. "I forgot to call Francisco, the guy who gave me a tour earlier."

"You promised to call him?"

"I should have told him I changed my plans. I meant to take him out to dinner tonight. As a thank-you, you know?"

"Oh, you are so German in your sense of duty! He'll get over it."

He knew she was right, but the way she said it was so…Rosa. Irresponsible Rosa. He was always defending something that was inconsiderate just because it was widely tolerated in her part of the world, back when they first met, even though she, too, must have been the occasional victim of this laissez-faire attitude. And to be branded as a German with sense of duty, as if every German had a strain of Bismarck in him!

"I really liked her," Rosa said out of nowhere.

"Liked who?" he quipped.

"Your sister. Can I tell you one thing she told me?"

Reiner strained his mind to remember the occasions the two women spent alone together in Greece, out of his earshot. "What is it?"

"It was about you. About how much she admired you, envied you for your mind."

"This is what you talked about? Me?"

"Of course! What else was there to talk about?" She laughed. "And there was one more thing. She told me she thought we were a terrific couple."

"We? Meaning you and me?" He was touched and felt a jolt of excitement that flowed through his body from his heart to his groin to his toes…and back to groin. He leaned over the table and squeezed her hands. "She never told me anything about that. You know, that wasn't done in our parents' house."

"Done? You mean you never talked about anything?"

"Well, trivial things like, 'Where did you put the corkscrew?' or, 'I saw a rabbit in the garden.'"

Rosa, who, in Reiner's estimation must have chatted freely about her feelings since the age of three with everyone she ever met, shook her head slowly and looked at him with sympathy. He stood up and excused himself to the restroom. He'd been meaning to do this for some time but was so intrigued by their conversation that an extra minute did not seem to hurt. But as he navigated around chairs and tables across the darkened room, he could acknowledge to himself that he left at that precise moment because he didn't want to be pitied by her as if he had some monstrous physical affliction like the Elephant Man. He also didn't want to blow it since *la noche es joven*—the night is young.

In the restroom, he looked at himself in the mirror and smoothened down his hair. Then he repeated, using muscle memory, the smile he'd felt on his face when he met her that afternoon. He decided he had to do better.

"How was Sitges?" she asked when he returned. "Did you see anything? I mean, except the dreary inside of this conference center?"

"Have you ever been there?" he asked. She shook her head. "Well, Sitges is such a special place. So, there is this hill that divides the town in two, and each side has its own beach. One part has a long promenade with rows of magnolia trees and a statue of a famous painter—"

"El Greco, no?"

"Yes, that must be him! The Greek. How did you know?"

"He is famous. In Spain, many towns have at least one bust of him on display."

"OK, so the other part has lots of boutiques and a famous bar, San Sebastian. Important people have visited it; poems have been written about it. On the hill, there are several churches and ancient government buildings, and one of them is used as a conference center. It hosts meetings on all kinds of esoteric matters like chaos theory and shamanic breathwork and, of course, the field I'm working in."

"I won't ask you what that is."

"Thanks, that helps! But, the really exciting part was the performance arts festival."

"Like what?"

"One of the events had to do with the eye: a woman dressed all in blue, selling blue cups, knitted gloves, and other blue whatnots in a blue stand. Next there was a man dressed all in yellow, selling yellow stuffed animals in a yellow stand. And so forth: green, red, purple. You could buy these things, but you could only pay for them with fake money, and to get the fake money, you had to go into a booth where actors dressed as doctors put an eye patch over one of your eyes to mark it as 'donated'."

"That doesn't make any sense." She emptied her third glass of cava and rolled her eyes.

"Did I say it would? Anyway, the theme of the *eye* was picked up in the final procession, which was headed by a giant balloon up in the air and strapped to two of the performance artists. The balloon was painted to look like—you guessed it!—a giant eye.

"And sometimes, the balloon got caught by a gust of wind and ran into a balcony and anybody who was on it would shriek and back away. Later, the straps got entangled in some store signs. It was funny because, as a giant eye, it should have seen what it was going to run into, so it looked like it was doing it on purpose."

As he described the procession winding through the narrow streets of Sitges, Rosa followed each of his gestures with her eyes like a puppy. The bottle of cava was clearly doing its job.

"Reiner, can I ask you something?" she said when he was finished, looking straight into his eyes. Her otherwise perfect tongue made her speech sound heavy.

"Anything, sure."

"Could we...can we possibly...?"

"Totally," he said, catching on to her meaning without further explanation. "I have this great place right by the water, and it's all covered as business expenses. I just had the same idea."

This wasn't exactly true, but it was actually an idea that had festered in his mind since the moment he ran into her that afternoon. In reply, she sent him an air-kiss across the table and the half-finished, still-steaming dish of paella.

It was strange, but the anticipation of this reunion had also made Reiner feel like he was approaching an encounter with Monika again, as if he might find her again in a crowd just as he did in Sitia after he and Rosa spent that blessed night in Mires and took the bus via Ierapetra. It was silly, but he couldn't brush it off, and with it came a wave of warm appreciation for the role his sister played in him crossing paths with Rosa. Weren't their present circumstances a replay, a divine correction of a wrong move that they'd made without any grand insight into the workings of *Schicksal?*

Why did Rosa go back to Spain so abruptly? Why didn't he simply follow her back to Salamanca? How often would something like this happen in their lifetime? Rarely once, and it was even less likely that it would happen twice—certainly never more than that. He'd been timid and stupid the first time around, but that was just a byproduct of his youth and lack of experience. No matter how he looked at it, this second chance was nothing less than a cosmic, existential opportunity, and as such subject to purviews and considerations entirely different than the ones he normally dealt with. That was a nascent thought he prepared and nurtured in his mind as a possible explanation to his wife sometime later.

His thoughts came to a halt when he noticed Rosa fixating on something on the wall just past his left ear.

"Oh my God! Holy cow!" she exclaimed. "Did you see the picture behind you? It's the Tiffany woman. What was her name again? Can you imagine? She was right here! She maybe sat on the same chair you are sitting on! Think about that!"

He turned in his seat and twisted his head around. Sure enough, there was the familiar, deceptively innocent-looking schoolgirl face in a black frame and with a crooked, left-leaning signature running across her blouse.

"You mean Hepburn? Audrey Hepburn!" he cried. "Did I ever tell you that she was a favorite of Monika's, too?"

Rosa stopped and looked at him quietly for a few seconds, then said in a slightly slurred voice, "Monika this, Monika that! I'm tired of this, you know? Can't we just focus on what we have *now?*"

She said it with such a sweet expression and her mouth puckered that it didn't sound nasty, but it hit Reiner like a bolt of lightning. His first impulse was to take offense, but then he caught himself; he didn't want to risk losing her. This entire day had been a miracle, a promise of reinvention. Somewhere in the back of his mind, engraved by a *Studium generale* philosophy class, was the blunt dictum of Lucretius about free will:

"If there is no atomic swerve to initiate movement that can annul the decrees of destiny and prevent the existence of an endless chain of causation, what is the source of this free will possessed by living creatures all over the earth?"

And with this swerve set in motion, he saw and couldn't deny what Rosa objected to. Wasn't it true that the idea of some unfinished business with his sister had followed him like an obsession? Purging her from his mind, at least for the short while he had to spend with Rosa, was perhaps the way to go.

"I guess you are right," he said with a shrug before raising his glass. "I can't wait."

Chapter 47

"I became a shadow

Don't ask me why, maybe in another life
I'll live in other moons
Don't darken the glances you took until yesterday
before I kiss you

Forgive me that I can't explain
the nights I cried in front of you
I turned my tear into a drink so that I get drunk
Guilts I hid in my chest

Don't forget hugs, and believe me it's not your fault
that I'm leaving in the dark
Don't run behind me and cry,
if you want, leave your secret stroke in my nights.

Forgive me I can't flap my wings
in the caves that, my soul, I closed myself.
Blind, but I was looking for a candle, maybe to trick the truth
But I was desperate

I became a shadow to come at nights at your life
To slide like a star in your body, I'm lost again
It became a shadow under your sheet,
but my kiss dawns in another hug."

—Mantinades, *Pantelis Pantelidis*

* * *

[Barcelonly airport. Re.: two nipples, etcetera]

–Ages-old mystery of women and men. Their firefly-like attraction to each other, crafted and programmed long ago by the gods, with a little help from evolution

–Stupendous emotional whirlwinds caused by the innately bipolar qualities of the human constitution

–Case to be made that a large part of it is caused by the way people are nurtured, not by nature. Babies fixate on the triangular constellation of eyes and mouth; then, as they grow up and enter adolescence, they fixate on everything triangular anchored by two prominent dots

–In the end, two nipples and the pubic bush become the ultimate promise of transcendence, of complete immersion in another person, just as the baby wants to be one again with her mother

–Btw, there is nothing original about that; other people have made the same observation throughout history

–Human beings tend to forget all of this whenever they get entangled in this miracle, and it happens over and over again in their lifetimes; their brains become inflamed as they are overtaken by a drive no one can properly account for

–Was there anything that has not been done in pursuit of this blind drive that mankind calls love? Starting from the beginning of antiquity up until the present. From heroic deeds like slaying dragons, all the way to general, avoidable tragedies – deceit, treason, murder, war

* * *

Something about the flight attendant who guided him to his seat reminded Reiner of her; perhaps it was the way she moved or the way she looked at him, but it was definitely something other than the fact that she was pretty in the same vein as other Mediterranean beauties, and that she had Rosa's finely chiseled nose and even the resolute curve of her mouth. But then he told himself that it was probably nothing but a projection of the previous night and his intense communion with Rosa's body, Rosa's mind, Rosa's everything, still permeating the ether around him: the very ether that was supposed to keep planets supported in their eternal motions, if one listened to the renowned medieval scholars. He would not have been surprised to find the outline of her face—or even of parts of her body—in the clouds they passed through as the plane climbed to the altitude necessary to scale the Alps.

Unfortunately, when he looked out the window, the plane was already well inside an intense fog, and it would likely be impossible to tell even in the air.

Rosa had left early in the morning because of an unspecified business appointment, and her sudden absence from the hotel room made him feel numb. The long breakfast he'd imagined, with lingering recollections of a night spent in close company, never happened. As he packed his belongings, he discovered the tidbits she'd left behind in her whirlwind departure: a tiny comb, a bottle of aspirin, a roll of dental floss. He put them all into the plastic bag reserved for his own toothpaste. He had tried to drink in her unique scent, but again, his sense of smell failed him in this most important task: another sign of getting old.

He took out the photograph she had given him; it was a passport-size color picture—and not a particularly flattering one—that showed her looking straight at him without blinking. It gave him a jolt to look at her in this miniscule, glossy-paper capacity, for it instantly invoked the memory of her living presence, as though through a mechanism of active hallucination. But, seeing the picture also revived his trepidations about a future without her, which seemed bleaker with every mile he got closer to home. So profound was this dread that he considered it a blessing that he would have to spend so much time navigating the maze of Heathrow to the shuttle bus that connected the airport to the Underground, and, by way of the train from King's Cross, steadily make his way home to Cambridge. This was why he'd dismissed the quicker and more comfortable option of taking a taxicab directly from

Heathrow to his home, a ride that would be astronomically expensive, but defensible as a routine business expense.

One reason he hated flying—and there were many—was that it bypassed the gradual adjustments, the transitions one made from exiting one territory to entering the next. Flying meant making shortcuts of a route involving many infinitesimal steps that were commensurate with the landscape and natural human pace. Johann Wolfgang von Goethe's actual Italian journey had taken the man weeks, including breakfasts, lunches, dinners, overnight stays, changes of horses, and unforgettable encounters with locals who accused him of spying because he had the audacity to take out his sketchbook and draw their ancient landmarks surreptitiously, without asking for municipal permission. Flying replaced all that with the unnatural *Strapaze*—the strain—of sitting in a narrow, fake salon, in the uncomfortably close company of strangers without any means of escape.

He greeted the man next to him on the right, who had black hair and close-set eyes, and wore a thick, blue flannel shirt. The urge to share his experience with anyone was overwhelming.

"Where to, today?" Reiner asked him.

"Liverpool, via Heathrow," the man said with a Spanish accent.

"I'm just going back to Cambridge," Reiner said.

"Nice place, Cambridge. From there you are?"

"It's more complicated. I'm German, but I live and work abroad."

"From Segovia, I am."

"And what do you do, may I ask?"

"Cars. I sell them. What picture you look at? A woman?"

"Ah, you noticed? Here, see for yourself." He leaned over to show his neighbor the little photograph nestled in the hollow of his hand.

The Spaniard took a quick look, gave Reiner the glance of a connoisseur, and said, "Beautiful."

Clearly, he was not a man of many words. Reiner made up his mind to try out his neighbor on the left once he was finished here.

"I was with her last night," Reiner said.

"With her. And now without her?"

"You seem to understand the quandary I'm in."

They were interrupted by the captain's announcement. "We are about to take off. Turbulence is to be expected, but nothing that a modern aircraft such as this and an experienced crew such as ours cannot handle. So relax, and enjoy your flight."

The announcement was repeated by the staff in fluent German, French, Italian, and Spanish, and by the time it was all finished, the man from Segovia was fast asleep.

Reiner turned to the man on the left, who had spent his time thus far inspecting the glossy safety instruction manual front and back. He sported one of those beards that had lately come into fashion, the kind that filled the area between his lower lip and the tip of his chin. Reiner gauged him to be a hedge fund manager or some other type of investor that dealt with other people's futures.

He showed him Rosa's picture after a brief introduction.

The man gave it a quick look, nodded, and pronounced, "She is eminently fuckable."

Reiner retracted his hand and recoiled into his seat at the crudeness of the remark, even though he had to concede that he'd tested the statement himself and had empirically proven it to be correct.

Chapter 48

Flight Attendant Kate

When one must take the same route going back and forth several times a day, day in and day out, one looks forward to distractions: like meeting passengers who don't fit the normal mold. It comes to the point that even negative experiences can be a brilliant distraction. Like this immense Japanese businessman, the other day: his £5,000 business suit got splattered with tomato juice when I opened a can across the aisle from him to serve another customer.

Or, I should rather say *sprinkled* since I saw just a few dark red spots on the white-striped, blue fabric. His face turned the same color as the juice, and he demanded an apology before I was even able to take a breath. What a wanker! He scoffed at the £50 cleaning voucher I presented to him; we have cartons full of these in the stowage bins, more than we have cans of tomato juice. What he wanted to see instead were curtsies and every other manner of public humiliation that fell short of having me fired and banned from the job of senior flight attendant for life. This may be what he is used to from similar incidents on Japanese airlines—tomato juice replaced by miso soup, I suppose—but I refused to play along. When I look back at it now, it was all rather funny.

But the incident I'm referring to now was of an entirely different nature. It took place during my last shift of the day, going from Barcelona to Heathrow. It was an experience of a kind I didn't enjoy at all, neither right as it happened nor afterward.

The bloke in seat 2B was handsome, of medium build, blond, and good-looking. He was in high spirits—maybe even high on a substance or something, but I'm not one to judge. He was all too keen to share his most recent experience with the strangers sitting next to him. He spoke English with a German accent, which I found a bit charming. Right after he boarded the plane, he started animated conversations with the passengers in the business cubicles on both his left and his right. One was a luxury car salesman from Valencia or Sofia or some other city ending in 'ia'. The other was one of those investor types. As far as the contents of these conversations is concerned, they were the usual macho chitchats about this and that regarding women: pretty much like anything else I've overheard over my fifty million miles on this job.

At one point, he went to bathroom number one; it's the one located right behind the door to the flight cabin. It all went pear-shaped from there. There was silence for the longest time, or at least what counts as silence on a plane, what with the engines constantly droning. Then, at least ten hectic flushes of the toilet in bathroom number one.

That in and of itself is unusual; the most I can ever remember hearing on a flight before then is five, and those were executed by a lady with a sick stomach. Afterward, she came out white as a bedsheet: probably chundered inside, poor thing.

This time, after the ninth or tenth flush, there was no further sound. Now, you must know that we have clear instructions to leave the occupant of a restroom in peace unless the conditions of the flight demand otherwise. This particular flight was smooth, so there was no reason to interfere as far as the European Union Aviation Safety Agency's (EASA's) rules were concerned. But after half an hour, it was reasonable that I should get worried about his well-being. So, I knocked on the door again and again, with no response. My fist might be small as fists go, but there was no reason why he shouldn't have been able to hear it from inside. I then used the master key to open the door. Here, I followed word for word the instructions I was issued two years ago, when the required time to wait before taking action was reduced from one hour to thirty minutes.

I was gobsmacked by what I saw: the restroom was empty! I felt like chundering myself right there on the spot. There were traces of recent activity—splashes of water, a torn piece of toilet paper—but no trace of the bloke who had clearly entered the restroom in front of several witnesses, including me, and who had to have produced the commotion for everyone nearby to hear.

I stepped back in horror and closed the door. I must have stood there for a minute or two, gathering my thoughts, as they say. Then I spoke to the commanding cabin manager about the situation. I might have used the nautical expression *man overboard*, for which I was later rightfully reprimanded by the captain. But at the time, it was a mere slip of tongue used to deal with a situation no training had prepared me for.

When word spread in the cabin, there was a lot of panic. I don't blame the passengers because I could hardly keep it together myself. They were reluctant to visit the remaining bathrooms after that, as though they were convinced that they all were portals to their doom!

Many children have this naïve idea that the loo on an aircraft simply empties into space. This is probably because of the enormous flushing noise you hear when you press the button. And it would make a lot of sense if you think about it. My dad once told me about the loos on the trains in the fifties and sixties that used to be open to the tracks. When you looked down, you could literally see the muck-splattered crossbeams flying by like the frames of a movie. So, maybe this is the way kids think of it here on the plane. But even if that were the case, there is no way a full-grown man would have fit through.

In my eleven years of flight experience, I've never experienced the disappearance of a passenger into thin air—pun intended, since at the altitude we were flying, the air outside is really a bit thin. Barely life-sustaining, like they say it is on Mars.

Naturally, we were concerned with the business of reconciling the passenger count with the flight manifest from the port of entry. 2B or not 2B? We knew quite well we were in a bit of a bind, and we didn't exactly look forward to the reception we were going to get upon landing, what with the airline representatives, not to mention—God forbid—MI5 and officials of the Civil Aviation Authority.

And oh, those bloody reporters—I almost forgot.

Epilogue

Several years have passed since I started this account and set the siblings in motion on their journey to the early playground of heroes, gods, and demigods. They stumbled from one place to the other, unable to discern what was left of the spirit of ancient Greece, but the sun, the sky, the land, and the people they met sang to them and bewitched them.

I took no pleasure from engineering Reiner's demise, but I felt something had to be done when he veered off the path I had carefully laid out for him. If this decision caused a commotion on the plane he took on his way home, then I console myself with the knowledge that the plane, along with its human cargo, was, at any rate, doomed and headed for obliteration at the very end of the book by virtue of it all being immaterial figments of my imagination.

The fact is, I stood with him all along, even up to the point where he re-bedded his acquaintance, girlfriend, mistress, lover—or whatever he might have called her at this advanced stage of infatuation—in his posh hotel suite in Barcelona near the waterfront at the point where he lost sight of his mission and his moral compass. Come to think of it, it was actually the evening before, in the restaurant, where he betrayed me and defied my clear instructions.

It is true, there were a couple of times when he was in need of corrective actions, but even then he was willing to go along and treat me with respect. But this last transgression was simply unacceptable. What I resented most was the cavalier way he treated the memory of my sister, who was the very reason for his existence as my stand-in. With freedom comes responsibility, and while he has been a model in that rubric for most of his journey, he faltered and failed all the more spectacularly at the end. Why this was so is beyond me.

In German, we have the expression, *"sich spatzing machen,"* or, "to take on the aggressive demeanor of sparrows." All over the world, sparrows are known as rambunctious, as creatures lacking respect. What the expression means is to have an attitude, to act ostensibly without considering others, to defy norms, to defy boundaries of decency and common sense. At one point, Reiner may have gotten too full of himself; he was imbued with too much uncontrolled life, perhaps due to a lack of the necessary calibration at the very start.

This happens with billiard balls, too; the smallest error in direction and velocity at the start will grow into a colossal mistake at the end of the ball's trajectory.

Reiner made it quite clear on several occasions that one important reason for his hatred of flying was the absence of a means to escape. Well, at least I am satisfied that I was able to grant him this wish. You may take issue with the exact way I engineered his exit. I suppose I could have made it happen right in his seat, 2B, and perhaps this would have been the easiest way, but I wanted to preserve some sense of his dignity during his final moments, and give him some privacy as well. These are common protocols of decency that are to be observed at someone's deathbed, after all.

* * *

My sister was vibrant; I could feel it even in her absence. What I learned as I tried to track her down and then follow her path was that sometimes a life is preformed at an early age, condensed like in a chrysalis.

If only I could, I would love to go back and do a few things differently: rent a donkey for the two of us and do the rounds through the villages. With great clamor, a gang of children might welcome us to each village in turn. True to the ancient habits of Greek hospitality, elderly couples would fight over the privilege of sheltering us and giving us a meal. I would never, ever fall asleep on the beach. We would also reserve a day to visit Phaistos, the second-famous Minoan palace.

With age comes an appreciation of the very dimension of age, of the silent presence of time—even of antiquity.

It is getting closer to winter again. All the flowers will soon be gone, but their building plan is wisely hidden in a virtually indestructible sequence of nucleotides in their DNA. That means we will see them again; another winter will pass, and it is just a matter of time.

Dear Monika, dear sister: I could tell you so much now that I didn't know when you were still with us. Just think about the weekly updates in the science section of The New York Times! I'm now in the habit of collecting stories about Crete. It's true that I've been a collector of a lot of things throughout my life, but it's no longer fool's gold in glass jars gained by knees getting bloody as they press into the gravel. Now it's news stories I find on the internet, the hard disk of my laptop as their receptacle, and a stiff neck as the result of working into the night. In a way, it is another manifestation of *Übersprungshandlung*. I'm still the bird in the corner, out of its mind.

For instance, I just read that six-million-year-old footprints were found on Crete, and that they were made by some prehuman ancestors walking upright on their earliest rendition of feet with toes, but that they were still flat-footed, still awaiting the formation of the arch that conveys springiness to our steps, and with it the propensity to take off and run at a second's notice. But here is the part that drew my special attention: at the time that the petrified footprints were made, Crete was still connected with Africa, forming a northern outpost of the Sahara. Is this where the palms in Vai came from? Perhaps those waiters had it all wrong with that silly idea of pirates dumping their coconuts on the beach.

Then, only a few days go by, and Crete is back in the news, this time with an earthquake:

"A powerful earthquake measuring 6.3 struck the seabed at 12:24 p.m. on Tuesday, local time, south of Crete. The quake had a focal depth of 8.2 km (5.09 miles), and its epicenter was southeast of the city of...Ierapetra."

God, no, it cannot be! Is my live-in tower still standing? What happened to my outlook high up in the sky? With so many changes around me, I want to hold on to something; is this too much to ask? And then

I read on:

> *"The USGS said the epicentre of Tuesday's earthquake at 09:24 GMT was Crete's eastern village of Palaikastro."*

I had to read it twice since I didn't believe my eyes. Right, of course, it *had* to be Palaikastro, *our* Palaikastro, where we slept under the open sky! This left me speechless.

At this point, nobody has seen this manuscript except for the people in my writers' group, who are sworn to secrecy. They would never, ever leak a live creation to other mortals, never mind gods they don't believe in. Still, I can't help but feel that someone out there, up there, has read this draft and now retraces the protagonist's path with divine wrath.

Palaikastro, I found out, was in fact the site of one of the Minoan palaces, and it perished not long after a good part of Thera, today's Santorini—an island seventy miles north of Crete—got obliterated in a volcanic eruption that extended sixty-three cubic kilometers up into the air with the force of forty atomic bombs. A tsunami wave taller than one hundred and fifty feet wiped out all life on the northern coast of Crete. The event dwarfed the 1883 eruption of Krakatau and changed the path of history.

Reading this got me calculating: sixty-three cubic kilometers equals fifteen cubic miles. Manhattan occupies twenty-two square miles. Imagine Manhattan as one solid block, carved out to a depth of two-thirds of a mile, then simply tossed into the air and pulverized. All those Starbucks coffee shops, the Met, Carnegie Hall, the Strand, the 9/11 memorial, all of Chinatown, Peruvian and Greek restaurants I love, St. John's Cathedral, the subway with all its rats and graffiti, the collection of the New York Historical Society, and all the consulates and embassies of friendly and unfriendly nations combined: imagine all this has turned to dust and will be circulating the planet for years to come! The sun would be a white blur in a permanently gray sky, and plant seedlings would shoot thin, yellow sprouts, desperate for light. Farmers would be forced to bury their last emaciated cow, and summer and winter would have become one continuous season: the season of dread.

The priestesses would shed their precious garments for sack clothing and join common folk in search of food. Grass would still grow, but slowly. Dried and ground to a powder, it can be baked into edible patties; there is not much nutritional value to it, but stomachs would feel filled for a while.

We also just learned from our daily paper about the detective work of molecular archeologists (yes, there is such a thing now!), which led them to conclude that the sculptures we saw in Greece were once painted in brilliant colors. Those sculptures are crumbling now, and they are bleached white like the tusks of the Cohoes Mastodon.

Monika, where is this going? What will happen to all our insights, our lives of continuous learning? The *Studium generale*? All the art you created? What lessons do we take with us to our graves? Is this all going to waste?

Monika, I'm bleached already; my hair is white as snow, and all its colors are gone!

If not as *your* keeper—a job I failed miserably—I have strived, belatedly, to live as the keeper of your memory. In writing this book, I have rebuilt you from fragments I found in the overlapping salt-and-pepper, patina films in my hippocampus, drawing from the picture of you looking at me from under the wide brim of the black hat that undulates along the rim like the side fin of an eel as it swims through its aqueous habitat. From there, I moved on to all the other pictures stacked up in shoebox number fifteen after I took them out of my clumsy albums. I liberally borrowed from your letters that I found in my Leitz binders—the ones that have traveled with me everywhere like precious jewelry. In the interest of full disclosure, I corresponded with your other living siblings, too, and they answered a few questions and sent me some letters from their archives and whatever else they could find to help fill in the gaps.

When we are children, we don't regard our own death as a serious matter. Everyone who reads this will think I must be kidding, because even at that age, it is likely that we have seen cars totaled, wrapped around trees, and can begin to grasp the idea that one can go from everything to nothing in the span of a millisecond, the blink of an eye.

But there is inertia everywhere in the universe. Things don't just stop, because where would that energy go? Not just energy, but information, too. And how about beauty, or love? All that can't simply disappear; the laws of physics are ironclad. Take stars, like our sun: they take millions of years to die, which would be a decent interval to prepare oneself, get things in order.

I realize I can only talk about myself—my thoughts, my fears, my feelings, my convictions—and can't put words into anyone else's mouth. We never had these kinds of conversations, Monika, and now it is too late. I should have just let you be when you were sick and tired of collecting fool's gold in the backyard instead of needlessly pressuring you.

I was the fool in this game, and you were wise beyond your years.

The End

Author's Note

Some parts of the story are autobiographical, others are totally invented. Ever since I set my foot on Crete I was smitten by the joyfulness of the people, the light, the atmosphere, and the ubiquitous presence of ancient history. Something about it resonates with my temperament, with the way I see the world. I did visit Crete once with my sister in the 1960s, and later realized that my memories of that trip were an important part of the way I remember her. The idea of the novel came, as in many plays and works of fiction, from my finding and re-reading a letter as I opened boxes after a move. The manuscript took years to finish as it gained contours on its way through three writers' groups.

Acknowledgments

I got very interesting suggestions from my writers' groups in New York. I will single out Ellen Conly, Carole Rosenthal and Susan Mellin for their most cogent feedback. Although Gene Garber never saw a draft, I must credit the framing of the story and use of an avatar to the inspirations I received from him, master of metafiction. I sent an early draft to my Greek-born friend Barbara Ritza Strüven in Hamburg to see if I caught the spirit of the island, and I was gratified about her enthusiastic response. I thank Stardust Atkeson for many encouraging remarks and steadfast support. Special thanks go to Nicholas Birns who kindly agreed to read the manuscript and gave me substantive, helpful comments.

I wish to acknowledge the professional help I received from Heather of First Editing in content. Thanks to my wife Carol for a critical reading of the proofs. Finally, my thanks go to Gordon McClellan, Suanne Laqueur and the rest of their team at Canoe Tree Press/DartFrog for their superb job of bringing this book into the final form.

About the Author

Joachim Frank is a German-born scientist and a writer living in New York. He has published numerous poems, prose poems and short stories (see franxfiction.com) and one novel, AAN ZEE. He is a Professor at Columbia University (joachimfranklab.org). In 2017 he shared the Nobel Prize in Chemistry with Jacques Dubochet and Richard Henderson.